D1135156

THE ASHES

BOOK III OF THE FEUD TRILOGY

KYLE PRUE

Cover design by Ashley Ruggirello www.CardboardMonet

Library of Congress Control Number 2020900702

The Ashes|Kyle Prue

This is a work of fiction. All characters, organizations and events portrayed in this novel are either products of the author's imagination or are used fictitiously.

❀ Created with Vellum

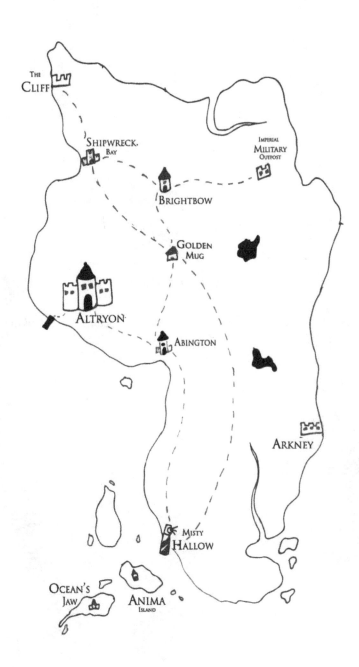

DEDICATION

For my Mother

My intrepid guide through all the fictional adventures and all the real ones too.

PART I

"The wound is the place where the Light enters you."

-Rumi

IMPERIAL MILITARY FORTRESS

NEIL VAPROS

The skin was going to come off. That was the only thing Neil knew for certain. Day in and day out the chains wore against his flesh, which was already softened and tenderized by the water around him. The skin on his knees was already long gone, and he was certain the wrists were next. He'd been transferred here over the course of a few weeks and held in this custom cell for three interminable days. He'd been quite the nuisance to his captors while they transported him, and he was sure that they were taking their frustrations out on him now.

Leaving someone chin-deep in water doesn't sound like torture, and it isn't. Not for the first day at least. The true horrors come the second day, when the skin ruptures at the slightest friction and the stress position tears muscles and damages ligaments. Sleeping was also out of the question. Every time Neil's head drooped in pursuit of slumber, his nose dipped into the water and he startled awake.

Neil's arms were chained to the floor. He could raise them, but not high enough to get them out of the water. And he could forget summoning a flame. He could only shoot fire from his hands on good days, and the lack of food and sleep served to make him too weak to channel his energy. Even if he did manage to summon a fireball, it would be born in the water and perish instantly. On the second day, he considered ending his life. But today, day three, was different. He'd grown used to the frailty and the pain. He no longer wanted to die. Today he wanted to breathe fire.

His first plan had been to simply materialize out of his bonds, but the way they dug into his joints prevented that. He'd been attempting this for days and found little success. He was finally able to channel energy into his mouth, but usually it just gave him a headache. He heard a latch open and realized that someone was finally coming to feed him. Or to kill him.

In order for a guard to enter his cell, he'd have to climb over a hatch and into the water. The cell door had a swinging top half, and it opened outward to reveal a disgruntled looking guard. He probably didn't enjoy getting thigh-deep in water just to feed their most annoying prisoner. He held a bowl of stew and had a few apples tucked under his arm. The apples were probably brought because they were buoyant, and Neil could spread them out over the course of a few days. It seemed Saewulf was going to weaken Neil before coming to see him.

It was an odd situation. Saewulf, the psychic, had finally revealed himself after laying low and pretending to be dead, only to disappear again. Neil could feel his presence though. Whenever Saewulf was near, the air felt thicker and harder to move through. Not that Neil was moving very often. He made a snap decision as the guard waded towards him. He wasn't going to wait for Saewulf to sap the life out of him. He was going to bring the psychic to him.

The guard dropped an apple. As he stumbled to get it, Neil filled his mouth with water. Then he concentrated his power straight into his mouth. He couldn't breath fire, but he was almost certain that he could boil water. The guard reached him and dipped a spoon into the bowl of stew. When he brought it to Neil's mouth, Neil leaned back. The guard frowned and leaned forward. This put his face right in range. Neil heaved his head forward and spat boiling water straight into the guard's eyes.

The guard screamed and threw his head back in pure agony. His eyes were glued shut, and Neil wondered if they'd stay that way. The guard struck at Neil a few times in retaliation, but Neil didn't care. He was growing tolerant of pain. Eventually the guard ran to the door of the cell and climbed out. He screamed many profanities and curses, but only one word really caught Neil's ear. *Saewulf.* He was going to get Saewulf.

Neil leaned his head back, almost in bliss. It was possible that he was about to die, but at least he could do away with the waiting. He didn't have to sit around for his destiny any longer, but summoned it. He heard guards arguing and footsteps running back and forth. The door had been left open, so for once he could learn a little about his captors. There didn't appear to be many guards, and the prison probably wasn't huge since he kept hearing the same voices. Even when there was a shift change, the new guards sounded familiar. Neil strained to hear beyond the walls and all remained quiet. Chances were he was being held outside the walls of the Industrial City. Chances were Neil wasn't yet in the city where he'd learned to speak and to walk. This wasn't the city where he'd lost two sisters and a mother.

Eventually Neil heard the guards vacate the hallways and then the familiar footfalls of his greatest enemy. Neil's hands naturally curled into fists. His spine would have straightened if it weren't already contorted in an unnatural state. Slouching for three days straight had damaged his ligaments thoroughly. Saewulf came to the open door and stared at Neil. It was hard to decipher his expression with half of his face burned away. But it wasn't friendly. "Saewulf," Neil said. "I've missed you. Care for an apple?"

Saewulf levitated into the prison cell, and Neil tried not to look impressed. That was new. He seemed to grow more powerful with every appearance. "Neil Vapros. You've been very unkind to one of my men." His voice was as bone chilling as ever. It sounded like stone scraping against stone. He looked down at Neil's crumpled form. "I hate that you still look like this." The honesty was apparent in his cold rasp.

"Like what?" Neil asked.

"We've both walked through the fires of this war." He pointed his hand at Neil, and Neil felt an immense pressure on his chest. "Those fires forged you. They strengthened your metal. You look older, like a man. Those same fires melted the flesh from my skin. I am dried skin over bone and here you are, undamaged. Unscarred."

"I have plenty of scars," Neil gasped as the pressure became more concentrated, like the head of a hammer.

"Not enough. Not yet."

Neil's rib cracked, and he tensed every muscle to keep from screaming. Saewulf's eyes showed satisfaction. He no longer had lips to do so. Neil waited until the pain subsided to a dull roar before trying to speak. "Why are you doing this? Why don't you just kill me?"

"I've been visited, Neil."

"I don't know what you're talking about."

Saewulf shook his head adamantly. "You've seen him too, right?" It almost sounded like begging. "The Man with the Golden Light visited me, Neil. He told me the prophecy. He told me about the Lightborn that would bring forth a new Altryon."

Neil gave way. "I've heard it too, but you don't seem religious, Saewulf."

Saewulf dipped his hand into the water and wiped it on his face. He breathed a sigh of relief. It couldn't still burn, could it? He'd been in the explosion almost half a year ago. "It makes sense though, doesn't it? *The Lightborn will be like a Phoenix. Reborn in fire. Forged in fire.*"

Neil stiffened. Hearing those words hurt more than feeling his rib break. The Wolf had said the same ones to him, verbatim. Either way, Neil didn't want to believe in a god who appeared to someone like Saewulf. "His life will bring about the new nation," Neil said.

Saewulf's eyes shifted too quickly. Neil had upset him. Saewulf pointed his finger and clutched Neil tight with his mind. "What did you just say?"

Neil found it hard to speak. "His life will bring about the new nation."

Saewulf glared at Neil. "Who told you that?"

Neil didn't see a point to lying. "Steven Celerius. He was visited too."

Saewulf maintained his eye contact for a while, then released Neil without warning. Saewulf laughed darkly, and it frightened Neil. "The honorable Celerius might have changed a word or two. I heard it differently."

"What do you mean?"

"His death."

Neil's tongue went numb. "What?"

"His death will bring about the new nation."

Neil didn't know what to say. Of course he believed the Wolf over Saewulf, but the Psychic wasn't budging. He didn't look like he was lying, but it was hard to tell with half of his face missing. "You think it's me," Neil realized. He remembered something from when Saewulf captured him. "You said that my life would never be as important as my death. You think killing me will... what?"

"Bring about the new nation. My nation." Neil wanted to vomit. "When I kill you, the revolution will die with you. The people's hope will die with you." Saewulf licked his teeth. "You are beloved, Neil Vapros."

"Thanks," Neil said.

"I never once dreamed I'd see the Celerius, Vapros, and Taurlum together, but one meeting with you and they decided to forgo two-hundred years of tradition. It's not the fire or the annoying attitude that make you dangerous, Neil. It's that. When you are dead the Lightborns will disband and the revolution will lose its figureheads."

Neil wanted to argue that his friends would never stop fighting, but Saewulf seemed more unhinged than usual. Neil didn't want any more broken ribs. "What does your new nation look like, Saewulf? A world without the Vapros, Celerius, and Taurlum?"

"I used to think so. I used to think it was those three families

7

preying on the weak and the innocent. Now I know better. It's all Lightborns."

Neil gasped and regretted it immediately. He hated that Saewulf had so much control over him. "There is no such thing as innocent rule. Every day during this war, I see Lightborns with gross amounts of power. They crush the normal people. The common people. A perfect world is clean of them. Clean of Lightborns."

Neil couldn't bear to listen anymore. "You seem to forget that you are a Lightborn."

"I will be the last one. The entire race will die with me."

Neil knew he was making a mistake before the words even left his lips. "All because of Barrick Vapros?"

Saewulf's jaw dropped, even though it looked painful for him. He seemed afraid for a single moment, then confused. Eventually it all gave way to fury. He lashed out with his hand and gripped Neil's neck up close. Skin on skin. "How *the hell* do you know that name?"

Neil stared him down. "I went to the island, Saewulf. I heard what they did to you. To your sister. You were chained, you were abused, you were their slave. They made you mine for silver and when your sister died…" He didn't need to finish. He and Saewulf both knew the conclusion to this story.

"You're lying," Saewulf said. It was a desperate prayer.

"I am no one's slave," Neil whispered. "You carved that into the walls of the mansion thousands of times. You wrote it in blood."

Saewulf dropped Neil and stared ahead blankly. It was clear that he hadn't been confronted with his past in a very long time. He slapped Neil with his mind and turned to leave. Before he left, Neil saw tears streaming down his face into the uneven lines of charred skin. He reached the door and gripped it with his hands. "What they did to me… What they did to her… It'll never happen again." He turned back to Neil with blazing eyes. "You want to know what my nation looks like? It's a place where no one will ever feel what I felt. Hopeless. Faithless. Powerless."

This time he climbed over the door instead of levitating, maybe to make a point. Or maybe using his powers tired him. He did use his powers to slam the door shut. Neil waited to exhale until Saewulf's footsteps faded. That had gone about as well as it could have. At least he knew a little more about why he was here and about Saewulf's plans. Although why was he still alive? Why hadn't Saewulf snapped his neck with a flick of his wrist?

He didn't want to think about what Saewulf had told him. Had the Wolf lied? If he was the Lightborn talked about in the prophecy, would he have to die? And what sort of nation would it bring about? It was all too much to think about and it felt like his brain was pushing against the inside of his skull. Luckily, Neil had lots of time to mull these things over. He wasn't going anywhere soon.

2

ABINGTON

LILLY CELERIUS

"If she escapes I'll have your heads!" General Carlin screamed with such ferocity that Lilly heard him several streets away.

She ran through Abington's alleys and cobblestone paths. It was the largest village outside the walls of Altryon, and Lilly estimated that even with her legendary Celerius speed it would take her several minutes to cross. She hoped she could weave through the streets quicker than Carlin could reorganize his men. Two soldiers tried to block her way, and she cut them down with her twin blades. She didn't even stumble. She could see the end of the street, and her objective sat a few miles away: the Courthouse. Abington's prisons were filled with rebels and outlaws, so they'd started storing the most rambunctious criminals in their courthouse.

She sped through a squadron of men and didn't leave a single one intact. She heard hoof beats behind and she knew that Carlin was coming for her. At other points in her life she would have faced him without hesitation, but things had changed in recent months. General Carlin had always been quick for a non-Lightborn, but he was now almost as quick as she was. There was no logic to it. He was probably skilled enough to cut through an entire army with his broadsword. He was also long past an honorable fight. If she decided to face him, he'd have archers and gunmen ready to tear her apart at the first sign of weakness.

The doors of the courthouse were several inches thick and made of solid oak. Once she reached them, she looked back. Sure enough, Carlin was barreling down the street after her. The wind tussled what was left of his hair, and his permanent scowl looked especially menacing today. She didn't have much time.

She tested the door handle. Locked, of course. She sheathed her daggers and placed her palms against the oaken doors, channeling her energy until the wood began to splinter around the locks. She could hear the hoof beats getting louder. Eventually the door deteriorated enough and she kicked it in. She was inside before the splinters landed on the ground.

Lilly ducked under the blades of the guards waiting in the entry hall. On a whim she bolted down the hallway to her right. In no time, she was browsing cells at lightning speed. She stopped when she found one occupied by an ashen-haired girl. "You're getting out early," Lilly said.

"Oh yeah? Good behavior?"

Lilly dug into her pocket and pulled out a long, smooth piece of metal. The rebellion had two chief engineers, James and Jack Jacobson. They'd done a lot of research on Imperial locks and had come to the same conclusion: they were shoddily built and simplistic. A lot of them were also identical. She hoped that their theory about this thin piece of lead was correct. She shoved it into the keyhole and focused her power through it. The vibrations were supposed to make the soft metal morph to fit the lock. After a few seconds, she turned the metal in her hand and the door clicked open.

Bianca Blackmore wrapped Lilly in a tight hug, and Lilly was slightly taken aback. She'd never been hugged by anyone outside of her family. "If you tell your Uncle that I was captured I'm going to hurt you," Bianca said affectionately.

Lilly pulled a belt from inside her blue military coat and handed it to Bianca. "I assumed you'd want these."

Bianca wrapped the belt around her waist and exhaled in relief. "You have no idea how much I've missed these. Felt naked without 'em."

They proceeded down the hallway, away from the entrance in pursuit of a back door. Lilly looked back. "Did it work? Getting captured?"

Bianca sprinted to keep up with Lilly's advanced speed, and Lilly slowed a bit to accommodate her. "It did," Bianca said. "They were going to use me as bait to capture Neil, but a messenger came and told them there was no need. Neil's been captured."

Lilly found the back door and realized it was locked. She fished through her pockets for another piece of lead. "Vapros is alive?"

"It seems so," Bianca said. "Hearing that might not please you in particular but—"

"It's really all right," Lilly said. "I'm happy for you."

She wasn't lying. Neil had lied to her about her brother's death, but that didn't mean she wanted him dead. She often thought of the last moment she'd seen him, hurling from the window of the Cliff, trying to save their lives from the hands of the evil Imperial Doctor.

Bianca looked at her feet. "There's one more thing." The tone made Lilly nervous. "Neil isn't the only one who's still alive. Saewulf... The guards have been whispering about him... He's alive."

Lilly dropped the piece of lead and turned to Bianca. She could hardly get the words out. "But Jonathan...."

"I know it's hard to grasp," said a voice from the other end of the hallway, "that your slave died for nothing."

Lilly gritted her teeth and palmed one of her swords. Maybe she and Bianca would have a chance. Maybe together they could defeat him. Carlin's sword was already out. "It was hard for me to accept as well," he said. "But if working with the Emperor's pet means scrubbing the earth of the Celerius family... Then it's a small price to pay."

Carlin had once spoken of the extermination of all Lightborns, but things were different now. His hatred had been refined. All he cared about was killing Lilly and her uncle, The Wolf. Lilly had the lead piece in the lock and was shaping it, but it would take time. "Can you...?"

"Hold him off?" Bianca asked. "We'll see."

Bianca threw two knives from her belt and palmed two more instantly. Carlin dodged the first and caught the second in his gloved hand. He twisted his malformed lips into a smile. "You're going to let your little friend have all the fun, Lilly?"

Archers filed into the hallway behind him. "You've freed her just to lead her to slaughter?"

He blocked two more knives without the slightest show of effort. Lilly didn't even see his blade moving. He advanced and his men notched their arrows. Bianca threw knives and took down two of his soldiers, but they were replaced before the next knives were in her hands. Lilly finally worked the lock and shoved the door open. As Bianca ducked through it, Lilly caught the two arrows shot at her. She threw them to the ground and followed Bianca. They slammed the door shut, and Bianca jammed a throwing knife into the bolt. Maybe that would stick the door shut for a few moments.

"What now?" Bianca asked.

"Split up?" Lilly asked. "Meet back at the Wolf's camp?"

"Is it in the same place?"

"More or less."

Bianca flung a knife into a soldier charging down the street at them. "Then I suppose I'll meet you there, rich girl. Thanks for the parole."

"Until we meet again, street girl," Lilly responded, smiling.

At one point those had been vicious insults, cast at each other with full malice, but things were different now. Bianca took off running down an alley and Lilly watched her ashen hair disappear. She split off in the opposite direction and drew her short swords. They would taste Carlin's flesh eventually, but not with his army at his back. He'd die alone. That was a promise she made to herself nightly.

3

IMPERIAL MILITARY FORTRESS

NEIL VAPROS

Neil awoke to the sound of the door opening. He groaned to no one in particular. He had no idea how long he'd been half-asleep. It could have been an hour or a week. It was hard to gauge time in this place. Especially since he was losing his mind piece by piece. His skin hadn't all floated away, yet. So maybe it was the same day.

A soldier entered, but something was wrong. His helmet was pulled way over his face and he held a giant metal pan instead of a bowl for soup. "Are you going to hit me with that?" Neil asked.

The soldier walked behind Neil and began shoveling water out of the barred window. He wanted to ask more questions, but he was just glad that they were changing out the water. Being part of a Vapros stew wasn't exactly a good time. "The water level is falling," said the soldier. "Let me know when you have the ability to lift your hands above it."

Neil was having trouble concentrating. "Why?"

"So you can summon fire and melt the chains."

Neil paused. "I get it. Keeping prisoners is hard, but—"

"I need your help, Neil Vapros. The one that I am sworn to protect is in danger."

Neil grasped at a memory back from his days in Altryon. "It's you," Neil realized out loud. "You're the man in the mask. The one who's been protecting Lilly."

Silence.

"You saved my life. The Pig was going to kill me, and you killed him first."

"He was going to go after Lilly. I had no choice."

Neil tried to lift his hands above the water, but he just couldn't reach. The soldier furiously scooped water and sent it out of the window. "Why are you freeing me?"

"You are in a military fortress near Abington currently. Lilly is there, in the main village, and she is surrounded."

"Lilly Celerius doesn't want my help." Neil said, trying not to sound too pouty. "She can take care of herself."

"She thinks she can, but she has much to learn. Please, Neil. I need your help. She needs you."

"Why aren't you there now?"

"I cannot fight an entire army on my own."

"And I can?"

"I'm just a man, Neil. I need the Phoenix."

Neil felt his power building in his chest. Even with his hands below the water, they began to warm. "Lower the water level and I'll go after Lilly," he promised.

Lilly's protector shoveled water out of the window for what felt like an hour. "Why not just break my chains yourself?" Neil asked.

"I want it to look like you escaped on your own, through your own sheer force of will. I don't want anyone to know that you had help."

"You should watch out for Saewulf."

"He's upstairs, in his bed," Lilly's protector said. "If you stay quiet, I don't think he'll be able to stop you from escaping."

"You think?"

"That's the best I can offer."

That was a good enough answer for Neil. Eventually he could raise his arms out of the water. That's all it took for him to summon the fire from within. Neil concentrated fully on his shackles, weakening them with his fire. Eventually the metal links grew red hot, and he slammed them together. His left bond shattered and then he focused on the remaining restraint. Eventually it became easy to break and he tore free. Neil turned around to get a better look at the soldier, but he was gone. Neil blinked in amazement. He'd been there a second ago. Maybe he'd left while Neil was busy breaking the chains. The man moved like a shadow. Neil felt bad for doubting Lilly's claims of being followed and protected. Evidently, someone was firing arrows into her enemies left and right.

Neil didn't have a moment to dwell. It was time to escape. The door was open, and Neil pulled himself through the top half with considerable effort. He collapsed the second his feet hit the ground. He was malnourished and hadn't stood in a very long time. Using his fire had also been a large drain on his energy. The feeling was familiar. He remembered being lost and exhausted in the Taurlum mansion about a year ago. Things had come a long way since then. Sheer adrenaline brought him to his feet, and he surveyed the hallway. His cell was isolated against one wall. A hallway ran in both directions. Neil painfully lumbered down the hallway on the right and once around the corner he found a steel door. Thankfully, it was unlocked and he slipped through. There were two guards waiting, but Neil dealt with them effortlessly despite his weakened state.

What Neil did not deal with effortlessly, however, was the guard that came around the corner and caught him in the act. The guard opened his mouth to scream and Neil launched a fireball into his torso.

The guard slammed into the wall and then to the floor. The metallic parts of his armor clanged and echoed off the stone walls. Neil cringed. He had to escape now. Saewulf might have heard that, and if anything was going to stand in Neil's way of freedom, it was the psychic. Neil dragged himself through two more doors and found himself outside in a small courtyard. There was a gate and a guard tower, but Neil's power of materialization allowed him to get to the top. Once he reached it, he eliminated the two guards manning it. This had been almost too easy.

Before Neil could pat himself on the back, a loud alarm bell rang out. He turned to locate the sound and realized there was another guard tower he'd neglected. It didn't matter now. He was on top of the gate and Abington was below, looming in the distance. The fortress was on a hill overlooking the village.

Neil heard the door to the prison fly off of its hinges, and he leapt from the top of the guard tower. Saewulf was here. If Neil didn't escape, he wouldn't live to fulfill his promise to Lilly's protector. Neil used his power of fire to fly down the hill toward Abington. Maybe fly wasn't the right word. It was more like guided falling.

Behind him the wall of the gate was obliterated by Saewulf's raw power. Showers of concrete rained down as Saewulf made his own exit. He roared in fury, but the noise was drowned out by the wind in Neil's ears. Neil risked a look back over his shoulder. Saewulf was a quickly vanishing speck on the hill. Neil knew that guards would die for letting him escape. He wondered if Lilly's protector would be among them when judgment came.

It wasn't difficult to find out where Lilly and Bianca were once he got to Abington. He landed on a high rooftop and watched the soldiers scramble. Clearly they were trying to out maneuver someone. Neil could see General Carlin in the distance commanding troops. Carlin sent them in opposite directions around the blocks of the city, evidence that they were trying to corner someone a lot quicker than they were. Neil used his fire to travel from rooftop to rooftop. He knew the risk of being seen was high, so he jumped without the aid of his powers when he could.

Before long Neil saw a blue speck darting through the streets with extraordinary speed. There was no doubt it was Lilly. He followed, but soon he noticed a problem. As she evaded capture by squadron after squadron, other groups of soldiers blocked off the area and moved inward through the streets. Soon she'd be trapped. Neil saw Lilly come to a full stop in the middle of a road. What a miracle it was that he'd recognized her. Her hair was short now, barely past her ears, and not flowing over her shoulders like it once had.

Soldiers came at her from both sides, armed with arrows and rifles alike. She turned back and forth with two blades drawn. That was new. Apparently she'd abandoned her long thin sword for two short swords. A few guards notched arrows, and Neil could see Carlin cutting through alleys and streets to get to Lilly.

Neil focused his energy. He could hear Carlin shouting below him. "Do not take her alive! Fire! Fire everything! Don't stop until she stops twitching."

Arrows and bullets flew, and Lilly dodged the ones she could. Neil let the fire explode out of his hands and propelled himself toward her. A bullet tore into her shoulder before he could get there, but that was the only damage she sustained from the soldiers. Neil tackled her straight through the decaying door of a nearby shop. They rolled onto the floor, and she howled with pain. He was almost sure he heard a crack. "You broke my spine," she said on the verge of a scream.

Guilt surged through him. This wasn't the first time he'd broken someone's spine. Lilly whimpered in pain while her spine healed itself. Miraculously, Neil was unharmed. Soldiers tried to stream through the doorway, but a few well-placed fireballs deterred them. Neil faced Lilly. "Are you all right?"

"You. Broke. My. Spine."

"I'll take that as a yes. We have to go."

He grabbed her by the hand and led her out the back door. They were in another street, which wasn't ideal, but at least they weren't dodging bullets or arrows. Neil knew roughly where they were from studying the streets from above, and he pointed down an alley. "Go that way and then take a right. If you move fast enough you should be able to get out of the city before the Empire locks it down."

Lilly's spine must have been fully fixed because she straightened it to glare into his eyes. "We have much more to discuss, Neil Vapros."

"I can't wait. Where's Bianca?"

"Other side of the city. She went running past the courthouse. She was trying to make it out too."

Neil focused his energy in his hands.

"You better not die before I get the chance to eviscerate you," Lilly said.

He grinned and bowed to her slightly. "Of course, Miss. Love the hair by the way."

He launched himself back up to the rooftops and without delay flew across the city in pursuit of Bianca. He looked for anomalies in the troop formations. He found them soon enough. There were three squadrons surrounding a stone building. They kicked down doors and broke windows, hunting someone inside. Neil flew to the roof and found an open hatch. What kind of building was this? It was stone and as tall as many of the buildings in Altryon. This was an anomaly for the villages of Volteria. He poked his head through the hatch and saw the seal of the Imperial Bank on the wall. Further down he caught a glimpse of ashen hair. It was her.

Neil jumped through the hatch and used his fire to land several stories below. He didn't fully take stock of the situation before diving in headfirst. Bianca was battling with four or five guards. They'd probably already been inside the bank when she locked it down. Neil started by going to the doors and melting the inside of the locks with one finger. With any luck that would slow down additional pursuers. Neil turned around to assist Bianca with the guards, only to see that one had his sword to her neck. She saw Neil for the first time, and he saw her. Her eyes welled up as he lit a fireball in his hand.

"Stand down Lightborn!" the soldier roared. "I will slice her throat if you make a move."

Neil's head was swimming. He was tired and sluggish. He hadn't eaten, hadn't rested, and was using energy he didn't have. "Trust me," Neil said to the soldier, "if there's one person that you don't want to be right now, it's the guy standing in between the two of us." He pointed at Bianca tiredly.

"You don't look so good," the soldier hissed. "Really think you've got the strength to put me down?"

"No," Neil admitted. "But I don't have to."

"What?" When he looked back to his sword, it wasn't against

Bianca's neck. She'd always been light-footed, so saving her was only a matter of turning someone's head. Before the soldier could adjust, Bianca launched a throwing knife into his chest. Neil followed it up with his largest fireball yet. The soldier was thrown into the wall so hard his armor cracked.

Bianca dropped the rest of her knives and stared at Neil. He was losing control of his legs. Every last drop of focus and energy had leaked out of him, along with the fire. He reached one hand out toward her.

"Neil?" she asked. "Are you...?"

He couldn't understand her after a few words. His face burned and the world went black. He hardly felt his body hit the ground when his legs failed him.

4

THE RUSTY WHEEL INN

RHYS VAPROS

"It makes no sense for warriors to grow old." Rhys pressed his pen against his wrist, desperately trying to dull the voice inside of his head. *"Fruit rots, animals grow senile, and warriors go soft... Or drink themselves to death."*

Rhys looked up from his book to the other side of the inn. Darius sat there, eyes fixed on *a Rough History of Lightborns.* It was possible that he was reading, but it was more likely he was just staring off into nothing. *"You're just jealous because you died young,"* Rhys shot back.

"Did I?" asked the Imperial Doctor. *"I have to say, I feel very much alive. I'm invigorated by the amount of information in your brain. I could spend all day learning up here."*

"Do it silently," Rhys commanded.

The young Vapros boy had considered all possibilities. Two had risen to the top of the pack, and in recent weeks they'd become his primary theories. It was entirely possible that the Doctor had driven him mad a month ago with the use of torture and manipulation, and now Rhys was imagining voices. It was also possible that the Doctor had used an enhanced ability to transfer his annoying mind into Rhys's head before his death. Either way, things were bleak.

If it did turn out that Rhys wasn't insane, the Doctor's constant commentary would certainly change that. He tried to focus on something else because clearly his books weren't helping. He looked back at Darius. His friend, the Taurlum giant, slurped down the last drops of ale from his mug. After losing both Josephine, who'd been like a second mother, and Anastasia, his love interest, he'd grown even more cynical and aggressive. It didn't help he hadn't been sober in a fortnight.

They'd been hiding out in Abington under the Empire's nose for weeks. There was rebel activity here and there of course, but they'd made the mutual decision to rest up and recover from the traumas of recent months.

Rhys stood up and approached the table, his small metal foot clanking against the floorboards. Darius looked up at him. They were currently living at this inn for lack of a better place to lie low, but they didn't speak much anymore. They'd made a silent agreement to be alone with themselves. "What are you reading?" Rhys asked. His own voice sounded unfamiliar in his mouth.

"The Lightborn book," Darius said.

"I know. Who are you reading about?"

Darius looked at the page again. He ruffled his blonde hair. "I guess I've forgotten," he said. "I've been... I've had too much of this." He rattled his mug.

Rhys leaned over the book. At the top of the page, the Wolf's neat writing said: *Nikolai Taurlum.*

"Oh," Rhys said.

Darius looked away, most likely to hide the pain in his eyes. The Imperial Doctor had been using his uncle Nikolai as a pet and a weapon to torture people. This was the primary reason Rhys hadn't told Darius about his new mental state. What would Darius say if he knew that the man who had turned his uncle into a monster was inside Rhys's head? *"I hardly did anything to Nikolai Taurlum. The man was an aggressive simpleton before I met him. He might have dropped ten I.Q. points, but he was well-fed at least."*

"That's repulsive," Rhys said. It took him a moment to realize he'd said it out loud.

"What is?" Darius asked. "I'm not allowed to have a drink?"

"No, no, no," Rhys said. He rubbed his temple. "The…" He looked down at the book. "The drawing is repulsive. It looks like the Wolf put more time into the other ones."

Darius looked at the book. "Oh really?" He paused for a second. "You could be right. The face is a little weird."

Rhys nodded. "I agree. Really weird."

Darius squinted at the paper again, focusing on the drawing this time.

He turned another page and Rhys glimpsed the entry. It was the page about Eric Vapros. This had been one of Rhys and Darius's favorites. Eric had the ability to drain power from other Lightborns and his lust for power eventually led him to drain his family members. In a rare act of collaboration the Taurlum, Vapros, and Celerius had put aside their differences to have him bound and killed.

Rhys always thought of this as evidence the feud could be overcome, but his last few weeks with Darius shook him. They seemed far closer to strangers than the friends they'd become since banding together to escape the Empire.

"Did you hear?" Darius mumbled. "Lilly was here. In Abington. Yesterday."

"What?"

"That's why the streets were all closed down."

"Oh," Rhys said. "Did she…?"

"She got away. Maybe we oughta think about…" Darius trailed off.

"Rejoining the rebels?"

"Right."

They made eye contact for a moment, then both looked off. "Or maybe we could wait a bit to—"

"Recover. Rest up," Rhys said.

"Right." Darius stared at his near empty mug. "Right."

Rhys knew what they were both thinking. Were they even any good to the rebels anymore? Darius was drunk and depressed all the time, and Rhys was crippled and insane. How had they fallen so far?

"Okay so... Maybe next week," Darius concluded with a final chug of his drink.

Rhys took this opportunity to return to his table and his book. *"You know what you'd love to read?"* the Doctor said.

Rhys didn't respond.

"The pain index is just sitting there, in my old lab. It's filled with decades of carefully compiled research and experiments. And the best part is, I was almost done."

Rhys didn't respond. His dynamic with the Doctor was odd. He had a choice of what to say and what not to say. If he didn't want the Doctor to hear his private thoughts, he wouldn't, which was very fortunate. Rhys desperately wanted to get a look at the pain index, and every time the Doctor brought it up it became a little harder to squelch his curiosity. Rhys wasn't exactly sure where this curiosity came from and he hoped that it wasn't the Doctor's private influence.

"We could go tonight. The fool is always either drunk or hung over," the Doctor said, louder this time. *"Don't you want to see? Was I just a madman? Or was I a brilliant scientific mind? Unappreciated and cut down before my time."*

"I thought warriors weren't meant to grow old."

"I was never a warrior," the Doctor persisted. *"I was a scientist, and so are you, Rhys. You understand the thirst to learn, to improve the world, and to make a difference... At any cost."*

"Not at any cost." Rhys wanted to make sure the Doctor understood that above all else.

"Not yet, I suppose. But you will."

Rhys pulled his book close and tried to fill his mind with the knowledge. He'd picked the most mundane book possible: *The History of Misty Hollow's Bridges*. Maybe with enough of it he could drown out the Doctor's voice. Despite his desire to do so, he knew it wouldn't work. The Doctor was spinning a web in his mind. And while it felt possible to clear the cobwebs, he knew if he ever stopped the Doctor might take control. Rhys shuddered and hoped that the Doctor couldn't feel it. If the madman sensed any fear he would exploit it. After all, that was his greatest talent.

5

THE SLUMS

HAROLD THORNE

Adam Gregory was called Iron Adam for a reason. Even though he wasn't a Taurlum, he might as well have been. Years of factory work had solidified his muscles and his wide shoulders added to his box-shaped form. Anyone watching him rifle through papers in this abandoned butcher shop might have found it funny. His shoulders were hunched over so his head wouldn't drag across the ceiling, and he struggled to organize the delicate parchment with his massive hands.

His face was enough to deter any comedy, though. His eyes sunk deep into his head and he looked at the people who had gathered, almost hopelessly. "Was anyone followed?" His voice was like the sound of a mountain moving.

"You're being paranoid," a worker said. He was a little too loud, and people flinched when he spoke.

"He's not being paranoid enough. Do you know what Thorne would do to us? If he knew?"

"He can't go around slaughtering his workers," Iron Adam said, seizing the attention of the room. "He's not royalty."

"He kills men every day," someone grumbled. "We either drop dead in his assembly line, or we die in the streets because he withholds our wages."

"We need to join the brotherhood," someone whispered.

"We need to start the union," Iron Adam persisted. "It's our only hope. We can't beg for power. We need to take it."

The people sat on the floor or in the few chairs that could be found. Their meetings were always cramped and uncomfortable, but maybe that was a good thing. It kept people awake. It kept them alert. "Thorne needs men to work in his factory. If we unionize, he can't force us to work. We can negotiate as a group."

"Thorne will lose profits."

The unenthusiastic voice came from a boy sitting in the middle. Iron Adam squinted and saw that it was the green-skinned boy. Many avoided him simply because of the way he looked. His skin had a pale verdant hue and thin red veins stretched over his whole body. Black messy hair swept over his forehead giving him a boyish look. No one knew what had made him this way, but it didn't stop the other factory workers from poking fun at him. They called him the "drowned one" because he looked like a body fished out of a river. Some called him "Moss," or "Leaf" and a few went with "Lizard." Iron Adam was partial to Leaf, because the boy never had a firm opinion on anything. He drifted. He always seemed detached from his own body. Or maybe he was bored.

"Of course Thorne will lose profits, Leaf," Iron Adam said. "I fail to see how that matters. The man owns every factory in Altryon. He's not going to starve if we are able to eat."

"You don't understand," Leaf said.

"What don't I understand?"

"Thorne is a businessman."

"Yes."

"The best business man in Altryon."

"Perhaps." Iron Adam was becoming annoyed.

"What's cheaper? Paying every worker in the city a living wage... Or making an example of twenty men?"

The papers crumpled slightly in Iron Adam's hand. "I don't..." He struggled to find his words. "He won't be able to make that choice. The union will be formed in secret."

Leaf reached into his coat pocket with skeletal fingers and drew out a small canister. "You don't keep secrets from Thorne. Thorne knows his business. Thorne knows every cog and every gear of his business. And you are his business."

Perhaps everyone was too shocked to react, but no one stopped Leaf from pulling the pin on the canister. Black smoke billowed from the top and the men around Leaf collapsed, wheezing and screaming. Leaf just sat there as he was engulfed in smoke. Not only was he immune to the weapon, it looked like he didn't mind that it was going off.

Iron Adam leapt to the back of the shop in an attempt to flee. He heard the front door being kicked in and tripped in his haste to escape. Before he knew it, two men grabbed him by the arms and attempted to restrain him. He threw one off and tried to run again, but cold steel slammed against the back of his knee and he heard it crack. The smoke was already dissipating when they turned Adam over to face his opponent.

"Adam Gregory. One of my finest employees. Such a shame you've decided to be so unreasonable." Harold Thorne removed his gas mask and patted his stylish hair back into place. His curled mustache had stayed annoyingly unruffled throughout his siege. "Thank you for providing an entrance, Leaf," Harold said.

Leaf shrugged. "Sure."

Leaf had done an admirable job. Thorne had only brought three thugs and even with his new invention, the revolver, they wouldn't have stood a chance against twenty desperate men. Leaf had considerably shifted the terms of the fight.

Thorne smiled at Iron Adam. "So I really am curious. What did you hope to accomplish here today? You thought my employees would betray me and unionize behind my back?"

"These men have no love for you." Adam spat at him, but it missed its mark. Thorne was unfazed.

"I've had my employees try to unionize many times, but I've never really understood the concept. Could you lend me a hand?" Thorne's eyes were empty and calculating.

Adam nodded slowly. He was skeptical, as he had the right to be. Harold Thorne understood unions well. At any sniff of them, he'd eliminate workers and potential threats. "So... we form a group and demand certain rights as a unit and not as individuals."

"And I can't very well fire my entire workforce, can I?" Thorne asked.

"No sir." Iron Adam tried to remain resolute.

Thorne snapped his fingers and his men dragged over a worker. "So let me just be sure that I understand... Mr....?"

"Thompson," the man blubbered.

"Mr. Thompson asks for a raise and for shorter hours." He pulled a revolver from inside of his jacket and fired a bullet straight through Mr. Thomson's forehead. "I can spare one worker." He craned his neck to observe the damage. "Clearly."

Iron Adam looked like he was trying to speak, but his tongue froze in his mouth. Thorne smirked. "So say you all decide to rise up against me. Every last one of you..." His men all raised their revolvers. Leaf pulled another canister from his pocket. "What am I to do? Kill every single worker? I couldn't possibly do that? Could I?"

Iron Adam heard the revolvers cocking. "Please don't do this," he whispered. "You were a good man at one point. You were charitable. You gave to the poor."

Harold nodded. "I was. But that was when I had competition." He nodded to his men, and bullets began flying.

When the smoke cleared and the terrible noise ceased, Iron Adam was all that remained of the workers. He lunged at Harold, but was struck to the ground by one of his men. "You are an evil, immoral man," Adam said while shuddering.

Harold's eyebrows narrowed. "Immoral? No, no, no, Adam. I'm afraid you don't understand good business. Good business isn't immoral, it's *amoral*. I don't hate you people. I just don't really care what happens to you."

"These people had families!" Adam was screaming now. "You call this amoral?"

"I call it risk management." Harold fired another shot from his revolver into Adam's face.

He paused and admired the havoc they'd wrought. "Risk is eliminated as it appears and gain is...?"

He gestured to Leaf.

"Maximized," the boy said.

"Exactly."

Thorne pocketed his revolver and turned to his men. One of them pulled a ledger from his pocket. "We can have these particular men replaced immediately."

"Good," Thorne said. "The revolvers have passed their initial tests and so has Leaf. Between these and Carlin's potions, we're about to make a killing. Schedule a meeting with the Emperor."

Harold approached Leaf and examined the boy for side effects of the gas. He looked unaffected, as per usual. "Boy am I lucky I found you," Thorne cooed.

"What should I tell the Emperor you want to speak about?"

"Tell him I feel like diversifying. I'm entering a new market." Harold touched his face and found that it was splattered with blood. He pulled out a handkerchief.

"Which one?"

Harold wiped away the evidence of his crime and shoved the handkerchief into his pocket. "Death," Thorne said, a small smile playing on his lips. "We're getting into death."

6

IMPERIAL MILITARY CAMP

THE MARKSMAN

Everything imitates nature. Victor Venator knew that better than anyone. Sure, civilized humans liked to think that their ways were best, but they had no perfect systems, not like he saw in the forests. Nature was perfect when undisturbed. The animal populations controlled each other, not for gold or power, but in pursuit of the most basic desire: survival. The Marksman let out a long shuddery breath. That's what he needed too. He needed to survive.

The military camps surrounding Abington imitated beehives, with workers streaming from tent to tent eager to satisfy the needs of the queen. In this case, the queen being Carlin. He heard the General go from tent to tent, assaulting and berating his men. The Marksman scoffed. Fear only drove men so far, and Carlin's lunacy would inspire desertion before devotion. "Sir we need to talk about these letters from the Emperor!"

SMACK.

The soldier would remember that, and it would keep him in line, for a time. But soldiers were not like worker bees, even if their bases were like hives. Bees would sacrifice themselves at a moment's notice to protect the hive and their queen. These men clung to Carlin and the Empire because it was the larger and more violent force. One side would not see the summer, and these men had gambled their lives serving a man whose brain was rotting away.

Carlin stormed into his tent and ripped his breastplate off. He threw his sword to the ground and screamed into his hands. The Marksman didn't need super human hearing to know that it was a roar of pure pain. "General," the Marksman whispered.

Carlin turned, eyes bloodshot, his deformed lip twitching. "You," he spat. "Victor Venator." He opened his arms wide, a taunt. "The last remaining member of the Pack."

The Marksman's remaining hand curled into a fist, but he controlled his breathing. No signs of weakness. Not in front of someone who consumed it to survive. "My brother, the Hyena, lives."

Carlin snorted. "For the son of the Imperial Doctor, you really are painfully unaware of the current events. The savage is dead."

"Dead?" How had he not heard this yet?

"Decapitated."

"By whom?"

"Lilly Celerius."

There was an extra heartbeat in that moment. The Marksman wondered if it was Carlin's hatred for his sworn enemy or a bold faced lie. "Speaking of..." the Marksman said. "I'm here today on very urgent business."

"You don't have any more business with the Empire. The Pack is dead and gone." He looked the Marksman up and down. "Maybe once we would have had use for you, but now..."

Carlin didn't need to remind him. The Marksman rarely thought of anything besides his missing hand. Bianca Blackmore had taken everything from him. "The world's greatest shot can never hold a weapon ever again," Carlin snorted. "That's ironic, isn't it?"

"Harold Thorne has prepared augmentations for me. They're being sent to this very camp." The Marksman didn't let anything show in his face. Carlin was out for blood from anyone who could provide it. "Soon I will return to fighting strength."

"You don't look at fighting weight," Carlin said. "You look thin. And sickly."

The Marksman nodded. There was no use in hiding it. "My father's injections."

Carlin's tent was massive and lavishly decorated. He even had a feather bed and soft silk blankets. The Marksman could smell the feathers. Carlin removed his gauntlets and tore off other parts of his armor as he spoke. "Ah yes. The Doctor's fabled injections. One month is it? Before you die?" Another taunt.

"Yes," the Marksman said. "I've searched every one of his hideouts for a recipe, but there is none. I managed to find another month's supply. I am to take it tomorrow."

"So why have you come here, savage?" Carlin asked. "Are you giving out invitations to your funeral?"

"No," the Marksman said. Carlin would be a tricky subject to blackmail. He had to apply pressure, but Carlin was brittle and coarse, like tree bark. He would not bend far. "General, I know what makes you so fast. I know what makes you so angry. I know how you catch arrows and move your broadsword as if it is without weight."

He heard Carlin's heartbeat racing. Pumping blood through his veins. Not all of it *his* blood though. "I don't know what you mean," Carlin said. There was a knife on his belt and he was holding it now, casually enough.

"Don't lie to me. I can smell it on you."

Carlin stood abruptly. "I will slaughter you, boy."

The Marksman didn't mind being called boy. No words from this man could bruise his ego. "You might not know this, but Lightborn blood all smells different. Your skin smells like common man, but you leak power. Power that is not your own."

Carlin unsheathed the knife. "Careful."

"I need some."

"I don't know what you're talking about. Keep your Venator tricks away from me." Saliva dripped though his torn lip.

"I need Anthony Celerius's blood."

The demand cleared the room. Carlin must have heard silence, but the Marksman heard the General's heartbeat racing wildly. He smelled the sweat on his brow. "I..." He sighed and returned to his feather bed. "It's not Anthony Celerius's blood. Not anymore."

"No?"

"No. Thomas Celerius. I had his body drained too." Carlin gritted his teeth when he spoke, trying to chew through his shame. "It works far better than his brother's."

The Marksman had been leaning on one of the supports, but he walked forward to stand in the center of the tent. "You inject it?"

"No," Carlin said. "It nearly killed me when I tried that. I had Harold Thorne make it into a potion, mixed with alcohol. It absorbs slowly and stays with me for longer."

"Harold Thorne? Why didn't you have my father mix it?"

"Your father mixed your medicines. Where's that left you?" Carlin looked vulnerable, but all humans oozed vulnerability when Victor looked at them. Sometimes they just didn't know it. "I can't give you any."

"Why?"

Carlin held up a gloved hand with two fingers up. "Two reasons. First of all, I don't have much left. I need it to fight the remaining abominations. I'm on a clock too, Victor. If I run out before they die I won't stand a chance."

"Why not?"

"The withdrawals are..." Carlin assessed the Marksman and Victor heard his heart skip a beat. "Powerful."

"What's the second reason?"

"Second of all, it doesn't heal." He waved his fingers over his upper lip. "If it did, I wouldn't still look like this."

"I have to try something," the Marksman said.

Carlin said nothing.

"I know how you feel, General." Was it possible to get on this man's good side? "You are at war with your insides. You hate the Celerius, maybe more than anyone has hated anything, yet you fill your veins with their blood. My body rots and I fight to keep it from expiring. You must feel the same chemical burn in your mouth that I do."

Victor didn't even see Carlin rise. Suddenly he was in front of Victor with the knife to his throat. "The Celerius do not deserve their gifts. I use it as a means to an end and nothing more. When they are all dead, their blood will be burned along with them. I gain no pleasure from this, but it's what I have to do."

That was a lie. This time it was much more obvious. Carlin's pupils dilated whenever he moved. He loved the power that rested in each and every one of his steps. "All right. Either way, I must try some to see if it will save my life."

Carlin laughed. "You're of no use to me, fool. You're a sickly, one armed, former assassin with one month to live."

"I am my father's son. I have information. Information that I will trade for one single sip."

"What kind of information?"

"I know how to kill Lilly Celerius." This was Carlin's greatest weakness, and exploiting it and applying pressure was crippling him. "She walks away from every battle with you because she can heal. The benefit of being a true Celerius."

"And you know how to stop that." Carlin's breathing was louder now. He couldn't hide his excitement. "You know how?"

The Marksman gave him a courteous smile. "I do," he said. "For a sip."

7

REBEL BASE CAMP

NEIL VAPROS

Every time Neil awoke, he awoke angry. He hadn't asked to be a prophet or a chosen one, and it wasn't exactly convenient. Not only had he been pushed from bloody conflict to bloody conflict, but if Saewulf was telling the truth, then he was also marked for dead. The least the man with the Golden Light could do was show up and offer the slightest bit of guidance.

Neil had drifted in and out of consciousness for days. Most of the time Bianca was there, holding his hand or running her fingers through his hair. Some days he saw glimpses of people with him. Once he even thought he glimpsed the Wolf's blue coat fluttering around the tent.

The day he awoke fully he received the visit he hoped for. However, this time Neil was almost certain it was a hallucination. Maybe it had always been some sort of dream. The Man with the Golden Light stood flickering by the side of his bed. Neil tried to reach up to touch him, and the Man placed a finger on Neil's chest over his heart. It felt sharp and dug deep into his flesh.

With a start, Neil's eyes opened and he gasped for air. Placed on his chest where the Man's finger had been was the tip of a long dagger. Lilly was balancing it with one finger lazily. "Morning."

"Morning," Neil said. "Bring breakfast?"

"No."

"Gonna assassinate me?"

She sighed. "No. Probably not."

"Disappointing. I feel like hell."

She lifted the dagger and leaned back in her chair. "Do you now?"

He did. His mouth had never felt drier and every part of his body ached, especially his ribs. He knew it would be a while before he could fight again. When he leaned up he realized his chest was bandaged tightly. So were his knees and wrists. He'd been confined to a small military cot in what he could only assume was one of the Wolf's military tents. "Where am I?"

"Rebel base camp. Somewhere between Abington and Brightbow, lodged between a forest and another forest."

"I thought Shipwreck Bay was base camp."

"It was," Lilly said, "The Wolf is anxious though. He thinks it's best to be on the move constantly. He says we're in the 'endgame.'"

"My, my," Neil said. He could tell he sounded disdainful. He and the Wolf had quite a bit to discuss. "What about the two of us?" He pointed to her sword. "This the endgame?"

"We're certainly never going to be friends, Vapros."

Neil paused, gears inside his head clicking away. "Well, then I should probably apologize."

"Really?" she asked with a little hostility.

"Yes. I'm sorry I kept the truth about Jennifer and Edward from you. I never wanted to hurt you, I just..." He struggled to articulate this feeling. "That love you have for Edward? That's the same love I have for Jennifer. But she might have been the least liked person I've ever met. People feared her, abandoned her, abused her."

"She was a killer. Through and through." It sounded like she'd said that to herself and not to Neil. She was gripping the knife though.

"You're right. And she killed Edward. And it ruined her. It killed her innocence. You might have loved Edward, but so did Jennifer. She loved him more than anything. And she lost herself when she lost him."

"So who's to blame?" Lilly asked, almost pleading now.

"My father? Your father? Whoever started the feud?"

"Unsatisfying," Lilly groaned. "That's so unsatisfying."

"So is all of this," Neil said. "The feud always has been unsatisfying. We'd kill you and you'd kill us and we'd sob and grieve, but we'd never feel any better. There's no satisfaction in killing."

Lilly seemed to perceive something in his voice. "Who'd you kill, Vapros?"

"What do you mean?" Neil tried to keep his mind from wandering.

"I know a lot about killing. I hear it. Who'd you kill?"

Neil thought of Mama Tridenti. "Someone who deserved it. Someone who would have killed me."

"So it was worth it?"

"No," Neil said. "I have trouble believing it ever is."

Lilly sheathed her dagger. "Well, if I had the chance to—"

"Kill Carlin?" Neil asked. "Everything would be better?"

Lilly glared at him, then softened. "It has to, Neil. It has to. I don't have..." She trailed off, tearing up. "It can't just be like this. Not forever."

Neil laid his head back on the pillow. He didn't know how to answer. He settled on changing the subject. "I met your protector."

"What?" Lilly asked, perking up.

"You were right. Someone is looking out for you. He broke me out of Saewulf's prison."

Lilly shifted, her eyes alight. "Who is it? Did you know him?"

"No. He sounded the same as when he killed the Pig last year. But I couldn't place the voice. Couldn't really see him either." Lilly didn't respond. After a few moments she pulled her short sword from her belt and ran a finger over the blade. "Who do you think it is?" Neil asked.

"Anthony," Lilly said without hesitation.

"Anthony Celerius?" Neil asked. "I know his voice. It wasn't him."

"I'm not convinced."

"He's dead."

"We never got a body."

"Yeah, but Carlin did."

She glared at him, and he tried to form an apology. She shook her head before he could. "It's fine," she said with an exhale. "I'm just... worked up."

Eventually Lilly sheathed her sword and stood to leave. "Do you hate me?" Neil asked before she reached the open flap of the tent.

"No." she said. "Which is remarkable because I have a never ending supply of that."

"Hate?"

She nodded. "I'm good at reading people, but only when they have something I have."

"And what do we both have?"

"Brokenness," Lilly said. She took a long, measured pause without looking at Neil. "I'm sorry for all of your losses."

"And I for yours."

She left without a final word. Seeing Lilly pained him. She was so full of passion and aching. He could tell she never knew where to put it. Except for her undying revenge plot against Carlin. Neil wondered if ending him would finally do something for her. He wondered if she'd ever be able to move on.

It was nearly an hour later when the Wolf arrived. He didn't look surprised to see Neil awake. Neil remembered that he could use sound waves to survey his camp. He'd probably felt Neil moving. "Neil Vapros, my good man," he said with a large grin. "It's been *quite* a while. You look shockingly alive."

"You're shocked?" Neil countered. He could see the Wolf slightly set off balance by his tone. "Aren't I the chosen one? I can't die."

"Ah," the Wolf said, "well, yes."

The Wolf looked as Neil remembered him. He was handsome, resolute, and strong with a straight spine and iron jaw. His beard had grown out a bit, making him look gruffer and younger.

However, something was different. Now Neil saw something new. The Wolf had a pair of strategist's eyes that assessed Neil and scanned him cautiously. The Wolf approached slowly. "You've taken quite a beating."

"Indeed. Saewulf was not kind."

The Wolf gritted his teeth. "So the psychic's still kicking."

"Yes indeed. Kicking quite hard."

The Wolf looked deep in thought. "That complicates things." He approached a far off table. "Want a drink?"

"Have any water?"

The Wolf pulled his personal canteen from his belt and passed it to Neil. He took a swig. "When we have the time I'd like to hear absolutely everything about how you came to be here," the Wolf said.

"Oh, we'll discuss," Neil said. "You wouldn't believe the things I've learned."

This one was a barb and the Wolf sensed it. "Feeling all right, Neil?"

"After Josephine's funeral you told me something that really stuck with me." Neil sat up. He was fuming.

"I told you that you were burdened with purpose," the Wolf said.

"You did. And you told me that the only way out of this was through it. That if I wanted to be with Bianca, I could fight my way through this war and be with her."

"Yes."

"And then you told me your prophecy." Neil was on his feet, despite the pain. "My life will bring about the new nation."

"Yes," the Wolf said.

"That's what you said to me."

"Yes."

"And that's how it was told to you? Verbatim?"

The Wolf clenched his fists. He lowered his head and Neil saw shame in his eyes. "Ah," the Wolf said, "I see."

"My life?" Neil said again, begging now. "My life?"

The Wolf was silent, and Neil could see those eyes again. Dissecting him. Looking for a strategy. Looking for a way out. "Do you know how much I've sacrificed?" he finally asked. "What I would give?"

"It's very clear what you would give." Neil's hands were smoking. "My. Life."

"May we speak with some civility?" Neil had never seen the Wolf afraid before.

"No," Neil said. "Civility landed me here. I don't want to be figurehead of a cause that's going to kill me. I don't want to be a pawn of a man who is leading me to slaughter. Speak with a little rage, Steven Celerius. Speak with a little honesty."

"Fine," the Wolf said, pivoting now. "Do you know how many men I see die every year?" Neil didn't respond in time. "More than you could possibly imagine. Last year it was thousands. The war was different. We sprang up two or three times per year. But now... Now that it's all out war, I see killing fields and hardly anything else. Do you know what I would do to see that stop? Do you know what I would do to protect these men and women?"

"What?" Neil spat.

"Anything. Anything short of surrender."

"You're not sorry?" Neil's ribs ached and he was wheezing. "No apology? You just do what you have to do?"

"I am sorry," the Wolf said. "I am sorrier than you could possibly know. I have an immeasurable amount of blood on my hands. More than anyone else you know, I'd say. And nothing has gutted me more than this lie has."

"More deception." Neil hobbled back in the direction of his bed. "More lies."

"Neil you must understand." He took a step forward, and Neil's hand ignited. The Wolf took the step back. "I'm not even sure if I believe in the prophecy. Or if it's you that it describes."

"Saewulf believes it," Neil said. "He wants to kill me for Altryon and you want to kill me for Volteria. What's the difference between the two of you?"

"I gave you a choice."

"No. No, you did not."

"Well, I'm giving you one now. You want to leave? Leave. I won't hold it against you. You want to hide? Hide. That's not cowardice. It's understandable. But if you want to stay, stay. This is not my rebellion. I just happen to be in charge of it. This is a rebellion of thousands of good people who want to be heard and treated like human beings. You can fight for them without fighting for me. But if you leave, you are fighting for nothing and no one."

Neil wanted to say that he'd never wanted to be a fighter, but he was exhausted. He stared at the Wolf, sizing up his former hero. Who was this man? Had Neil ever known? He thought back to the first time he'd seen the General fight. He'd bobbed and weaved through sword swings like a dancer and bent out of the way whenever he felt resistance. He changed directions seamlessly when he realized his current one wouldn't serve him. Now Neil could see that this is how he spoke as well—with an inherent need for survival at any cost.

The tent flap opened, and Bianca peered in. He wondered if she could feel the tension in the room. When she saw that he was awake, she ran to him. She wrapped an arm around him, but stopped when he winced in pain. "How are you alive, you idiot?"

He smiled at her, trying to shake off his rage. "I seem to continue on. Against all odds." Neil threw the last bit over her shoulder to the Wolf.

"What are you two discussing?" she asked, turning to look at the Wolf.

"The future," Neil said, drawing her attention back. "Where I'll be after this is over."

"With me, hopefully."

"That's what I told him," Neil said.

The Wolf's eyes were on the ground. "I'll leave you two to talk." He approached the flap. "Neil let me know what you decide. About where you want to end up."

"Wolf," Neil said.

"Yes?"

"Can you find someone to give me a tattoo tomorrow?"

The Wolf assessed him. "Yes. A burden on your soul?"

"Yes."

When Neil was alone with Bianca, he silently pulled her close to him and they spent the next moments clinging to each other. Neil had never been angrier or more confused, but Bianca was his anchor. She was the only thing he was really certain about. And as far as where he'd "end up," he knew he wasn't going anywhere he couldn't feel her in his arms. Not if he could fight it.

Neil leaned back eventually and closed his eyes again. He could feel Bianca watching him, skeptical about the frigid air in the room.

Neil lowered his hand over his heart. Lilly's dagger was gone, but he could still feel it. He looked at Bianca and wondered if he'd ever have to leave her, or if this weight would ever leave his chest.

8

IMPERIAL PALACE

HAROLD THORNE

Harold Thorne was exceptional at most things, and if he wasn't exceptional at something you could bet that he'd figure out how to be. He'd grown up short and feeble, so he researched muscle groups and nutrition until he'd transformed his body into that of an athlete. Once a woman had remarked that his timing was off when he danced, so he studied the waltz for months until his dexterity turned him into the centerpiece of every ball. A man once made fun of him for not understanding the rules of Backtrack, a card game, so he had the man killed. He didn't have time to learn everything.

One thing Harold was especially unexceptional at was delegating. As his slew of factories and shops grew, he had no choice but to allow his subordinates to take control of certain operations. Even though he confined himself to three hours of sleep per night, he was only one man, and one man only had time for so many things. One thing he had never relinquished, however, was acquisition. Whenever he took over other companies, Harold was always there. This was because he liked to pride himself on his ability to sniff out the slightest scent of trouble. When a business was on the verge of collapse or money was going missing, Harold could always tell.

This was the case as he casually surveyed the Emperor's waiting room. Thorne had been allowed to bring three men, and they hung back anxiously. Two guards waited by the door to the throne room in silence. The guard on the right was extremely tall and muscled. His partner had a long scar under his eye. "Lavish isn't it?" Harold mused to his men.

"Yeah, boss. Walls are pretty," said one.

"Well, it was built by the Lightborns when they were in power," Thorne said. "And those dynasties were built on gold and silks and delicacies." He tapped his polished shoe on the floor. "Listen to that echo... Gorgeous." He glanced at the taller of the Imperial guards. "Must be a nice place to work, huh?"

The Imperial guard glanced at his companion, unsure of whether to answer. "It's very nice, sir."

"Must be stressful, no? With a war going on?"

"No war, sir," the tall soldier said instinctively.

"Right, right," Harold said. "There's never been a war." He winked at one of his men. The Imperial guards looked uncomfortable. "Anyway, nice accommodations right? Keep your wives and kids in the Military District?"

"Yes sir," said the scar faced guard.

"At number 606 Shallow Bank, right?" Thorne asked casually.

The guard gasped. The tall guard stepped forward. "Listen, Mr. Thorne, you may think-"

"And you're at 811 River Road yes?"

The guard was speechless.

"I like the road outside your house. Most of this city is cobblestone. It's tough on the knees."

"Sir, I don't understand the—"

"I'm sure you don't understand much, so why don't you listen?" Thorne whispered in a soothing tone. "I don't want to hurt you or your families. I just want the slightest bit of inside information before

I make quite a large investment in the Emperor's campaign outside these walls."

The guards looked at each other. "You don't know how powerful he is," the scarred guard said in a voice that almost went unheard.

"I know he's sick," Thorne said. "Mentally or physically, it doesn't really matter to me, but people say he doesn't bathe and he locks himself in his chamber for weeks at a time."

The guards didn't answer, but the tall one nodded slightly. Thorne's men didn't seem to have any interest in the extortion happening in front of them. They milled around aimlessly. "Where's the Empress? No one's seen her in months."

"Alive."

"I bet," Thorne scoffed.

"No, she is," the taller guard insisted. "She's just…"

"He beats her, right?" Thorne said. "I mean he beats everyone."

"He used to. When he first starting going after the Lightborns, she had giant purple bruises on her face. She was caked in makeup for months."

"But not anymore?"

"No."

"Weird," Thorne muttered. He was tracking a theory, but he couldn't figure out how the Empress fit into it. "Anything else? Anything you'd want to know before getting involved with the Emperor?"

The guards shared a look. "Nothing sir. He's a noble and powerful leader." They said the last part in unison.

Harold laughed out loud, and everyone jumped. "Sorry, I'm sorry." He waved a hand dismissively. "Well, thanks for your help gentlemen. I'll have the boys drop you off something nice for your discretion. I appreciate you keeping this between us."

The doors to the throne room soon opened and Thorne entered without delay. He kept his face neutral, but the Emperor really did look sick. They'd once interacted quite a bit, but in recent years the Emperor had shut the nobles out of decision-making. The Emperor's face had always been colorless, but now it was a faint yellow and his eyes were misty. His head dangled lazily to the side as if it was too great a weight to bear. "Where's your crown?" Harold asked.

"Show respect." Saewulf was there, standing tall and strong, and Harold avoided looking at him on purpose.

"My apologies. Where's your crown, your highness?"

"Saewulf is having it cleaned." The Emperor's voice was low and slow. Lower and slower than it had ever been.

"Right." Thorne glanced over at Saewulf. The man was a sight to behold. Harold could see his teeth through his cheek. Most of the skin looked healed, but certain parts were never going to look right. Thorne knew that for certain. He ran factories and he was no stranger to burns.

"I won't waste your time, you're a busy man." Thorne paced a bit. "I think you need a strategist and I would like to apply."

The Emperor lifted himself in his chair with a fluidity that made Thorne uneasy. Maybe the sickness was an act. "Bold of you. Bold of you to assume I need a strategist. And bold of you to assume I would choose you, Thorne."

"May I make my case?"

"Go ahead." The Emperor's eyes opened a little wider.

"Your military is strong, but you're being outmaneuvered outside Altryon. The Wolf knows the terrain better than General Carlin. I would mince words, but I don't want to waste the time. Carlin controls the superior force, the Wolf controls superior intelligence."

"And intelligence wins out against force?" the Emperor asked.

"Undeniably," Harold insisted. "Always."

The Emperor put a hand against his chin. "And you're here to even the scales? Offer your big old brain?"

"I'm here to offer a two-pronged approach," Thorne said. "One: I'll assist Carlin, offering nuanced strategies the likes of which have never been seen. And two: I'd like to take over as your personal advisor."

The Emperor's head rolled around to look at Saewulf. "Why do you want to do that?"

"If I may, sir..." This was the riskiest part of Thorne's pitch, playing hardball. "Your Empire has endless might. You have the largest army, the fastest ships, the biggest guns, and your friend over here." He pointed to Saewulf. "But there's a difference between might and power and you do not possess power." He expected an interjection but didn't receive one. "Might is sheer strength. Power is your ability to effect the most change with the least amount of effort."

"Oh, that's fascinating." The Emperor's eyes grew dim.

Thorne was sweating now. He couldn't afford to lose his audience. "You fight two forces. A rebellion inside these walls and a rebellion outside. A mighty empire would crush both."

"Good strategy," the Emperor said.

"A powerful empire, however, would use the people against each other, the men inside the walls to fight the men outside the walls. Limited action on your part, maximum results." He was impassioned now, speaking quickly. "Let me write a few speeches. We can crush your enemies with your enemies. We can turn your mighty empire into a powerful one."

The Emperor began clapping without warning. "Oh my. Oh wow." He looked jovial for a moment, but it passed. "I suppose there's no wasting time is there?" His men approached Thorne from either side. "What do you plan to do first?"

"I'll find the rebel camp," Thorne said, determinedly. "It's been slipping through Carlin's grasp for months, but I know how to find it."

"Oh, he's already got plans. Brilliant." The Emperor's men began leading him out. "I'll have someone take you through the gate. You'll convene with Carlin within the next day."

Thorne bowed. "Thank you sir." He was beaming. That was easier than he'd thought.

"Oh, and Harold?" The Emperor's voice was little more than a whisper.

"Yes, s-"

Before Thorne could finish he was being dragged across the floor, kicking and gasping in panic. He tried to write a formula for escape but knew there was none. Saewulf wrapped his hand around Thorne's neck and placed the other on his face. He peered into the inventor's eyes, with his glowing ones.

"You're absolutely right about power and might, my good man. I appreciate the lesson." The Emperor's head flopped lazily to the side. "I am positively bewildered by your strategic genius."

Thorne was gasping, but his eyes scanned the room. "I have a few lessons in return. Look into my man's eyes," the Emperor continued. "You're a powerful man, are you not?"

Saewulf dropped Thorne and he collapsed to the floor. "I am." He sputtered after catching his breath. Saewulf grabbed him again as soon as he was done speaking.

"Sometimes all the power in the world can't defend you from true strength. True might." Saewulf lifted Thorne and dropped him again. The Emperor chuckled. "It's true what they say, right? That your brain will be studied and dissected for science when you're dead? Well, a brain is only as safe as the skull that houses it, and you can be absolutely certain that if you betray me I'll have Saewulf crush yours." Thorne suppressed a shudder. The Emperor hadn't stopped speaking. "You dare come into my throne room and insist that you're the only one playing multiple angles? See, you think you're playing chess while the rest of us play like children. Believe me, I am playing chess. Just not against you. You're merely one of the pieces." The Emperor giggled. "Have the camp destroyed in a week or you'll be executed. No deliberation, no second chances, no nothing. This is your trial, Harold."

Harold Thorne found his feet and stood teetering. He looked at Saewulf as he responded. "I understand, sir."

Saewulf and the Emperor shared a look. "Well, well." The Emperor's voice was alight with interest. "Maybe you're actually as smart as you think you are."

Thorne stood with his spine held straight as he left. "I've already put a plan in motion to find the rebel camp." The death threats didn't set him back a step.

"Oh really?" the Emperor called after him. "How are you going to do that?"

Harold Thorne gave a half smirk over his shoulder. "You have your servant, and I have mine."

He rushed out of the throne room and his men flanked him as he exited the palace. He was hyperventilating, but kept it hidden well. Soon his breathing returned to normal.

On the walk back, one of his men posed the question he'd been asking himself. "Uh...Boss?"

"Yes?"

"Why are we...uh... why are we doing this?"

Thorne slowed and turned back to his man. "Do you know what percentage of factories I own in this city?" He didn't wait for an answer. "Ninety-Eight. I used to have sixty-four. Guess what changed?"

"What?"

"Businessmen started going missing. Left and right."

"Missing?"

Thorne pointed behind his man's head. The man turned and squinted.

"They were dragged through those gates and they never came back out. Why? Maybe they were kind to Robert's rebels. Maybe they'd been a little too rude to the wrong person. Maybe it doesn't matter."

He lowered his hand, eyes still transfixed on the palace. "If I fail I risk losing everything, but you know what? I could also lose everything if Saewulf wakes up one day and decides I should. I put on a brave face in there, but that *thing* is the future. If I run from the future, I'll be crushed under its boots. I've got to make myself a part of it."

"Got it," the man said looking a little unnerved.

"There's two parts to expansion," Thorne said. "One is gaining power; the other is protecting what you have. We're doing both."

He'd gotten what he came for. He was now employed, if on probation. He also acquired a valuable tidbit of information. For he'd gone into that palace knowing that something stank. He just didn't know what. Now he did. And as he packed his bags to join the larger force in a bloody war, he realized he didn't mind the smell.

9

STREETS OF ABINGTON

RHYS VAPROS

Rhys was dreaming that he was trudging through tar. He took step after heavy step and sometimes imagined that hands were pulling at his pant legs. At one point he reached down and dipped his hand into the thick mess. When he pulled it up, it was stained red.

His eyes opened with a start, and Rhys looked around to realize that he wasn't in his room at the inn. He was in the streets of Abington in the dead of night. *"How did you do that?"* Rhys demanded.

"You were sleepwalking," the Doctor responded.

"I don't believe you."

"Fine. You went to sleep and I decided to stay awake."

Rhys tried not to let that terrify him. The Doctor was getting stronger, and Rhys didn't know his limits. Had he had this power all along? Had he simply been biding his time? *"Where are we going?"* Rhys asked.

"Just wanted to peek at the pain index," the Doctor said. *"It's in my lair."*

"Lair?"

"Lab. I meant lab."

"Sure you did."

"The pain index is just sitting there, Rhys. If we don't find it, it'll probably go undiscovered for generations, which I don't need to tell you, would be a crime against science and humanity."

"All of your work is a crime against humanity."

"But not science?" The Doctor laughed and the noise travelled down Rhys's vertebra. *"You can't tell me you don't want this for us. For our world. We could develop a quantifiable measuring system for pain. It could really help people. Understanding pain means treating it."*

"I don't believe you." Rhys was fighting hard now. Something gripped him. He'd been able to control the Doctor, silence him before, but now he found that he couldn't.

"You may critique my methods. They are critiquable."

"You turned my friend's uncle into a flesh-eating monster."

"And you know what? I'm sorry. That one's on me." He certainly didn't sound sorry.

Rhys found his vision blurring and darkening. He began shaking his head to rid his mind of the Doctor's control. He felt as if someone with immeasurable strength was gripping his skull. He heard a metal scraping noise and imagined it was a scalpel being dragged down an operation table. It wasn't until his vision cleared that he realized it was his foot dragging across the moonlit street. Was he still walking?

"You're trying to distract me." Rhys was shaking his head rapidly now, trying to free himself.

"I am not."

"Yes, you are."

"Did you know Jennifer is still alive?"

"No she's not."

"I'm a good doctor."

"We turned her into ash, and she floated away on the wind."

"I'm a very good doctor."

Rhys tried to sigh internally so the Doctor would hear it. *"STOP!"* Rhys demanded. His body slid to a halt and his vision cleared. He was no longer on the street, but in a darkened condensed space. It didn't take him long to recognize the Doctor's lair. Rhys's skin grew hot at the thought of this place. He'd been tortured here. Sitting on the table in front of him was the pain index, dressed up in dust. Rhys lowered a hand to it.

"What's the harm in reading a bit, Rhys? What the harm in hearing me out?"

"I-"

Rhys heard something rattle. He ducked down behind the worktable and peered out to see what had made the noise. Across the room, dozens of feet away, he saw the hunched over form of a man tearing through cabinets. *"Is that?"*

"Victor?"

Rhys wanted to hide, but his confusion got the better of him. His foot was metal and he couldn't get around without difficulty. Had the assassin really not heard him enter? The Marksman still had his Venator super hearing, didn't he? Rhys made tiny movements, getting closer to the Marksman as he ripped open cabinet doors with fury. Eventually, he stopped, panting. "I hear you," he said.

Rhys rose to his full height. "Victor Venator. Looking for something?"

The Marksman shrugged off the question. "You don't have to worry about me killing you. I don't take things personally."

Was this real? It certainly didn't feel like a dream.

"Okay," Rhys said. "What are you looking for?"

"What do you think?" The Marksman turned to face him. The man had been taking the Doctor's injections and now he was without them. He looked just like Anastasia had before she died. His skin was greying and sunken around his cheekbones. "I've got very little time left, certainly not enough to deal with you."

"Fair enough."

When Rhys turned to leave, he saw a figure lying on the floor several feet away. *"My body,"* the Doctor said with amusement. *"Well my last body."*

"I always thought I'd be the one to do it." The Marksman laughed. "I always thought he'd push me too far, and one day I'd break and kill him. Sometimes he'd speak and I'd hear his voice fade out and imagine what his forehead skin would look like parting for a bullet."

He opened a new cabinet and started rummaging. "I guess we all thought about that quite a bit. Killing him. I know Anastasia did. Even Lester had his tantrums. The Doctor was too smart for that though. He made sure we knew the cost. If he died, all of us died with him. And there he is, lying in the dirt, with no one who cares enough to bury him."

"Ouch." The Doctor sounded amused.

"And here I am. The last member of a dead family."

"The Venator are alive and well," Rhys said.

"Not that family. The Pack. His family. Our family." The Marksman stopped. He stood, jaw quivering, feverish. "Can you believe I still call it that? A family? He'd think that was so funny."

There was silence now. The Marksman looked wild and lost. The man had finally shed the human around the animal and was growling and pawing at his head. *"So now you enter the void, Victor."* The voice that left Rhys's mouth didn't sound like his own. It was slurred and deeper.

The Marksman's once vacant eyes became sharp again. His spine straightened, and Rhys could see him making calculations. He looked over Rhys's shoulder to the body of his father. "Oh." He opened and closed his mouth a few times. "Oh, I see."

"What?" Rhys asked.

The Marksman pulled a knife from his belt and made a small incision on his arm. Rhys knew about this from the Lightborn book. When Victor bled, he became something else. Not quite a human, and not quite an animal. "Oh, no." The Marksman's skin began to tighten and hair grew on his arms. His nails began to jut from the fingers on his remaining hand and his teeth shifted in his mouth. "I'm not talking to the boy. I would like to talk to the man piloting him."

Rhys wanted to run, but he felt the Doctor fighting that. "You're hallucinating."

"No," the Marksman growled. "He used to say something like that. Just like that." A spool of saliva dripped out of his mouth. "I thought he was insane, but he was right. He put his mind inside your head. He brought you here for his precious pain index. He's still doing his work."

Rhys began to tremble. He wanted to lie, but he couldn't. He stood, feeling suddenly bound by his captor. "Well, that's very fortunate for me, for two reasons. First, I very much wanted to say all that to his face."

"And second?" Maybe there was a way for Rhys to get out of this alive.

"Second, that mind has the formula for my injections. And you are going to give it to me."

"I'm not," the Doctor said, resolutely.

"Why not?" Rhys screamed back in his mind.

"He hasn't been very nice."

"What's happening?" The Marksman was pacing now.

"We're having a bit of a disagreement up here," Rhys said.

The Marksman scoffed. "If I hurt you, will he feel it?"

Rhys wasn't sure. "No."

The Marksman leapt across the room and caught him in his claws. "I don't believe you," he spat through his jaws.

Before Rhys could be eviscerated, he felt strong arms tear the Marksman's body from his. With a groan, Darius heaved the Marksman's body across the room and into one of the workbenches, where he sat groaning in pain. "Victor," Darius panted. "You look horrible."

"I know," he said through pained pants. "I'm dying. What's your excuse?"

"I'm off the wagon," Darius said with a shrug. "I don't think that'll stop me from ripping off your other hand."

"I liked your uncle better." The Marksman dragged himself to his feet. "He talked less."

"Let's go see him." Darius's eyes had something new in them. Something dangerous. "I'm sure he'd love to get his hands on you."

The Marksman jumped without warning, this time clawing at Darius's eyes and neck. Rhys wanted to materialize closer to help with the fight, but he was afraid to get within clawing distance. Darius finally found a handful of the Marksman's coat and slammed him into the ground, ending his furious flurry of attacks.

Darius teetered on his feet, and Rhys realized his friend wasn't completely sober. "What are you doing here?" Rhys asked.

"You bolted out of the inn like a maniac. I've been looking for you for an hour. What are *you* doing here?" Darius demanded.

"Sleepwalking." He desperately wanted to tell Darius the truth, but something stopped him. The Imperial Doctor had done unspeakable things to Darius. Would he be repulsed to know that the madman now lived inside Rhys's head?

Darius's eyes didn't leave Rhys's. He looked suspicious. "Well, good thing you were, huh?" He lifted his foot. "We get to tie up a loose end."

Rhys found himself unable to look away as Darius prepared to crush Victor's skull with his foot. Then Rhys noticed something.

A single drop of blood fell from Darius's body and landed by the Marksman's unconscious form. Darius hadn't gotten out of the fistfight unscathed after all.

Rhys saw Victor's nostrils flare, and the assassin startled awake. He rolled out of the way of Darius's foot, which landed uselessly where his head had been. The Marksman's animalistic features began to fade and Rhys could see that he was reaching for a firearm. Both of them knew the danger. Darius's skin had been pierced. When this happened he'd be vulnerable until the wound clotted over. Even worse, the Marksman's bullets posed more than a health risk.

The Marksman pulled a pistol from somewhere in his coat and fired off a shot. Darius lifted his hand to stop it and Rhys remembered that he'd recently come into his advanced ability: moving metal with his mind.

Unfortunately, in this particular case he only succeeded in shifting the bullet a little. It grazed his shoulder, and he seized in pain. Without warning Darius grabbed Rhys by the arm and pulled him through the nearest open doorway. Another bullet landed in the wall near Darius's head. "So I can't stop bullets. That's good to know," Darius grumbled.

Rhys and Darius exited into the night air, but not before hearing the Marksman calling in the distance. The sound morphed as it echoed in the chamber. Rhys was almost sure he'd heard "I will find you!"

"What did you do to him?" Darius asked as they made off into the night air.

"Nothing, he's insane," Rhys panted.

Darius took stock of their surroundings and finally nodded. "Okay, we have to see the Wolf."

Rhys could tell his face was going pale. "The Wolf? Why?"

"We need protection. There's no telling how much time that maniac has left. And he's fixated on the two of us for some reason."

Rhys paused, taking this in. "You're right. We need protection." It was convenient that Darius thought the Marksman was coming for both of them. Rhys was against telling Darius what was happening to him, but the Wolf was a different story. The Wolf would know what to do.

Also, Rhys was relieved to see some life in Darius's eyes. He'd been sullen and quiet since Anastasia's death. This action seemed to bring him back to life. Maybe this was something they both needed.

Rhys kept waiting for the Doctor to chime in, but he didn't. He remained eerily silent. Whatever. Some alone time would be good for Rhys's sanity. It didn't take long for them to collect their things and acquire a carriage toward the outskirts of town. Rhys tried to keep a brave face. He could tell Darius was doing the same, but once in the forest they jumped at every cracking twig and howl of wind. They were being hunted now. Rhys had given the Marksman something to live for. And that was a very dangerous thing.

10

REBEL BASE CAMP

HIGHEST HONOR

THE WOLF

This had never happened before. Not only had the Empire never sent a negotiator to meet the rebels, they'd never sent a negotiator to meet with anyone. Up until now, the Emperor had seen it as a sign of weakness. If someone from the rebellion wanted to talk terms, they did it with General Carlin or the Emperor himself. They were usually killed before the end of the meeting. However, today was a landmark occasion. The Imperial negotiator entered camp around midday when the sun hung directly above the Wolf's tent. Two soldiers escorted the negotiator to the Wolf.

He'd taken every precaution to keep the negotiator from knowing their location. The boy had been collected in Brightbow and brought here by way of several secret paths and roads, all while blindfolded.

The Wolf could tell by feeling the air that the negotiator had full pockets and a knife sewn into his coat, but he didn't have them confiscated. No one was quick enough to get the jump on Steven Celerius, especially not a non-Lightborn.

Still, the soldiers looked him up and down to make sure he wasn't a Lightborn. He didn't have the Taurlum's golden locks or the auburn

Celerius hair. He didn't have the strong jawline and black hair of a Vapros, and he lacked the razor-sharp gaze of a Venator. He was plain and unintimidating. Except for the curious green hue of his skin.

When the negotiator entered the tent, he looked around uninterestedly. The Wolf smiled at him faintly. He tried not to show any weakness to his guest. He'd even considered putting makeup around his eyes. It was paramount that he not look tired. He was the General of the Rebellion, an unshakeable force, a hurricane. He couldn't look exhausted. Even if he was. He pointed to the chair across from him and the negotiator sat in a deep slouch. The Wolf poured the boy a cup of wine. "The Empire doesn't usually do house-calls. Your Emperor must be getting very nervous."

"He is Emperor to all. Mind your semantics." The boy's voice was colorless. He sounded like he might be reading a script. "I'm also here under the advisement of the Imperial Strategist, Harold Thorne."

"Harold Thorne the businessman?"

"He has many talents." The boy swiped his fingers through his oily black hair. "You may call me... Well, whatever. Most call me Leaf. I don't mind."

The Wolf stared at him, sizing him up. Something already felt off. This boy was odd and dispassionate. This was also clearly not the cry for mercy he'd hoped it would be. "Why is your skin green?"

"Dunno. I was born green."

So much for small talk. "Have you brought me an offer?"

"I have. The Emperor is willing to very generously grant independence to Arkney and Shipwreck Bay. Provided they still pay taxes to the Emperor for his protection."

The Wolf stared at him. "Arkney and Shipwreck Bay are already free. The only village you control is Abington."

"For now." He had a stunning lack of interest in what he was saying.

The Wolf began trying to sense the lands around the camp. This felt wrong. This meeting was either a trap or a stark insult. Was Harold Thorne really making offers that would certainly be laughed at? For what reason?

"As you know, our armies are larger." Leaf continued. "They are better equipped. They are better trained. How long can you hope to keep your grasp on those cities? We are offering you a definite way to keep them."

"I have twice as many villages now."

"And you'll have none if you keep this up."

The Wolf scratched his chin. He'd shaved in preparation for this event, but now he regretted it. This was a joke. He was negotiating with a child. "And his only demand is that we pay taxes?"

"No." Leaf seemed even less enthusiastic about bringing up this next point. "You will also hand over all Lightborn fugitives to General Carlin."

The Wolf stared at the negotiator in awe of his audacity. "Including myself? Including my own niece? The boys I've seen growing up?"

"The contract states that you may be free, provided you do not father any more children."

The Wolf took a long sip of his wine without breaking eye contact. "Why are Lightborns so important to you?"

"They're not. They're important to the Emperor and General Carlin." He paused. "And those close to the Emperor."

"Carlin and his daddy drawing up treaties together." The Wolf sighed. "What a fun father-son activity."

The negotiator didn't acknowledge the reference to Carlin's parentage. "Will you accept the terms or not?"

"I'd hand myself over to the Emperor in a second if I believed it would make my people better off. At this stage, I don't see that happening. When I was general of your Emperor's army, I watched as the people of these lands were slaughtered without trial for the smallest offenses. I watched as their properties and goods were seized without justification. I watched as they were forced to live at the mercy of the Emperor's random mood swings and whims. And now, as leader of the rebel army, I watch it all the same. Your Emperor is not fit to lead these people. You know what we really want."

"It's off the table."

"We want liberation. And we'll do it peacefully if possible."

"It's off the table."

The Wolf finished his wine and licked his lips. The manners were gone. Steven Celerius was leaving the negotiations and the Wolf was coming out. "So you came all the way here just to spit in my face? You came all the way here to continue to treat us like nothing?"

"I understand that you're angry."

The Wolf was smiling now. "We're not angry anymore, soldier. We stopped being angry a long time ago. You have made us something else. You have made us… hungry."

"I'm sure we can arrange a way to get you more food. Trade convoys, embargo's lifted—"

"Not for food," the Wolf said. "We are starving for basic human rights. We are thirsty for the blood of our oppressor. Your Emperor."

"I'd heard you were a civilized man," Leaf said.

"When you treat someone like an animal for long enough, you shouldn't be surprised when they bare their teeth. You shouldn't complain when they resort to instinct. You and your Emperor made us this way. Savage." Leaf was silent. "Get out of my tent. Negotiations are over. Your Emperor wants mercy? He can beg for it when the walls come down around him."

Leaf sat for a moment, then stood without a word. He turned with no gesture or word of courtesy. The Wolf followed him. As the soldiers began to escort the boy to the edge of camp, the Wolf felt vibrations coming off of him. This was his special ability, and it was the same one as his niece, Lilly. He could send and receive powerful vibrations and the negotiator was shaking. Something had broken his icy cold exterior. The Wolf stood tall, even though he knew what was about to happen. He was nearing the center of camp, but that was okay. He wanted people to see this.

Leaf pulled out a foreign looking pistol and darted away from his escorts while firing at the Wolf. The Wolf had never seen a gun like this one. It didn't need to be reloaded after the first shot. Leaf kept firing away, randomly, wildly. The Wolf bobbed and weaved when necessary so that the bullets wouldn't strike his heart or his head.

After firing six shots, the pistol clicked empty. The Wolf caught the boy by the lapels but before he could subdue him the boy crushed one of his back molars between his teeth. In an instant his mouth filled with foam and his body shook. The Wolf dropped the corpse that had once been Leaf.

The Wolf's men stared at him, mouths agape as the bullets popped out of him and the skin healed itself over. He kneeled down and closed the boy's eyelids. "This is why the Empire will lose this war. They have had chance after chance to kill me. They've taken shot after shot, but they've always missed. They've always been off course. They've always strayed. I don't need more than one shot, and I guarantee you, the second we get our chance, we won't squander it. Those walls are coming down and the Emperor's head is coming off."

His men cheered and grunted in agreement. He didn't take time to bask in their admiration. He picked up the negotiator's gun and turned it over. Six shots had been fired. The Wolf had never seen anything like it, but this boy had one. This meant that the Empire now had them in their possession, and if that was true... The Wolf didn't want to think of the consequences. He could heal from six bullet wounds, but his men sure as hell couldn't. He just hoped he wasn't leading them to slaughter.

Far off he saw Barlow Venator watching. The drunkard swaggered over. "I heard that little exchange."

"A slap to my face," the Wolf said.

"Right. But he'd free Arkney."

"A temporary measure made to keep us off our guard. That peace would never last." The Wolf eyed the body of the green-skinned boy. "Tell me, can you hear his heartbeat?"

"No," Barlow said. "It's dead. What's with the skin?"

"I'm not sure." The Wolf turned the boy's head slightly with his foot. "He mentioned Harold Thorne."

"I heard. Harold Thorne the inventor?"

"Yes. Made me nervous." The Wolf used his advanced ability to feel the expansive lands around his camp. The Wolf signaled to a young soldier. "Have him searched, head to toe. I want all of his possessions smashed."

"Yes sir."

"And then have his body buried."

"Yes sir."

"Have it buried deep."

"Yes sir."

He watched as Leaf was carried away. "Jumpy, Wolf?" Barlow asked.

"Just being safe," the Wolf said, which was a lie. He felt incredibly unsettled by the news that Harold Thorne was strategizing for the Empire. Carlin he could deal with. Carlin thought like a general. But Thorne was a visionary of the highest order and he knew he'd have to grow accustomed to dealing with some unorthodox military maneuvers in the coming months.

As he returned to his tent he couldn't forget the image of the boy shaking and dying in his arms. How many times could he see something like that and maintain his sanity? Would he ever know a life where men didn't drop dead around him? He was sure something like that would make Carlin feel like a god. It made him feel like a plague. As he poured another glass, he imagined the boy's face had been that of Josephine's son. And then of Neil's. On some days the Wolf felt like a king, leading his people to their new world, into Volteria. On others he felt like a shepherd. The shepherd of young dead men.

OUTSIDE ABINGTON

RHYS VAPROS

"It must be dangerous to be a highwayman in Altryon." It had been quite a while since the Doctor had responded, and Rhys would sometimes desperately send him an inkling of a thought. This was not because he missed his companion, but because silence was far scarier than incessant chattering.

Rhys had transmitted this particular thought less than a day into their journey when they found their path blocked by a pack of rough looking individuals. *"You never know who you might be robbing. You might accidentally rob a Venator. Or a rebel. Or a flesh-eating assassin."*

"Out of the wagon, boys," the bandit in front demanded.

"Or a Vapros and a Taurlum," Rhys thought.

Darius smirked at Rhys and hopped off his perch where he'd been controlling the reins. The sound of his feet hitting the ground made a dense thud, giving a hint of his true weight. "You gentlemen don't want to do this. Trust me."

"Oh yeah?" The same bandit now pulled a pistol. It didn't look like it bothered Darius. His skin had healed since his scrape with Victor.

"You and peg leg want a fight?"

"You're going to rob a kid with no leg?" Rhys asked from the perch.

"The Gibson Gang robs indeterminately. Kids with legs. Kids with no legs. Men. Women. Whatever."

"That's very egalitarian of you," Rhys said.

"So in the spirit of equality, leave all your goods in the wagon and take a walk in the opposite direction." He pointed with his gun for emphasis.

"Are you the titular Gibson?" Darius asked.

"*I wish.*"

"All right, not Gibson." Darius did a little turn. "Any idea what part of the forest we're in?"

"Right between Abington and Brightbow. Gibson territory."

Darius's face broke into a grin. He put two fingers in his mouth and whistled loudly. It was harsh, air from his iron lungs escaping through gaps in iron flesh. "Sorry boys. But the land between Abington and Brightbow doesn't belong to the Gibson Gang."

"And who does it belong to?"

The ground began to tremble and Rhys began to realize what, or who, was coming. The bandit at the front of the pack began to shake. He redoubled his grip on his gun. "Whose territory?" He fired a shot that bounced off of Darius's chest. "Whose territory?" He was whispering now.

"My uncle's."

The tree line broke apart and the hulking form of Nikolai Taurlum appeared. There were five men and all five managed to fire off a shot before the majority of the group was crushed to death. Nikolai grabbed one and used his body to batter the others. Two took off running into the distance. Nikolai eventually grew bored of the bloodshed and dropped his club. He turned to look at Darius. "Hello, my friend," Darius said with pain in his eyes.

Nikolai shifted back and forth, assessing his nephew. How many times had Darius been out here? Eventually he held out his enormous hand and Darius shook it. "Looks better doesn't he?"

Rhys nodded dumbfounded. The armor had been torn off and Nikolai's once shaggy hair and beard had been cut down to something reasonable. His skin was no longer stained with dirt and his eyes looked a little more human. "Is he... Does he..."

"He doesn't talk," Darius said. "He tries though."

Nikolai looked over at Rhys with curiosity in his eyes. "Harbasidguf," Nikolai said as if to demonstrate.

"What did that mean?" Rhys asked.

"I think he wants to know if he can eat you."

"Can you tell him no?"

"Yeah," Darius said. "I'm trying to get him to learn to eat animals again. And plants. It's slow going. He *really* likes people."

"I see."

"He always was a people person."

"Well you are what you eat," Rhys mused.

Nikolai was kind enough to help them clear the road. Darius attempted to move the carriage back to create room. The horses, surprisingly enough, were not too fond of Nikolai's presence and Darius reined them in with great difficulty. Rhys's job was to make sure Nikolai didn't get hungry and devour anyone. As Nikolai lifted one of the robbers he groaned. *"Grow big and strong."* Rhys said in a voice that wasn't his.

Suddenly Nikolai's eyes lost their understanding. He grabbed the man and began slamming him against the ground and roaring in fury. The horses, dozens of feet away, squealed in fear. Darius leapt from the carriage and socked Nikolai in the side of the head before he could dig into the robber's flesh. Nikolai turned back and roared with rage. Darius held his hands out. "Calm."

Nikolai roared again. "Calm," Darius repeated.

Nikolai was shaking, his eyes locked on Rhys. The glare was filled with bloodlust and Rhys understood. He'd tear himself apart to get at the Doctor too. "Calm." Darius's voice kept getting quieter.

Eventually Nikolai dropped his stare and turned away, pouting. Darius patted his back a few times. "Calm," he said again.

Eventually he ushered Nikolai back to the deeper parts of the forest. After a quick word, Nikolai lumbered back into the trees, toppling them as he went. As the noise of trees falling faded, Darius turned to examine Rhys. Silence. "What did you say to him?" Darius asked cutting through the space between them.

"I didn't say anything."

"It didn't sound like nothing."

Darius was approaching now, building speed. Rhys was desperate not to take a step back or show any kind of weakness, but he knew that nothing could stop a charging Taurlum and staying in place might mean getting trampled. Darius caught his arm and Rhys materialized out of the hold. "It was nothing," Rhys said as honestly as he could. "I just said he was big and strong."

"And that was it?"

"That was it." Darius took another step in his direction, and Rhys evaded again. "You're scaring me." Rhys was shifting tactics now. "I didn't do anything."

"It didn't even sound like your voice," Darius said more to himself than to Rhys.

Rhys gulped now and prayed Darius hadn't seen it. "You're imagining things. You're... It's seeing Nikolai. I bet it brings up harsh memories which..."

"Don't deflect," Darius said. "Is that thing in your head?"

Rhys was still, staring a hole through Darius's head. "I..."

"The Doctor wanted to transfer his mind into yours," Darius said. "Barlow Venator said that was his 'life's work.' Did he?"

Rhys would have rather been one of the highwaymen lying a few feet off. He felt the hot sting of embarrassment in the back of his brain and the weight of fear pulling on his chest. "I'm just not all better yet. I was... He had me down there for a while. I'm upset. I have the right. I'm missing a part of me, Darius." He lifted his little metal foot.

Darius studied him. His features were softening. "You didn't answer my question. Is he in your head?"

"Of course he is," Rhys said. "I can't stop thinking about him or his experiments or his evil lab. Is he controlling me? Is he puppeteering me? No." This was true enough, excluding a few moments.

"Do you need help?"

"I think so," Rhys said. "I just... Let's go see the Wolf okay? I need to keep moving or I'm going to suffocate. All I want is action."

"Okay little buddy." Darius pointed at the wagon. "Let's keep moving, eh?"

Rhys nodded and materialized back up to the perch. He waited until they were moving to recede back into his mind. *"What was that?"* he asked. *"What did you do to Nikolai? Was that a command?"*

There was no answer to those or any of the other questions Rhys asked. When the sun began to fall, Rhys in a desperate attempt asked one final question. And this one received an answer. *"Why won't you talk to me?"*

"I'm past talking." The Doctor was louder now, as if growing closer. *"I'm like you, Rhys. All I want is action."*

REBEL BASE CAMP

NEIL VAPROS

When Neil lived in Altryon he'd often been preceded by his family's reputation. He'd walk into bars and the sight of his coat would bring a flood of hushed whispers. He'd always loved that as a younger man, but now he resented his reputation. He hated how the rebels looked at him. They would gaze at him as he walked through camp, and when he arrived they'd hurry out to gawk at him. At one point a woman approached him and earnestly shook his hand while saying, "I know you're here to help."

The more people believed in him, the more people placed their hopes in him, the more people needed him, the harder it was going to be to leave. And Neil desperately wanted to leave.

He'd never signed up to be the Wolf's sacrificial lamb, and he certainly didn't like being carted out for strategic meetings and speeches. The Wolf always requested, through Bianca, that Neil show up to all important events despite his coldness. He didn't contribute and usually didn't listen, but he knew his actual purpose. When the Wolf's men were seized by anxiety they could look up and see not only Neil, but also Lilly Celerius and Barlow Venator. The message was clear. No matter how bad things got, the Wolf still had the Lightborns.

Today Neil was on his way to a "troop-repositioning meeting" when he was flagged down by a messenger. He clearly wasn't of the rebellion; his clothes fit well and he wasn't covered in the dirt that came with striking from the shadows. "Sir Vapros?"

"Neil Vapros. Yes."

The messenger dug into a pouch and removed a letter. "Someone paid a lot of money to have this sent."

"Curious," Neil said as he retrieved the letter. "I don't have many wealthy friends anymore."

The messenger bowed and left. Neil looked at the seal. It was copper colored, but he couldn't make out the shape of the crest. Maybe it was a scythe? He broke it and removed the letter while he left his tent. Sure, he had to be wary of the occasional assassin, but being in a rebel camp offered him something that he hadn't had in a while: allies surrounded him. Even Shipwreck Bay was thick with Imperial presence when they'd been there. This was the first place Neil felt that he could finally roam without the urge to cover his face or hide behind every corner.

He pulled the letter from its envelope and looked for the signature. A smile spread across his face. *Alex Tridenti.* He'd tried not to, but it was impossible not to miss the Tridenti and their carefree nature. The friendship between them had been so pure. They hadn't liked him because he was a Lightborn, or because he was a noble, or even because he was "the Phoenix." They just simply liked him. Or at least, they used to. Neil remembered the reason he'd had to flee their island at the break of dawn. He never expected to receive any letters at all, not after killing the old matriarch and accepting the burden of pretending to be a spy.

Dear Mamba,

I hope this letter finds you in good health and in good spirits.

The air was warmer than usual tonight and Neil walked off in the direction of the nearby lake. Best be by water when reading a letter from Alex Tridenti. The air buzzed with an unrecognizable sound, but it made Neil's chest feel warm inside. He scanned the letter further, almost in a trance.

Somehow I've managed to keep the Tridenti family together despite their constant efforts to destroy themselves.

The warmth in his chest expanded, and he felt overcome.

I'm not sure if this should worry you, but last month Serena vanished from the island with our fastest ship. She still doesn't know about our mother's deception, and I assume she's going somewhere to sulk. Either way, I'd steer clear of giant pirate ships.

That spoiled it. Neil looked down at the snake tattoo on his forearm. The Wolf had brought in the rebellion's tattoo artist (who apparently existed) and had the serpent inked the night before. It made Neil's arm feel heavier. The very sight of it made him feel sick, but it was a burden he had to carry. He'd chosen to kill Mama Tridenti, the mother of his friends, and it only made sense to carry that choice with him, no matter the weight.

The Wolf's voice brought Neil back to reality. "Neil, we're skipping the meeting today."

Neil turned and eyed the General. How long had he been standing there? "We are? Why?"

"I've got a surprise for you."

The Wolf hadn't seemed particularly joyful of late, so the glint in his eye sparked Neil's curiosity. "Lead the way."

Things were still cold between them and Neil was doing his best to hold onto his anger. His life depended on being able to resist the Wolf's charms. The General led him through camp, picking up people along the way. He waved Lilly over from where she was sharpening her sword and Bianca from where she was delegating to a few soldiers. They joined without hesitation. "Where are we going?" Bianca asked.

"The Wolf has a surprise," Neil said. He tried to sound cheerful, but he came off sounding bitter. He still had no clue how he'd tell her about his predicament. Hell, about anything. It had been hard just to share the stories of his experiences with the Tridenti at the Ocean's Jaw.

71

"How's the tattoo healing?"

"It's fine. Stings a bit."

"Is that…?" Bianca noted the letter in Neil's hand.

"From them? Yeah."

Bianca crossed her arms. "We've been trying to get in touch with the Tridenti for months. They won't respond to us."

Neil could tell where she was going with this. "There's been a bit of a changing of the guard. I can't see Alex plunging their family into a war."

"Well maybe if you wrote him…"

Neil shook his head. He couldn't do that. Not yet. He wasn't strong enough.

The small amalgamation of Lightborns arrived at a tent near the edge of the camp. Neil noticed that it was in no short supply of armored men. Something important was being kept here. The Wolf nodded to his men and they parted the canvas covering the door. Once inside, Neil found it to be a sort of makeshift interrogation room, complete with a man tied to a chair with a canvas sack over his head. Tables held weapons and other devices used for torturing prisoners, but Neil hoped they were just for show. The Wolf might be guilty of hiding the truth from Neil, but he didn't seem like the type to dismember people for information. When Neil drew closer, he realized the prisoner was missing a hand. "You cut off his hand?"

"What? No," the Wolf said. "He was missing that when we got him."

Bianca's eyes flickered over the prisoner. "It's not…?"

"It's not the Marksman, no."

"Have you seen the Marksman?" Lilly asked. "This man's twice as thick around the waist."

"If everyone in Altryon would stop calling me fat, I'd love that," said the prisoner.

Neil recognized the voice, but he couldn't place it. The Wolf grinned. Neil approached and slowly pulled the bag from the prisoner's head.

"Just kill me," Quintus said. "Please just kill me."

Neil grinned. "God, I've missed you." He admired his old enemy's clothing. "You're a foot soldier?"

"You and your friends saw to that, Neil Vapros," Quintus blubbered. He sounded a little different and Neil noticed his tongue was slightly discolored. "You Lightborns. You took everything from me. Mr. Vapros over here burned down my home and got me demoted. That assassin, Anastasia, tortured me and got me demoted again. Then I got demoted because I accidentally lost track of a few cannons." He paused. "That might not be your fault, but I suspect you're all involved in some way."

"We are," the Wolf admitted.

"I used to live in the most expensive home in Altryon and do you know what I do now? I sleep on a military issued blanket on the ground in a squadron of eight-hundred men. I don't even have any friends." Quintus had a small tear in his eye.

"Small price to pay for the..." Neil paused. "Is genocide the word?"

"Mass imprisonment?" Bianca offered.

"A lot of people were killed," Lilly noted.

"Not enough of us to be a genocide," the Wolf said.

"Fine. Small price to pay for the mass killing you orchestrated," Neil clarified.

"I won't apologize," Quintus said defiantly. "You Lightborns were out of control. Saewulf has the right idea."

"Extermination?" Neil asked.

"That's the word," the Wolf said.

"Look at you Lightborns," Quintus said. "You fight for the people? That's what you say anyway. Well, where are all the normal people? Looks like the Wolf's inner circle has a whole lot of Lightborns."

"So does the Emperor's," the Wolf said. "What do you think Saewulf is?"

"A psychic," Quintus said.

Everyone in the room exchanged a look.

"We picked Quintus up a couple days ago. Evidently we have ourselves a deserter," the Wolf said.

"I'm not a deserter." Quintus shook in his chair as he flailed his

73

legs. "In the Imperial Military you serve until death. And I fulfilled that requirement, therefore my service to the Empire has ended."

Everyone in the room slowly turned to look at him. "You..." Bianca eyed him suspiciously.

"You died?" Lilly asked.

"Yes indeed." Quintus sat up straighter, looking a little proud. He lifted his head, jowls flapping and exposed his neck, which had a deep scar across it. "Nearly cut my head clean off."

"Who?" Neil asked.

"The clowns."

Everyone turned to look at the Wolf. "Been a weird day?" Bianca asked.

"Oh yes," the Wolf said.

"So let me get this straight," Neil said. "You were murdered by clowns?"

"Yes," Quintus said.

"All right." The Wolf went to his weapons table and selected a club. "We need to speak in private. Quintus would you mind taking a nap?"

"Well, if you want I can—"

Before he could finish, Quintus was knocked out cold by the Wolf's club. His head hung down and a hearty drop of drool spilled from his lips. "We appreciate it."

"We shouldn't knock people unconscious," Bianca said. "It causes brain damage."

"Really?" Neil said. "We do that all the time."

Bianca nodded. "And Quintus needs everything he's got left."

The Wolf interrupted. "I know Quintus's story sounds a little preposterous, however, I'd like you all to hear me out." The group was silent. "I believe Quintus was murdered by the Dead King."

"Volteria has a king?" Neil asked. "A dead one?"

"Volteria has someone who claims to be a king." The Wolf placed the club back on the table. "He's a Lightborn. I'm not sure which kind, but it's said that no one can die in his presence."

"And the clowns?" Lilly asked.

"The Dead King is the head of a travelling circus. The Brotherhood of Merriment has been going village to village for decades and even played shows for the last Emperor a few times."

"Why is this important?" Bianca asked. "You want to recruit him?"

"He's been slaughtering Imperial Squadrons one by one and setting their men free. I've also heard rumors of him crumbling buildings with his mind."

"Sounds like Saewulf," Neil said.

"He's most probably a Lightborn," the Wolf said. "Either way he could be very useful to us."

"In bringing down the wall," Bianca realized aloud.

The Wolf pointed at her. "Exactly. At this point the revolution has two objectives. We need to take Abington and force the Emperor out of these lands, and then we need to bring down his walls. If we can manage that, we can unite all peoples fighting for freedom."

"What was he saying about cannons?" Bianca asked.

"I intend to create a three-pronged attack on the wall. Firstly, with the Dead King, if he can be coerced into joining us. Secondly, with these cannons, and finally with an invention the Jacobson's have cooked up."

Lilly rolled her eyes. "You mean the catapult?"

"It's a trebuchet," the Wolf muttered. "But yes."

Neil had only encountered the Jacobsons in passing, but they didn't exactly fill him with confidence. The two mousy brothers had been named Chief Strategist and Chief Engineer for the rebellion. In recent weeks they'd been hammering away at a giant contraption on the edge of camp and delegating to soldiers twice their size. They seemed capable enough, but they had the strange quirk of nearly always being coated in gunpowder. This made Neil nervous.

Before they could ask any more questions, the flaps of the tent parted and a lone soldier entered. "Ms. Blackmore, your guerilla force has returned. They'd like to brief you."

"You have a guerilla force?" Neil asked.

"I have two," Bianca said with a wink as she exited with Lilly in tow.

"Doesn't seem like you've told Bianca about my deception," the Wolf said after a moment.

"No. She looks up to you. The way I did. I'm not sure why, but I don't want to take that from her."

The Wolf stared at Neil. "I thought it might be because you hadn't decided yet. Whether or not to stay."

Neil didn't meet his eyes. "Yes," he said eventually. "That too."

The Wolf pointed across the room. "If you're curious about death, you might want to ask an expert."

Neil approached Quintus's snoring form. He slapped him, which brought him back to consciousness with a scream. "I hate you all… *So* much."

"You died," Neil said, humor gone. "What was it like?"

"It was only for a moment," Quintus said after what seemed a genuine moment of reflection. "I lifted up out of my body and heard thousands and thousands of voices ushering me forward. And then a golden light."

Neil looked back over his shoulder at the Wolf. The truth was becoming harder to ignore. "And then what?"

"I was pulled back into my body. Suddenly, I was alive again, staring into the face of some man with long hair. I don't know what you all call him, but he calls himself the Dead King. He told me he was searching for a boy with green skin."

The Wolf eyes narrowed. "What? Why?"

"What?" Quintus said.

The Wolf began to turn restlessly. "What about the boy with green skin?"

"He said he had a responsibility to destroy the boy with green skin. He said the boy—"

The Wolf didn't wait for Quintus to finish. "Men!"

Two men entered on command. "I had a young man buried on the outskirts of camp the other day. I need you to find him now."

"What's happening?" Neil asked.

The Wolf brushed past him, weaving through the flaps of the tent.

"I've made a mistake. A colossal error." He seized, rage and frustration sending his muscles into a flurry. "I was outplayed."

"How big? How big is the mistake?" Neil was running now to stay in speaking distance with the Wolf.

The next sentence was muffled by the wind and the activity of the camp, but Neil was almost certain the Wolf said, "I might have killed us all."

"What?"

The Wolf stopped outside the entrance to his personal tent. When he turned, Neil saw a flicker of panic cross his face, only to be masked again. "I didn't say anything. Gather the inner circle. The Empire is coming."

"And we're fighting?"

The Wolf shook his head. "We're running."

OUTSIDE ABINGTON

HAROLD THORNE

You can only move troops so quietly. Men going to war need weapons and armor and those things are heavy. Whereas the revolution could sneak through brooks and forests without much worry—their army was made up of odds and ends cobbled together—the Empire boasted overburdened men all the way down to their military-issued steel-toed boots. They won battles they could get to, but in years and years of fighting the Empire had never managed to crush Volteria and its leaders because the rebels could always outmaneuver them. That was before Harold Thorne. Before a man who could locate the camp. Before a man who forced half of the military to exchange their metals for leathers. Before a man who knew how to turn camps into slaughterhouses in the moments before the dawn.

He decided not to hold anything back. Thorne had called in favors and staked his entire reputation on the siege of this camp. If the war ended it would end tonight in a clearing just outside of Abington, right under their noses. "Anything else?" Thorne asked.

Leaf, who was coated head to toe in a thick layer of dirt, shook his head. "That's most of it. The Wolf's tent is in the center. If we move from the outside in-"

"We can trap him." Thorne nodded. "How was your nap?"

"It was fine." Leaf never said much about the moments when he had the life ripped from him. "Standard. They buried me pretty deep though. Must have suspected something."

"Well, you are weird looking," Thorne noted.

"Indeed. Weird."

Thorne continued taking notes. The two of them were alone in a small tent staked down in a bank a few miles from the clearing. Thorne liked getting his hands dirty. He'd once worked on a shop floor and forever missed the feeling of grit under his fingernails and the sense of accomplishment that came from a job well completed. "Tell General Carlin he's cleared to lead an offensive in from the South. You and I will take the West, and Saewulf will take the North."

"And the East?"

"He'll be here soon," Thorne said.

As if hearing that, The Marksman hobbled into the tent with expert dramatic timing. "Thorne." His skin was grey.

"Victor. Looking well."

The Marksman collapsed onto the ground and coughed up a thick glob of bloody mucus. "Need healing," he managed between shuddery gasps.

"Right, right." Thorne went to his trunk and removed a syringe. "This is far from being the real thing, but maybe there's a week in it. I can't give you whatever you need to live, but I can make you expel the toxins that are killing you."

"A week sounds good."

The Marksman looked worse than most corpses. Thorne estimated he might have less than an hour left. "Fine then. However, I just want to make sure we discuss terms."

He placed his boot on Victor's chest and pressed down, encouraging a bout of bloody coughs. "This is not done out of the goodness of my heart. This is an investment. You take my medicine, you trade for it with your loyalty."

79

"Made that bargain quite a few times, Thorne," the Marksman hissed. "Just do it. I'll kill whomever. Whatever."

"Good boy."

He inserted the needle into the side of Victor's neck and with one thumb pushed down on the plunger. "I'm no doctor, but that should do the trick."

The Marksman rolled over onto his belly and vomited, hard. "Dawn is in four hours," Thorne said, "which means we lay siege to the rebel camp in three. More than enough time for your body to purge itself of toxins. Then you've got a lot of killing to do."

"Like I said," The Marksman said. "Whomever. Whatever."

"Good." Thorne went back to the trunk. "You know I can't stand seeing beautiful things destroyed. There was a statue on my commute to work when I was a child. It was of a woman in a hood. To this day I have no idea who it was or what it was for, but I passed her every day and ran my hand across the smooth marble. The same way I can't bear to see beautiful things destroyed, some men can't bear to see beautiful things exist. I came by one day only to see that the sculpture had been defaced. Fingers struck from its left hand, hood cracked, knees shattered." He eventually found what he was looking for and removed a metal contraption. "So when I had the money I bought the block and therefore the statue. I had it repaired and made pristine and, in a way, took ownership of its beauty."

He fastened something to the stub where Victor's hand had once been. "That statue's purpose was to be beautiful and I returned it to its purpose. Your purpose is to kill, Victor. And now I have returned your purpose to you."

Victor pulled his arm away only to see that it was fitted with a long metal weapon. A revolver built into his body. He turned it over, amazed. "Six shots at a time, one handed reloading, low caliber bullets as I know that's your preference. Not a bad range if I do say so myself."

Victor's eyes welled up. Thorne hoped it wasn't just the sickness. He laughed aloud and patted the Marksman on the shoulder. After a couple moments Victor stood and admired the specs on his weapon.

He pulled the hammer back a few times and let the chambers revolve. "It fires six shots?"

"Yes sir."

Victor rotated his arm getting used to the weight. "How do I look?"

Thorne smirked. "You're beautiful."

And then the Marksman left to fulfill his purpose. Thorne didn't know much about the Venator, but he knew of their code. One of the most important rules was not to kill for sport. That didn't sound like a problem. When Victor killed, it wasn't sport. Victor killed to live.

REBEL BASE CAMP

NEIL VAPROS

There was a pervasive guilt that filled Neil's body whenever he thought of Rhys. He'd begged Bianca for every piece of news, but she had painfully little. Rhys had been tortured and lost a foot, but he was rescued and sent with Darius for safekeeping. Other than that, Neil had nothing. Although he wanted to run off into the distance and protect his little brother, there was nothing he could do. He didn't even know where to start looking.

That's why when Rhys and Darius pushed their way through the entrance of the Wolf's camp during the middle of their evacuation, the mix of emotions Neil felt was complicated to say the least. At first, joy. He materialized to his brother and wrapped his arms around him with all the strength his cracked ribs would lend him. Then, when he pulled back, concern. Rhys's hair had grown out into a mess and the bags under his eyes were a deep purple. "You're alive." Rhys sounded grateful and his eyes looked slightly glossy.

"You're alive," Neil responded.

"And me too." Darius said.

Neil pulled back. "I never thought I'd be this happy to see you."

Darius chuckled. "Honestly, I feel the same way."

Darius looked over Neil's shoulder. Neil had completely forgotten that Bianca, Lilly, and the Wolf were here. "Miss Celerius!" Darius called. "You are also alive."

"So are you." Lilly didn't look up from the war map she was studying. "I'm mildly pleased."

"That's better than I expected," Darius whispered to Neil.

"Tell me about it," Neil said.

Bianca rushed over to hug them and compare notes about their recent weeks, but the Wolf continued to shove papers and plans into bags. "I'm thrilled to see you boys, but we don't have time for a reunion," the Wolf said. "We're evacuating. This camp is compromised."

"To be fair so are we," Darius said. "The Marksman is after us."

Bianca made quick eye contact with Neil, and he could tell they were thinking the same thing. Both of them looked awful. Darius was doing his best to mask it, but he looked wounded. And Rhys hadn't said much of anything. "You okay?" Neil asked.

Rhys nodded, but there was a certain dullness to it. *"Just need some rest."* Rhys's voice sounded deeper this time and not entirely his own.

"Rhys?" Neil asked.

He stumbled forward toward the center of the tent. *"Tired. Just so tired."* Neil saw him slip his hand into his coat. *"This is where the heart is,"* Rhys said. *"Good. Good."*

Without warning he pulled a knife from his coat and stabbed at the Wolf's back. As if anticipating it, the Wolf spun and disarmed the boy handily. With the same motion he gripped him by the coat and swung him onto the table. Rhys tried to lift his arm, but the Wolf stabbed the knife into the sleeve of his coat, pinning his arm to the table. "Doctor. I'm afraid I don't have time for this. Release the boy. Now."

For a moment the room was totally silent. Then it erupted into chaos. Lilly restrained Rhys's other arm, Darius thundered over to stop things from escalating, and Rhys shook violently, spitting and screaming. All Neil could do was watch on, horrified and useless. "Release the boy. Now." This time the Wolf's voice shook the tent.

"Or you'll do what?" Rhys asked in his new voice. *"Remove his head from his body? In front of all his friends?"*

The Wolf slammed his fist onto the table. The Doctor laughed. The Wolf turned to glare at Darius. "Did you know?"

Darius shook his head. "He's been acting weird but never... Not like this." He paused. "I had my suspicions."

The Wolf looked down on Rhys and then at Neil. Neil hadn't realized it until he was under the Wolf's gaze, but he was crying. "I will fix this," the Wolf breathed in a quiet promise.

Neil nodded numbly. He'd thought he had his brother back, but in yet another cruel twist of fate, his brother was farther away than ever. "Plans have to change," the Wolf said.

"Do tell," the Doctor said.

The Wolf socked Rhys in the face, rendering him unconscious. "Once again we really shouldn't do that," Bianca said.

"If anyone can spare the brain cells it's Rhys," Lilly said quietly.

The Wolf went to the wall of the tent and cut down the fabric. He removed Rhys from the table and wrapped him tight in a complicated knot. "We have to split up. I know someone who can help Rhys, but it's in the exact opposite direction of where we need to go."

He pulled out an inkwell and dipped a finger in it, circling a patch of land. "Rhys needs to see the Grand Master at the Venator Lodge, while we need to find the Dead King."

Neil was hardly listening. He approached Rhys's body and placed a hand on the side of his head, smoothing out the wild hair. This was the boy who'd been afraid of the dark all his life? What had the world done to him?

"I believe the Dead King to be a man by the name of John Cartwright and I've tracked him to-"

"Wait," Bianca said. "John Cartwright the writer?"

"Yes," the Wolf said.

"The poet?" she asked again, incredulous.

"Yes."

"You think the romantic poet John Cartwright is an impossibly powerful Lightborn that makes it so men can't be killed."

"Yes," the Wolf repeated.

"Didn't John Cartwright write Little Billy?" Darius asked.

"Yes." The group stared at the Wolf, a heavy blanket of skepticism weighing on the tent. "I know it sounds odd. But I've kept correspondence with Cartwright over the past eight years. He's all but admitted it to me in this most recent letter."

He held up a stack of papers. "So some of us need to go see Cartwright here out by Arkney." He drew another circle. "And some of us need to go to the Venator Lodge by Shipwreck Bay to get Rhys cured of this particular affliction."

"Affliction?" Bianca asked.

"If the Doctor is taking over Rhys's body, the culprit is most definitely hiding in the mind. No one knows more about the mind than the Grand Master."

"I'm going with Rhys," Neil decided.

The Wolf grimaced. "It would be much easier to convince Cartwright to join us if you were there, Neil."

"I don't care," Neil said. "My brother needs me."

"Understandable. Darius?"

"I'm with Rhys."

"All right. Darius and Neil will take Rhys and the rest of us will go to meet with Cartwright. The rest of the rebels will slip into the shadows and wait for our siege on Abington. We must leave immediately though."

Neil looked over at Bianca. His heart was torn. He'd finally be with his brother, but he'd just gotten her back and it was impossible to know when would be the last time. She looked back to him. He realized she was thinking the same thing. Suddenly Neil saw a ripple pass through the tent, starting with Lilly and moving to the Wolf. "Oh no," she whispered.

The Wolf shook his head. "We're too late."

"Where are they approaching from?" Bianca asked as she readied her knives.

"All sides," Lilly said. "We're going to have to fight our way out."

"We're not ready." The Wolf drew his sword. "There are still…" He looked around the tent wildly until he made eye contact with Neil. "I need you to do something for me." His eyes came to Lilly next. "Both of you."

"Yes?" Lilly asked.

"We were drawing up plans on the south side of camp yesterday morning, remember?"

"Yes," Lilly said.

"There are three tents I need destroyed by any means necessary. They have letters to Cartwright, not to mention strategies on how to take Abington. If they find it, they might very well win the war."

"Why us?" Neil asked with one more glance at Rhys.

"Lilly is the fastest and you can fly."

"I can't fly," Neil said. "I can fall kind of slowly."

"Well, you can throw fire and that's what I need right now."

Neil looked back at Bianca. Then at Rhys. Then at the Wolf. "Ready?" He asked Lilly as she bolted to his side.

She drew her swords and nodded. Without another word, they exited the tent and walked into the open air where clouds of smoke were blooming. Then the ground shook, the rebel camp becoming a killing ground.

REBEL BASE CAMP

HIGHEST HONOR

LILLY CELERIUS

Running never felt like running anymore to Lilly. It felt like soaring. She never felt the ground underneath her feet and the world would blur around her until she decided to stop. Now she weaved around men's blades and sliced through them without stopping to see where they fell. She reached the tent long before Neil and took stock of the situation. There were Imperial soldiers about two hundred feet away and advancing quickly. She had limited time to act. "Miss Celerius?" There were two guards in here, and judging by their torches they were thinking the same thing as the Wolf. "Are we being attacked?"

"Yes," Lilly said. "Burn these documents. Then burn the tent."

"That'll take a while."

"No it won't. I brought you a friend."

Neil landed outside the tent in a burst of flame, scarring the grass beneath him. "You're faster than I remember," Neil said to Lilly.

"You're just slow."

"Cracked ribs." Neil motioned to his bandaged torso.

"You were slow before the ribs. These men will help you burn the tents."

"Hi boys," Neil said.

"Move quickly," Lilly said. "We're running out of time."

"Yes, Miss Celerius," one of the guards said as he lit the documents on the table in front of him.

Lilly made a decision. "It's Lieutenant Celerius."

Neil threw a fireball at the center of the tent and the documents ignited. "Did you just promote yourself?"

She shrugged. "File a complaint."

She stepped out into the open night air and watched as the wave of Imperial soldiers marched in her direction. She saw something else too. A small wave of dust hurtling in her direction. Something was coming at her. And it was coming at her fast. She knew it was Carlin before he arrived. He slowed to a stop and a gust of wind came with him. "I have a question for you," Lilly said, holding her swords at the ready.

Carlin grinned and opened his arms wide. "Yes?"

"Are you a Celerius?" Her voice quivered a bit and she resented herself for it.

Carlin spat on the ground. "No." That was confusing but a relief. "I am much, much more than that."

Lilly glanced behind her. Neil was throwing fireball after fireball, turning the tent into an inferno. "What's in the tent?" Carlin asked.

"Fire," Lilly said. "And not much else."

She wasn't sure how, but Carlin breezed past her reaching the center of the tent in an instant. He sliced both of the guards in half and swung once or twice at Neil, who evaded clumsily. He threw a fireball and knocked Carlin backward. "General Carlin."

"Vapros."

"It's been too long. Last time I saw you—"

"You lit me on fire," Carlin interrupted.

Neil laughed. "Oh yeah. I forget about that sometimes."

Carlin lashed out, but Neil was surprisingly good at staying out of his way. Lilly took this opportunity to swing at his back, which he blocked as if sensing the blade cutting through the air. "Get to the other tents," Lilly commanded.

Neil saluted and escaped through the back of the tent. "Other tents?" Carlin asked.

He swung wildly, which she blocked without response. He parried her next blows and kicked one of her blades out of her hand into a burning patch of grass nearby. After exchanging blows for another minute, she managed to rake her remaining blade down his sword arm. He seized in pain and dropped his weapon. The cut wasn't deep enough for him to lose the arm, but a trickle of blood travelled from his elbow to his wrist. She waited to see if he would heal, but he didn't. If he wasn't a Celerius, then what was he?

Carlin retreated to the other side of the tent and pulled her blade from the grass. It glowed red from the heat. "What have you named this one?" he asked.

"Thomas."

"Another way he'll aid in your death."

He attacked her with the blade, but she could see he was slowing now, half as fast as he was before. She found herself not only on the offensive, but winning. She delivered cuts to his hand, then his leg, then to his chest. He dropped the blade and groaned in agony. "What does that mean?" she demanded. "Thomas never did anything to hurt me."

Carlin pulled a flask from his coat and downed it before she could stop him. A drop of red liquid fell from his mouth. "Not on purpose, no." And with that his speed was back.

Before she could process what was happening, Carlin reclaimed her sword and raked it across her chest all the way up to her chin. She fell screaming to the ground. He stood now, teetering back and forth. She waited for her wounds to heal, but they wouldn't. She stared at him as he approached, trying to make sense of what had happened. "That drink makes you fast," she realized out loud. She thought about what he'd said earlier and she gasped. "It's blood. It's his blood."

Carlin chuckled and stood tall. "Yes, Lilly. Yes, it is." He looked her over. "You're not healing."

He admired the sword in his hand, still glowing. "Burning you..

That's the answer isn't it? You won't heal if your skin is burned. The Marksman was right."

She said nothing, but knew he was right. That was a well-kept secret in the Celerius family. Cauterized wounds took weeks to heal. She reached for his blade, and he put the burning one to her neck. "Don't move," he said.

Her eyes filled with tears. She'd never felt rage like this before. "You took his blood?" she asked in disbelief. "You took my brother's blood?"

"Anthony's too."

She couldn't imagine letting him do that to her. She couldn't imagine him using her blood to fuel his murderous rampages. "Do it," Lilly said. "Kill me. Do it now."

Carlin eyed her, and gritted his teeth. She could see him thinking hard. "Don't say that. Don't ask me to do it."

"You won't use me." She was crying now. "Not like you used them."

A few soldiers entered the tent, led by a man with shoulder length dark hair. It took Lilly a moment to recognize Lieutenant Virgil, Carlin's right hand and Anthony's former protégé. It had been a long time since she'd seen him and she hated the fact that he was here. He'd sat by and watched her brother killed like a coward. Would he do the same here? She couldn't fathom how much death he'd stood by and condoned. "Sir," Virgil said eyeing the General. "You're wounded."

"Yes. Take this woman into custody."

"You're not going to kill her?" one of the men asked.

Carlin looked as if he was weighing his options. "No. She'd like me to. But I'm not giving her the satisfaction." He used the sword to pin her coat to the ground. "She's got a bigger purpose."

"Any other orders, sir?" Virgil asked.

"Yes. Find Neil Vapros."

REBEL BASE CAMP

NEIL VAPROS

The rebel camp had been partially evacuated at the time of the attack, but as Neil gazed upon the destruction from above he wondered if the remaining rebels knew how bleak the situation was. After all, Neil was flying, or falling slowly, and he could see everything: Carlin and his men coming from the south, Saewulf razing tents and advancing from the north, men with gas masks followed by plumes of yellow gas from the west, and endless gunfire from the east. Neil saw bodies falling everywhere and tents collapsing over men like funeral shrouds.

He landed farther to the center of camp and made quick work of another tent. This one was easy. He had rage to spur him on. He didn't know whom it was for, but seeing this much death around him made his entire body hot. He reached the last tent without impediment, and found it occupied by a few Imperial soldiers. Neil made quick work of them, but before he could burn the documents a figure filled the entryway of the tent.

Neil turned to let free another fireball, but was out of energy. He'd been flying and roasting entire sections of camp and needed to rest.

The soldier at the entryway had an arrow notched into a bow and piercing eyes that look vaguely familiar. "Neil Vapros."

"We haven't met."

"No? My name is Virgil."

The silence and tension between them was palpable. Why was this man so familiar to him? There was something about his voice and complexion that Neil found familiar. Neil pointed at the arrow. "You going to let that thing loose?"

Virgil didn't say anything. He just waited. Neil felt his energy returning and eyed his enemy. "Why do you look so familiar?"

"I'm not sure."

"What's your last name?"

"Servatus."

"I don't like it," Neil said. His energy returned and with a burst of fire Neil catapulted himself toward Virgil, closing the distance immediately. They collided. Neil felt pain radiating through his chest, but he ignored it. Virgil tried to grapple with Neil, but Neil deterred him with a few well-placed jabs. Eventually Virgil tried to wrap his arm around Neil's and pull it from its socket. Neil was ready for that. He'd seen that move before and twisted around and delivered a solid kick to Virgil's nose, sending him onto his back. "Virgil Servatus," Neil breathed as he made his way to his feet. "No ring to it."

"No?" Virgil asked as he pulled a knife from his belt.

"No, not like say… Virgil Venator."

Silence fell on the tent. Neil held Virgil in his gaze. There was a millisecond long twitch in Virgil's eye, and Neil knew he was right. "You going to use that knife?" Neil asked.

Virgil lowered it.

"You a rebel?"

Virgil shook his head.

"But you're not Imperial either?"

Virgil waited, and then shrugged. "Real hard to tell these days."

Neil understood that. He was going to ask a few more questions before another figure appeared in the doorway. Virgil, true to form, threw his knife at Neil. It lightly grazed him, which was probably intentional. Neil responded by throwing a fireball that extinguished once it hit Virgil's chest.

Their intruder wore a gas mask, but removed it upon his entrance. He was a well-dressed man with an impeccably styled mustache, removing a revolver from his coat, he fired it casually at Neil. The shot went wide. "Neil Vapros, in the business, we call that a 'warning shot.'"

Neil stared the man down. He too looked vaguely familiar. "You recognize me? I'm a old friend of your father's. My name is Harold Thorne."

Neil had met Harold Thorne a few times as a child, when his father had been looking to expand his alcohol business. The man certainly looked different from the grime-stained industrialist Neil had once known. This man, even in the harsh terrain looked impeccably styled. "This tent full of plans?" Thorne asked. "Quite a find, eh?" He grinned at Virgil who grinned back.

Neil looked back at the boxes of documents lining the room and made a few quick calculations. Could he kill Thorne before he was shot? Could he destroy the documents before he was shot? Was he willing to try? "I get it," Thorne said. "Complicated choice. Everyone says they want to die for the cause, but it's not so easy to back up that kind of talk. You ready, Neil? Are you a martyr or a coward?"

Neil saw a flash of white light in the darkness behind Thorne. "I'm a coward." He paused before adding, "But she's not."

A knife imbedded itself in the back of Thorne's shoulder. When he tried to lift his arm he found it useless. Bianca kicked him from behind. When he tried to stumble to his feet, she kicked the back of his head, driving his face into the earthen floor. Blood spurted from his nose, coloring his mustache. He changed hands with his gun, fumbling messily. Neil took the opportunity to throw a fireball at the documents with his right hand. With his left he launched himself in Bianca's direction, carrying her from the tent into the open night air.

Neil and Bianca landed in a calmer area a few feet off. "Where's Rhys?" Neil breathed.

"They were heading east right?"

It was hard to breath and harder to see. The air was filled with a yellow smoke that billowed around their feet and burned to inhale. Neil tried desperately to orient himself, but everything looked more or less the same when on fire. "I don't think I can fly again."

Bianca nodded and looked upward. It took Neil a moment to understand she was using the stars to determine which way was east. Neil kept watch as she did so. Eventually a figure appeared a few yards off in the smoke. He didn't look like much, with green skin and short black hair. Was this the boy that the Dead King was searching for? "Bianca," Neil said quietly.

The boy stared at them and wordlessly pulled a canister from his coat. He pulled the pin, and it began to release more of the yellow gas that filled the air. He didn't seem bothered by the fumes enveloping him. He tossed the canister in their direction, and Neil lifted his hand to throw a fireball. "Wouldn't do that," the boy said, without color in his voice. He lifted a hand to point at the canister. "Flammable."

Bianca kicked the canister away, but its work was done. She began coughing violently. Neil held his breath and grabbed one of her knives from her belt. He was no marksman, but his throw landed square in the boy's chest. He waited for the boy to fall, but he simply took the knife from his chest and dropped it. "Neil," Bianca choked. "We need to go."

Neil grabbed her again, but this time he was unable to summon fire to fly. He ran with her in a random direction. After a dozen paces, he needed to breathe and the sting of air deprivation was replaced with the sting of poisonous air. Neil's arms got heavy and the blood pooled in his toes. He struggled to lift Bianca. His eyes began to burn and water. He finally found a patch of grass where the air was clear. With a shout, he launched them high into the air.

Neil piloted as they slowly fell together. He held her close, the wind threatening to carry her away. Neil realized that this was always how it had been, Neil and Bianca struggling to hang on to each other despite what tried to rip them apart. Her eyes fluttered open and filled with fear, only subsiding when she realized he had control of things. He landed with her slightly outside of camp and collapsed, wheezing.

Bianca stirred at his side and laid her hand on his back. He eventually rolled over, eyes transfixed on the canopy above them and the stars beyond it. He felt delirious. Then his eyes shifted to her and the concern in her eyes. "Don't worry," Neil said as his vision went blurry, "nothing in the world could take me from you."

REBEL BASE CAMP

RHYS VAPROS

Darius wasn't known for his ability to carefully assess situations. He was more of the "rush into battle and assess afterwards" kind of guy. However, Rhys always thought that reputation was unearned. Darius had a quiet intelligence and situational awareness that many missed. At least, Rhys believed this until he awoke being carried in the direction of Saewulf Anima. The psychic was in the distance, leaving crumbled ground in his wake. "Whoa, what are we…"

Darius turned and they sped in another direction. "We're cornered," Darius said, breathing heavily. He lowered Rhys down in an abandoned tent. "I tried to go west, but there's too much smoke. I tried to go east but the Marksman was waiting and he's had a little makeover."

"And now we're moving…?"

"North. But that's not going so well either."

"Do you think Saewulf spotted us?"

Suddenly the tent was ripped away and there stood the Emperor's psychic, glowing with dark energy. "Yeah, I'm almost certain," Darius said.

With a brush of Saewulf's hand, Darius and Rhys went flying, their bodies rolling across the ground. Rhys realized he was wrapped in what looked like a blanket for some reason. For the first time he wondered why he'd been unconscious in the first place. The last thing he remembered was setting eyes on Neil. He often felt bad about not making a more conscious effort to continue the search for his brother, but he didn't remember how he'd reacted to seeing Neil alive.

Saewulf pulled the two of them back into his purview and cocked his head. "Lightborns?" he asked as he noted their appearance.

"No," Darius said.

"Saewulf lifted Darius into the air and slammed him into the dirt. "You feel heavy."

"That's rude," Darius groaned.

"Taurlum heavy," he said as he slammed Darius down again and again.

Darius tried to stand, but the force around him was too great. Rhys shifted and strained against his binds to no avail. He'd been tied tight. "Taurlum and Vapros working together," Saewulf said scornfully. "Heartwarming." He turned his glowing eyes to Rhys and dragged him closer. "I know this one. We met briefly."

"We did," Rhys said. "You were killing my sister at the time."

Saewulf's smile fell. "Regrettable. But necessary."

A rage appeared in Rhys's stomach that soon consumed his body. Without understanding how, Rhys undid his binds, finding the lack in tension and where to bend. Darius noticed Rhys shifting and attempted to stand again. Saewulf, though powerful, struggled against Darius's strength. Saewulf slammed him down again, but this time Darius raised his arms. Saewulf's body jerked back. "Fancy outfit," Darius said. "Those metal bracers?"

Saewulf tried to move his arms, but found them restrained. His expression changed from confusion to frustration. "I think I do remember you." He lashed out with his hands and the ground shook. "You were at the gate, right?"

Darius didn't answer. His forehead was lined with sweat from trying to contain Saewulf's power. "I remember you being too weak to stop the gate from closing, too weak to save the Celerius servant, too weak to stop us. You ran. You're always running." Saewulf gained control of his arms and with difficulty he brought his hands back in front. "So strong, but always too weak. Frustrating isn't it?" Darius groaned in pain. "Are you weak on the inside too?" The earth crumbled around Darius's legs. "You know war isn't for everyone. Hardship isn't for everyone. It breaks people."

Darius crumbled, his body pressed against the earth. It didn't matter though. Rhys had freed himself and materialized behind Saewulf, grabbing him by the back of the neck. Rhys channeled his energy and Saewulf shook. It had been a while since Rhys had done this trick, but something didn't feel right. Saewulf was fighting the urge to sleep, and no one had ever done that before. Rhys's brain began to throb from the pain and he soon heard the Doctor screaming within. Saewulf wouldn't sleep, but he was distracted and that was enough.

Darius lunged from his spot on the ground and delivered a hard swing to Saewulf's chest, cracking the ribs. "Funny," Darius swung again. "I feel strong enough."

Saewulf roared and Rhys's head felt like it was about to split. "Get him away!" Rhys begged.

Darius grabbed Saewulf by the arm and with a mighty heave threw the psychic across the rebel camp. Saewulf slowed himself dozens of yards away and landed without a noise. He paused, then lowered his hand to his chest with pained breathing. "I've never hit anyone that hard before." Darius heaved.

"Most people you hit…."

"Die, yeah."

"So…?"

"We run," Darius said. "We run."

They made it to the tree line before they realized Saewulf wasn't pursuing them anymore. Once they course corrected to head east, Darius broke to take a breath and Rhys watched him. "I can't believe we lived through that."

"Me either," Darius replied. "Can't believe we landed a shot on Saewulf."

"Think we should have stayed behind and fought?"

"No," Darius said after a while. "I think he was just getting warmed up." He sat on the ground. "And I'm out of..." He paused. "Well, everything."

Rhys sat down beside him. "Still. Excellent work."

"If I don't tie you up do you promise not to, I don't know, stab me to death?"

"Yeah, of course." Suddenly Rhys's stomach dropped. "Wait, why? What did I do?"

"You tried to kill the Wolf. Or, *he* did."

Rhys stared at Darius, trying to grapple with the fact that all his secrets had spilled out. "I... did? Is he okay?"

"He's fine. The old man is a lot of things, but none more than perceptive."

Rhys didn't know what to say. He was racked with guilt. He settled on, "I'm sorry. For hiding it from you."

"You know I'm your friend, right?"

The night air had a sort of cling to it. Rhys felt it like a blanket, sweltering him in his shame. "Yes."

"I'm not going to kill you to kill the Doctor. I don't know much, but I know that won't bring Anastasia back. And I know it's not your fault."

"Isn't it?" Rhys was tearing up.

"No," Darius said flatly. "What you do is who you are. What's done to you is not. That's what I believe. That's how I do right and wrong."

"Okay." Rhys wiped a tear from his eye. "Thanks."

"Always, Rhys. We're a team."

"Okay team," Rhys said when he could. "Where to?"

"Onward. As per usual."

And they ran again.

18

REBEL BASE CAMP

HIGHEST HONOR

THE WOLF

From the hill where the Wolf stood he could see the entirety of his camp. Half of it was consumed by noxious yellow gas, the other was demolished into a smoldering pyre. Giant tendrils of smoke climbed toward the sky, like giant hands reaching to the stars for rescue. He watched coolly with a few men at his back, the ones who fought through with him. James Jacobson, one of the chief engineers stood at his side, marveling at the horror. "Where's your brother?" the Wolf asked.

The boy pointed into the camp wordlessly.

"We'll get him back."

"If there's anything to get back," James said.

The Wolf clenched his jaw. "Yes."

The Wolf had always had a rule about war. He never looked at the faces of the men he slayed in battle. His kill count was much higher than most and he couldn't bear to know the ages of the men he killed. Snuffing out old men wasn't so hard. Killing boys was enough to chip away at the soul. He hoped Jacob Jacobson was off somewhere alive. He hoped he hadn't killed that boy too.

Once in Shipwreck Bay a woman had told him that she could see ghosts. Humoring her he'd asked, "Are any with me?"

She'd placed his head in her hands and said, "They are all with you."

At the time, he found it preposterous. These days he didn't know.

"Did we lose?" James said after a while. "I don't want to be the one to say it. But did we lose?"

"No," the Wolf said, a gut reply. "Volteria is not a place." He spoke loud enough so that all his men could hear his voice. "It was born in basements and bars and it lives in the hearts of men who believe they deserve a life free of shackles and oppression. Volteria flees into the woods with the people."

His men gave an impassioned noise of agreement and it felt like a blade to the chest. That's how it always felt. Blades to the chest. The more men who followed him, the more men would die. He was worried. Worried that they *had* lost. The revolution wasn't just bars and basements anymore. It was thousands of men in the open. A real force that could be truly crushed.

The Wolf extended his hand and felt for life around them. There were two figures not so far off, and he knew them at once. It was his right hand and his Phoenix. He signaled for his men to move in that direction. He'd been trying to keep his thoughts away from Neil Vapros, but they were always there slamming on the door. He found it a source of endless guilt, but that was his lot in life. Would he let Neil die to end the ceaseless killing that he saw everywhere? He hoped he was strong enough to lose one lamb to save the herd. When they approached Neil's unconscious form, with Bianca standing over him, he had to once again grapple with the hardest part of being a human, and a killer.

People were not cattle and never had the Wolf once seen death and felt that it was right.

19

IMPERIAL BANK OF ABINGTON

HAROLD THORNE

Most people feared death. Understandably. What could be scarier than taking steps into darkness, not knowing the terrain? Harold Thorne, however, was not most people and often fantasized about death. He knew the processes his body would go through as he lost consciousness, but what excited him was what would happen after he died. Specifically, the removal and dissection of his brain.

He'd been approached as a young man and asked to donate his body to Altryon's Scientific Society after his demise and agreed without a second's delay. He knew his legacy would far surpass his life. The thought was a supreme comfort.

It's also what confused him about Jack Jacobson. If things ended for him here in this makeshift dungeon, it would be the end. He'd have no legacy besides a hodgepodge of mediocre creations made for a failing rebellion. Why didn't he fear death? Why would he reveal nothing? Thorne lowered his red-hot tongs in frustration. "We found your tent," he said drawing out the syllables, letting the suspense build.

"I swear those drawings are uh… someone else's."

Thorne turned on his heels, body full of fury. "Stop! You're not charming. You're not funny. I don't like your jokes."

Jack didn't say anything, he just frowned. "Words are the real torture," he finally muttered.

"I found these," Thorne said, pulling a tattered piece of parchment from his coat. "Plans for a siege weapon. You really think you can bring down Altryon's walls with a catapult."

"Actually it's a trebuchet."

"What's the difference?"

"Oh boy, where do I even begin?"

Thorne lowered the parchment next to his tongs. "Is there no end to your optimism? Or your foolish bravery."

"No," Jack said.

Thorne gestured to his large array of torture devices. "I might end up using these on myself."

"That's fine. I'll wait."

Thorne grabbed a saw. "Most business men aren't creative. They don't innovate. They find satisfaction and even fulfillment in doing things exactly the way they've always been done. There are few businessmen remaining in Altryon, and every single one of them manages one of my shops. This is because I was willing to do things that kinder men never even dared consider."

"Monologuing for instance."

"I will execute you!" Thorne spat. He sputtered for a moment. "Damn it! I lost my train of thought. The point is that I'm creative. And I'm about to show you why I'm the only remaining titan in Altryon."

He slammed his closed first on the door. Eventually two soldiers came to the door holding a man in rebel clothing between them. "This man tells me his name is Arnold. That's probably made up. His name doesn't matter though. What matters is that you probably know him."

They pulled him up by his hair. Thorne saw the slightest light of recognition in Jack's eyes. "You might not be friends, but maybe you've seen him around. My point is, there's a difference between oppressors and oppressed soldiers. Oppressors have had their empathy sapped away." He gestured to his chest. "But the oppressed fight in no small part for empathy."

"So you're going to...?" The humor had leaked from Jack's demeanor.

"I'm going to decapitate this man with my saw. Starting with the front of the neck. Most people start at the back, but I am not most people."

The soldiers threw the rebel to the ground and held his arms down by his sides. He lashed and screamed, but was unable to come up with a single articulate word. "It's so easy to call yourself a hero when you take the pain and the mutilation for your people. But what about when it's someone else? What then Jack? What then?"

"Stop," Jack said.

"Tell me the Rebellion's next move," Thorne spat as he lowered the saw against flesh. "I have an entire hallway of lambs to lead to slaughter. You tell me how many you can watch die. You tell me, Jack."

A thin drop of blood appeared on the rebel's neck, and Jack groaned in discomfort. Thorne sawed deeper. The rebel made a furious scream for help.

"We're liberating Abington!"

Silence fell and Thorne stood tall. "How? When?"

"We're going to destroy the bridges between your bases and Abington and then surround it."

Thorne's eyes narrowed. "You don't have enough men to surround Abington."

Jack was silent.

"Or do you?" Throne asked.

Jack was silent.

"Handy information," Thorne said. The soldiers threw the rebel out of the room and Thorne followed them out. "My, my Jack," he said over his shoulder. "You were so funny a few moments ago."

He ascended the staircase and the two soldiers led him to the main floor of the Bank of Abington. Thorne gazed at the giant marble pillars and ornate etchings. Why hadn't they set up here months ago?

Saewulf was in the center of the bank, hands planted on a desk as two field doctors wrapped his body with bandages. The pervasive rumor sweeping the ranks was that Saewulf had taken quite a beating at the camp but had used his powers to reassemble and patch his broken bones. Thorne wished that wasn't true, but even now the bruising looked to be fading. "Sir, you're looking better."

"I heal quickly," Saewulf said, no small measure of pain in his voice.

Thorne noted the burns. "Is that a new thing?"

"Yes," Saewulf said.

How was Saewulf getting so much stronger? The riddle plagued Thorne's waking moments.

"Fantastic," Thorne said. "I know what the rebels are up to. If you're up for hearing it."

"Yes?"

"They believe they can't take Altryon without first uniting all five villages and forcing the Empire completely back behind our walls."

"They don't want us spread out?"

"No."

Saewulf waved his hand and the medics left. He took his shirt from the table and slowly brought it around his bruised, still significantly burned torso. "Do they plan to starve us out?"

"I can't imagine the Wolf would sacrifice the innocents."

Saewulf smirked. "I'm not sure. Seems to be his only move these days."

Thorne nodded slowly, entertaining the idea. "Maybe they think more bodies within Altryon creates more chaos."

"We can control anything the slums throw at us," Saewulf said.

"Do you live in the slums?"

"I live in the palace."

"Right. Well, I work there. You'd be surprised what they can throw at you."

Saewulf bowed his head, deep in thought. "So what now?"

"How strong are you?" Thorne asked eventually.

Saewulf cocked his head. "What?"

"Could you level a building?"

"Absolutely."

"A block?"

"I imagine so."

"A village?"

Thorne saw Saewulf processing that. "You want to…"

"Have you ever wondered why the rebels are so obsessed with taking Abington?" Thorne approached and took a seat next to Saewulf though it made him nervous. It was paramount that any fear or weakness be hidden. "They've never fought for any other village as hard as they do for this one. Why?"

"Because it's the biggest?" Saewulf asked.

Thorne shook his head. "It's the closest to the wall."

Saewulf stood now and paced around. For the first time Thorne noticed that he favored the foot farthest from his burns. "And having the closest village will help them how?"

"It's full of food and supplies, and it's easily defensible. If the Wolf takes Abington…"

"He mounts his siege from there."

The two finally met eyes and shared a silent conversation. Saewulf was the first to speak. "I can't level Abington. Thousands will die. This war is about exterminating Lightborns. There aren't any Lightborns in Abington."

"You know how many thousands of people will die in this war? This is the lesser of two evils."

"Crushing innocents makes it hard to believe that we're in the right."

Thorne couldn't help it. He laughed aloud. His cackles reverberated off the marble walls. Before they could return to Thorne's ear, he realized Saewulf was serious. Thorne *knew* they weren't the good guys. It was obvious from where he stood. It just didn't matter so much to him. With all the blood on Saewulf's hands could he really still consider himself a hero?

It was clear that the laugh had offended Saewulf. Instead of his usual rage, Thorne saw a deep pain reflected in the psychic's eyes. "That will be all, Thorne." He summoned his coat with a wave of his hand and it wrapped itself around him. "Your suggestions will be considered."

Thorne thought about pressing the issue, but decided to exercise patience. He bowed and retreated back to the basement, leaving Saewulf alone to brood. On the way down, Thorne imagined the sound of his boots echoing was the sound of his laugh. He'd damaged his position with the man in charge, but gleaned a valuable piece of information. Saewulf *actually* believed in his cause. He was intent on ridding the world of Lightborns.

When Thorne thought of his legacy, he thought of industry. He saw factories as far as the eye could see, and his products in the pocket of every well-to-do citizen. He imagined scientists with impeccable facial hair standing over his body, studying the brain that had guided their nation into the future.

Did Saewulf have fantasies like that? Did happiness exist in his new world without Lightborns? Did love? Did peace? Thorne reminded himself to be careful around his leader.

One thing Thorne knew from business was that men with desires were on the market, ready to be bought and traded. But no one alive could move men who believed in their cause. He was glad he had joined this faction, as he'd initially considered the possibility of joining the rebellion. At first he'd taken up with the Empire because they seemed like they were on the winning side, ready to lead the new world. Now Thorne knew that wasn't the case. Saewulf was the new world.

20

IMPERIAL MILITARY FORTRESS

LILLY CELERIUS

Lilly had been waiting for footsteps. It had been hours and her eyes hadn't adjusted to the darkness at all. She'd once escaped Imperial imprisonment by breaking the bones in her hands, but she knew that wasn't an option here. Her limbs were strapped down in various places and a thick strip of leather held her neck firmly against the dense oaken table. Without room to move the slightest fraction of an inch, Lilly had no choice but to wait for the sound of footsteps. And she feared those footsteps would carry a fate worse than death.

When Carlin came, he let the door drift open slowly. The light stretched over Lilly's cell and seared her eyes. She held them tight until she could bear it, then she watched as he gloated, taking his time descending the staircase to her table. He looked her up and down, examining the straps, making sure she hadn't tampered with them. Seeming satisfied, he stood at attention by her side. In his hand he clutched a stack of faded letters. "So," he said satisfaction dripping from his disfigured mouth, "Cartwright is cozying up to revolutionaries, eh? You can't trust anyone these days."

Lilly contemplated spitting on him, but she knew she wouldn't be able to reach him. She'd never felt despair like this. Neil's mission to burn the documents had evidently failed. If Carlin knew about Cartwright, he knew where to find the Wolf.

"I'm not a fan," Carlin continued. "I mean Little Billy is objectively hilarious, but his poetry, the stuff women swoon over, has always felt so silly to me. As a young man I used to comb through them, trying to see what had garnered so much attention. I always left confused. Cartwright brags. He brags and he brags and he brags. Every poem, a new woman." Carlin paced and his hands were curling and uncurling into fists. "He talks about this consumption. Being consumed. He talks about how he'd meet women and they would consume him head to toe. He'd have nothing else to think about. Nothing else in his life but the sight of them behind his eyelids. Nothing but the smell of them. I always thought that was so stupid. I always found that so trite." He paused with his back to her. "That was until I met Anthony Celerius."

She felt the silence clutching her throat beneath the leather strap and waited, passively begging him to continue. "Hate and love are one and the same. My mother used to say that." Lilly listened with reluctant interest. She had never heard this kind of pain in his voice before, but always heard him screaming or groaning or spitting. Never lamenting. "I met Anthony Celerius and I hated him when I set eyes on him. I had clawed through the ranks, spilled blood, and cracked my bones bettering myself. And this man, this *Lightborn*, came along and filled the army with his presence like ink through water."

Lilly couldn't be certain, but she thought Carlin was shaking. If she could turn her rage into energy, she would have long since ripped her shackles free, but she couldn't. She wished he'd do it already. Finish her.

"He didn't train like I did. He didn't want it like I did. He didn't even need to serve." Carlin turned to face her, a familiar sneer appearing on his face. "I was a bastard born in the slums and raised with the knowledge that I descended from royalty. I fought to serve my family. To serve my father. Anthony fought for what? Glory? Honor? You've seen what my men do. What this army does. Do you think there's any honor in it, Lilly?"

She glared at him, scratching against the leather straps with her nails. Carlin kept talking. "I hated him day and night. I hated him awake and I hated him asleep. Cartwright used to say that love is a well you can drink from that has no bottom. And I felt that way about hate. I drank from a well of hate, bathed in it, and found only more anger." He paused, musing slightly. "You must feel that way about me. Right, Celerius? You must hate me like that." He looked to her expression and nodded. "It pains me to tell you that there's no end to it. I put a sword through Anthony's chest and my hatred didn't stop. It simply moved. To Thomas. To you. To your uncle. To all of you. It's a well with no bottom. No end to it."

"There'll be an end to it." Lilly let her first words come out strong. They echoed. "When I end you."

"You think that now, but if you could kill me you'd understand how I feel. You'd understand how unsatisfying revenge is. I've gone through a lot of phases, Lilly. I've wanted you dead because I hated your kind. I've wanted you dead because I thought a god might want me to extinguish your kind. I've wanted you dead out of jealousy. But now I know that there's only one thing that will actually make me happy. There's only one thing that will actually empty this well of hatred. I hated Anthony because I wanted to be like him. And for a while now, I have been."

"You will never be like him." Lilly was flailing as much as she could, pressing her skin against every restraint. "Anthony was good. All the way through."

Carlin shook his head. "I don't want to be good." He sneered the last word. "I want his power. That speed. I want to cut men down like he could cut men down. His blood made me everything I wanted to be, but with Celerius dying out at an alarming rate, and my reserves running painfully low, I'm met with an interesting dilemma. Do I kill them all, as I've always wanted, and run out of the most precious resource imaginable?" He pulled a knife from his belt and balanced the tip over Lilly's heart. "Or do I tap you. Take your blood, use it, and make myself into the man I've always longed to be?"

Lilly thought of how she'd balanced a knife over Neil's heart and made a silent vow to apologize to him if she lived. There was nothing like this feeling. The potential and heat at the tip of the knife threatened to drive her insane. A few pounds of force and it would be through her heart, and that would be the end of it. "But since hate is an endless well, I choose to be the man I want to be. I choose to find happiness in taking the gifts you never deserved. I will come to you often, take your blood, and then you will heal and make more for me." Something pricked at his mind and he grinned. "You will be my never ending well, Lilly."

Lilly struggled harder now, trying to channel her strength to vibrate the straps or fracture the table, but she found it impossible. "I've wanted to kill you for so long, and I know it'll be quite strange to hear you beg for death."

He sheathed his dagger and began to ascend the steps, one at a time, savoring his walk. "But your cries will fall on deaf ears. You see... I've grown Lilly Celerius."

She was screaming now, desperate not to hear his next words. She knew it would be agony to listen to him for a second longer. Despite her best efforts she heard him laugh. "Oh yes. I've grown."

Lilly flailed desperately until she was exhausted. It was back to the silence now, back to the dark. She waited once again for footsteps, but this time with a vast terror, because when she heard them, they wouldn't bring her death. They wouldn't bring an end to her suffering. They'd bring her something much worse.

21

THE VENATOR LODGE

RHYS VAPROS

Darius and Rhys found the lodge at the crest of dawn. They'd been separated from Neil and Bianca after the Empire's surprise attack and decided the best course of action was to follow the Wolf's orders. All they could do now was hope the others had made it out safely. Rhys couldn't bear to think of the alternative now that he'd finally been reunited with Neil.

Rhys turned his attention back to the lodge. From the road it looked unassuming, but as they approached the small dirt path they realized just how large it really was. Seeming to be two stories, the lodge was actually connected to a vast network of bridges and tree houses that stretched far into the canopy.

Rhys remembered how his family had built their home underground with small corridors to deter intruders. Some in town had called it the "Snake Hole." He imagined the ropes course far above was a similar tactic. One wrong step or slip would mean a fatal fall.

Besides the jungle above, the Lodge looked defenseless. Save for one man who stood out front eyeing them from afar. He was clearly a Venator, with long hair tied into a bun and visible skin worn and scarred. He looked too young to be the "Grand Master" that they'd heard so much about. He had a bow in his hand and once they were close enough Rhys noticed that he had a hand on his quiver. The Venator had superior senses so Rhys knew their arrival had registered with the lookout long before he and Darius had spotted the Lodge.

"That's far enough," the Venator yelled.

"We're not here to fight," Darius called. "We need to see the Grand Master."

"He doesn't take walk-ins."

Rhys could see Darius's eyes flickering about. "You're the Horseman, right?"

Rhys had never seen a Venator look surprised, but the man's eyes widened a millimeter and then narrowed. "I am."

"So I assume you're not all that consists of the welcome party."

The Horseman lowered his bow and closed his eyes. He took a deep breath and the moment after the forest came alive. A large brown bear climbed over a boulder and into view, protecting the Horseman's right flank. An owl landed silently on his left shoulder, piercing them with its yellow gaze. Rhys turned to see the road behind them, only to have it blocked by the largest horse he had ever seen, a monument of glimmering muscle. "I smell your blood on you," the Horseman called. "Your kind is not easy to kill, but neither is anything in these woods." He placed a hand on the bear's neck. "I make do."

"Well, you couldn't 'make do' with Carlin, could you?" Darius asked.

This he knew from the Lightborn book. Carlin had killed the Horseman's sacred deer and the conflict turned bloody. Carlin won. The Horseman lived, but many of his animals didn't.

The entire forest seemed to stand on end as the animals drew closer, boxing them in. "That was many years ago," the Horseman said. "And I am no longer the young man I once was." Wolves appeared on either side of the path, snarling. "The man I once was would have killed you for that slight."

"We're here on behalf of the Wolf," Rhys said.

The animals stopped and a few even looked to the Horseman as if to say "Uh oh." The Horseman took steps forward and the owl flew to a branch near the front door. "Is this true, Taurlum?"

"Yes," Darius said.

"Then why arrive with so few pleasantries? We are friends after all, the Wolf and I." He paused. "Despite some tumultuous years."

"I've read all about it," Darius said, referring again to the fight with Carlin. The Wolf and Carlin had both been part of the Imperial Hunting Squadron in those days. Rhys sometimes forgot that the Wolf and Carlin had once both fought for the Imperial Army. The Wolf had been Carlin's superior when Carlin killed that special deer; he had tried to broker peace and clean up Carlin's mess. Apparently the relationship with the Horseman was strained for a time after that incident, but it seemed they'd gotten past the ordeal.

"We need to see the Grand Master," Rhys said. "I don't mean to press, but this is urgent."

It was. The Doctor had been silent for a few days now. At any moment he could reappear and Rhys didn't know what would happen the next time he steered the ship. "What does this concern?"

"A rogue student of his."

"Ah." The Horseman waved his arm and the animals receded into the bushes. "Where is he?"

Rhys gulped. "He's... uh..." He pointed to his temple. "He's right here."

The Horseman looked confused for a moment, and then his eyebrows dropped. "Oh, he did it. He was right."

"We think so," Rhys said.

Without another word they were led into the main building. The structure was entirely constructed of rustic knotted wood. Animal heads adorned every wall. Some species were completely unfamiliar to Rhys, and he remembered how little he'd truly learned in Altryon.

Eventually they reached a wooden ladder that led out of an open hatch. "Follow me, Vapros." The Horseman turned back. "Based on the way the boards creek..."

"I'll stay below," Darius said. "I don't do well on bridges."

"I can't imagine you do," the Horsemen said.

The Venator were certainly masters of subtlety. Rhys climbed the ladder and materialized through an obstacle course of rope bridges and wooden ladders. They reached the biggest house connected to the largest tree. "I assume this is it?"

The Horseman nodded. "You may go in. He knows you're here."

"How?"

The Horseman laughed.

Rhys pushed the doors open and immediately caught his breath at the size and intricacy of the room. Everything was intricately crafted with the kind of care that only went into hand-made things. A deep polish had clearly been undertaken on every inch of the room, giving it a glossy brown shine. Sitting at the far end of the room in a bent wooden chair was a frail man in a robe with milk-white eyes. "Vapros, eh?" he said in a voice that sounded as old as the woods themselves.

"You heard?"

"No. The sound of your blood flowing is different. Your hearts beat so quickly. Always anxious. Always ready for action, you Vapros."

"Yes," Rhys said uneasily.

"And the Taurlum. The heartbeats are so loud. It's deafening."

There was a pause as Rhys shifted slightly, checking to see if the old man's eyes registered anything. "Yes," he said finitely. "I am blind. I hear you shifting your weight though. I feel the vibrations in the floor."

Rhys approached now. "I come from the Wolf."

The old man nodded, a smile stretching across his face. "The Celerius and the Venator. Such an odd alliance. I quite like their kind. Principled."

"I'm here because of a former student of yours."

"The Doctor?"

"Is it usually about that?"

"It's always about that. He or his murderous Pack." He lifted his bones into a standing position. "A branch of our family tree, rotted and better lopped off. There are currently eight Venator roaming the realm, protecting their lot of land, but all I hear about are the bad ones. Victor. The Doctor. Even Barlow has his problems."

"He's..." Rhys paused. Would the Grand Master kill him to kill the Doctor? He was unsure. The man seemed brittle enough, but there was no way to be certain. "He had this theory."

"So it's your mind, eh? That's where he ended up?"

"Yes," Rhys said, words heavy with desperation. "And I need him *out.*"

The Grand Master approached, and Rhys realized how thin the man was. His skin looked thinner than his silken robe. "I cannot pull him out of your mind. You must do it yourself."

"And how will you-"

The Grand Master placed a hand on Rhys's body and Rhys lost control, flailing his limbs at the old man. The Grand Master dodged the swings without using an ounce of unnecessary speed. He was surgical and precise. He caught Rhys's hand and twisted his thumb, prompting a scream that wasn't his.

"Doctor. Even after all you've done to escape me, your own vessel brings you to your judgment."

"My vessel has brought me to your end," the Doctor hissed from Rhys's mouth.

Rhys materialized behind the Grand Master, but it didn't matter. He fought enemies from behind as well as the front and he'd never seen the boy in the first place. He delivered a solid kick to Rhys's chest that sent him sliding across the polished floor. "Why take the boy? For this purpose? If so, I am quite flattered."

"For Altryon," the Doctor said. *"For science."*

"And my assassination is?"

"A perk."

Rhys materialized into close quarters, but the Grand Master caught or dodged every assault. He caught Rhys in a tight hold. "I speak now to the boy. There is no killing the Doctor in the material world. This parasite lives within your mind and that is where you must go."

"I don't understand," Rhys said in his own voice.

"This weed must be pulled at the root."

Then he placed a thumb against Rhys's forehead and breathed in, focusing his energy. When he exhaled, everything went dark and Rhys realized he was plummeting into himself.

THE DARK WHIRLPOOL swirled into the vague outline of a room, oozing with black viscous material. Rhys landed on his feet and ripples stretched out from around his feet, further clarifying the space. Had he really been sent within his own mind?

The details of the space became clearer as he walked and the dark slime soon started to look like concrete and stone and wood. Before long Rhys recognized the space as the Cliff, the place he'd first met the Doctor. "Hello?" he called.

"This is quite the surprise." The Doctor's voice was clearer now and booming with incredible gravitas. "I never thought you'd slum it with me down here. Most can't bear to enter the darkest corners of their minds."

"I have a trespasser," Rhys said. His voice was loud here too.

"Trespasser? Look out the window Rhys."

Rhys saw the floor to ceiling window and went to it, expecting to see the ocean but instead saw endless avenues of other rooms and spaces he'd come to know. His childhood home, the Inn at Abington, the Golden Mug. However, something was wrong. The black ooze leaked into these places, gripping at floors and walls, changing colors and shapes into hazy black shadows. "This place is more mine than it is yours."

Rhys looked around, panicked. The Doctor's voice sounded closer. Why did the Grand Master think he could win this fight? Behind him a tendril of black ooze formed into the light outline of a man. "Is that... Are you...?"

The man grew larger and larger, tendrils of ooze from the floor and ceiling adding to its volume. Eventually Rhys recognized the copper jaw and the different colored eyes. "Am I here?" the Doctor asked. "Am I now gifted with everything I was deprived of in life? The Grand Master is a fool. He sent you to the one place I could imprison you. He thinks your problems will be solved with a battle of the minds? My mind is all I've ever had."

He reached out toward Rhys, but in that moment Rhys felt something in his hand. He swung his arm in an arc and splattered ooze over the walls. The Doctor roared in pain. Rhys looked down and saw his blade, willed into consciousness. "I feel the same way," Rhys said.

The Doctor charged at him and the ground shook, sending drops of ooze everywhere. Rhys lost his nerve and ran in the direction of the window. Could he jump from it? Could he die from falling in a dream? There was no time to debate the logic. He felt the glass shatter as he barreled through. The air swirled around him as he fell.

Rhys landed in a space not completely coated with shadows and slime. He'd thought of this place as he fell. It was the Golden Mug. He heard the Doctor's voice calling from a distance. "You cannot hide from me Rhys. I will trace you to your infancy if I have to."

Rhys examined the space. It was empty, save for the body of Josephine propped up against the bar. This was the part enveloped in shadows. Something in Rhys knew that the Doctor had put this here. He approached and put a hand on her shoulder. To his surprise, the shadows faded, releasing her in a shower of glittering light. "Ah," Rhys heard the Doctor say. "There you are."

The Doctor appeared, but he was smaller this time. "Running Rhys? Don't you know it's healthier to face your demons?"

He slammed his fist into the bar, and Rhys covered himself to avoid the splinters.

"I wonder where I should stick you, Rhys," the Doctor said, crushing Rhys's limbs with his tentacles. "Where's the very darkest patch of your mind? Where have you buried all your guilt?"

Something about that triggered an idea in Rhys's mind. He channeled all his strength and materialized back to the Cliff. The Doctor looked around in confusion. He knew Rhys was no fool. "I only grow stronger here."

The ooze puddling at his feet made him grow in size. "Is this a plea? A plea to be crushed?" the Doctor asked.

"You've been here, a parasite, feeding away long enough to forget whose mind this is." Rhys felt his power return and prepared for the jump. The Doctor's tendrils wrapped themselves around Rhys. "You are whole here, you're strong here. But so am I."

The Doctor seemed to sense Rhys's strength building and he pulled more ooze from the walls, growing larger still.

"I thought I could crush you. Squeeze you into a box and hide you, but you only grew. Because ideas are intangible and they cannot be killed." Rhys now knew why the Grand Master sent him here. "But now we're together, Doctor. And I can teach you this lesson in person."

He felt stronger than he ever had before.

"You cannot crush an idea," Rhys said.

"No?" The Doctor asked, squeezing tighter.

"No," Rhys said. "But spiders? *Those* you can crush."

Rhys made the jump, materializing to the place he knew best of all. The Vapros Bunker. His childhood home. Specifically, one of the hallways. In life, the Doctor might have liked this cramped, damp, fortress. But now, as a giant creature of shadow and slime, he was crushed by the confines of the building. He roared in pain as all of his bones cracked against each other. Rhys just managed to materialize out of distance.

The Doctor screamed gutturally and the cramped walls of the hallway twisted his cries into a distorted wail. "You cannot be rid of me, Rhys." He groaned. "I will always be here."

"I know," Rhys said. "And I will be back again and again. You see, this is not your kingdom, Doctor. It's your prison."

The Doctor tried to budge even the slightest inch, but his malformed body was stuck now, incapable of even the slightest movement. "It's a shame you're never going to finish that pain scale, Doctor. I'd sure like to know how much this hurts."

He waved and closed his eyes, pulling himself from the Vapros Bunker, soaring higher and higher until he found himself inhabiting his body again. He blinked a few times and saw the Grand Master, still with his thumb on Rhys's forehead. His eyes glowed and Rhys realized he was still leaving the trance.

Something was very wrong. There was a figure standing behind the Grand Master. "Everyone has blind spots old man," the Marksman said, cocking his revolver. "Even you."

There was a loud noise. Rhys gasped, face coated in blood.

22

THE VENATOR LODGE

DARIUS TAURLUM

Darius's neck was starting to ache from looking up so much. The more he looked, the farther the lodge seemed to expand into the distance. It made him miss the Taurlum Mansion in Altryon. Standing on that roof was the only opportunity he ever had to stand above anything and see far into the distance. Out here he was anchored to the ground by his tremendous weight and iron skin.

He glanced over at the Horseman and felt a little envious. He'd never swing branch to branch like they did. "You know quite a bit about me," the Horseman said finally. All his animals had gone, but the horse was back to have its shoes cleaned out. "How is that?"

"The Wolf wrote extensively about every Lightborn he's ever met. There's quite a long chapter on you."

"Yes," the Horseman said. "I once tried to kill him. I once tried to kill *quite* a lot of people."

"Over a deer?"

"Yes," the Horseman said. "I can handle seeing animals killed. I understand that humans are the way they are. But Carlin killed my deer for sport. And it enraged me."

Darius thought of Anastasia. "I understand." The Horseman finished cleaning the horse's hooves and then brought the animal's face close to his. He stared deeply into its eyes and it fidgeted. "How did you finally become like this?"

The Horseman didn't answer. The Horse began kicking and flailing, but the Horseman kept just out of distance of the tantrum. The horse tired and slowed. Eventually its eyes opened wide, flickering back and forth in a rhythm. Darius watched transfixed until it traveled off into the woods. The Horseman finally turned back to Darius. "Like what?"

"Calm? How did you overcome your loss?"

"I stood in the woods and watched the cycles of nature. I watched life and death happen thousands of times all around me. So many Venator stray from their code, but I never have. I believe that nature is the instruction manual for a meaningful life. Nature knows not revenge, so I chose to forget it."

"Would you kill Carlin if you met him again?"

The Horseman gritted his teeth. "Well, I am a man. And men are weak."

Darius smiled. "I know."

"You lost someone?" The Horseman's owl flew to him and the Venator began the same process again, staring into its eyes.

"Yes," Darius said. Even saying it released a torrent of pain. "How did you know?"

The Horseman was quiet again until the owl finished its tantrum and flew off. "Your heartbeat speeds up every time you speak of death."

Darius placed a hand over his heart instinctively, as if he could silence the sound. "The Doctor took someone from me."

"He's taken quite a few people." The Horseman looked up at the lodge. "We're all responsible for that. The person you lost. Was it long before their time?"

"A lot of things went unsaid," Darius admitted. He could feel the letter he'd written her in his breast pocket.

"Did she know?"

"What?"

"You might not have said it, but did she know it?"

Darius took a long time to consider. "Yes."

"Whatever happens after life, I can't imagine the dead want regret from us, Taurlum. Just as nature doesn't know revenge, it doesn't know regret. It knows change. And you won't be happy until you do too."

Darius wanted to respond, but let that moment last. The bear lumbered out of the forest toward the Horseman. "I hate to interrupt, but what are you doing?"

"I'm reconnecting with my animals."

"This is your ability? You can talk to them?"

"No, I wouldn't say that." The Horseman waved his hand. The bear gave a minuscule shrug and sauntered back into the forest. "I train them over a series of years. Eventually they learn to respond to suggestion."

"Why do they get upset when you 'reconnect?'"

"It's uncomfortable. I can't imagine anyone rooting around in your mind being pleasant."

"Could you do it to a human?"

Darius hadn't meant for that to sound sinister but the Horseman eyed him cautiously. "Why do you ask?"

"I just... Rhys has the Doctor in his mind. Maybe you could... pull him out?"

The Horseman shook his head adamantly. "An animal's mind is a simple machine, like a..." He looked Darius over. "Like a hammer. A human's is something far more complicated. Like a watch perhaps. Endless gears and machinations clicking away. It's much easier to break a watch than a hammer. I'm certain I'd be too clumsy to leave a human's mind intact."

"Could you take out a memory?" Darius asked.

The Horseman looked at Darius with pity, more emotion than he'd shown thus far. "Accept the change, Taurlum. Accept the nature of things."

Darius sighed. There really were no easy ways out.

"You're the second man to ask me that. If I could do this to a human."

"Who was the first?"

"Saewulf Anima." He tensed and the entire forest seemed to inhale. The birds and bugs stopped singing and the animals they'd seen earlier bounded to the Horseman's side.

"What's wrong?" Darius asked.

"I smell something familiar."

"What is it?"

"Venator blood."

"Well you're–"

"No." The Horseman drew his bow and slipped an arrow from his quiver. "It's tainted. Diseased. I know the smell."

"Who is it?"

The Horseman charged back toward the house leaving Darius with his animal cohorts. "Victor," he called over his shoulder. The silent flapping wings of his owl followed.

23

GRAND MASTER'S LODGE

RHYS VAPROS

Rhys wasn't exactly sure how it happened. Sure, Victor had ample time to sneak up on the Grand Master during the vision, but how did he slip past the Horseman? There was a man in the corner, dressed in similar Venator hunting gear, and Rhys deducted that he must have been a hunter, come running to save the Grand Master. This had gone poorly for him. The evidence of that was clear from the man's bleeding corpse in the corner. The Marksman looked worse still, bones jutting from his body, and creating a harsh outline on his greying skin. "Formula, Vapros. *Now.*" He pressed the barrel to Rhys's forehead.

"You've just ruined your only chance of getting it," Rhys said. "I shut the Doctor away. I don't think I can get back to him without the Grand Master who you have just—"

The Marksman looked at the Grand Master's corpse and back to Rhys. "Try. Try to make him speak."

Rhys did. Nothing came back. "He's shut away. Too deep."

"Then I have no need for you, do I?" Victor prepared to pull the trigger again, but a sudden flash of white appeared, digging talons into what remained of his damaged arm. He pulled away, trying to shoot at the owl but missed. The door to the hall was kicked open and the Horseman charged across the room, colliding with the Marksman. They stood, sizing each other up. "Victor," the Horseman said. He observed the Grand Master's body on the ground. Rhys saw him shudder with rage. "You fool."

"Ezra," the Marksman said.

"You must be truly desperate to come here. You know what we will do to you."

"You and what leaders?" the Marksman asked. "The Venator are a dead race."

"Not while I stand." The Horseman pulled a knife from a holder by his thigh. "As acting Grand Master, I sentence you to death, traitor."

"That sentence came long ago. I still stand."

The Horseman leapt over the body of his former master, slashing at the Marksman who hastily attempted to stay out of the way of the blade's path. After the first few misses, the Marksman pulled a blade from his belt and they disappeared into a flurry of vicious silver.

Rhys materialized to the window, desperate to make it out of the fray. He glanced down and saw Darius look up, far below. Rhys turned back, watching the combat and decided he could offer nothing. He materialized to a branch below, then to another until he was on the ground. "It's—"

"Marksman?" Darius asked.

"Yes."

"Where's the Doctor?"

"Back in the box," Rhys said. "For now. We're going to need a different way of reaching him if he ever comes back."

Before Rhys could recommend fleeing, Victor was flung out of the window. He handily caught a few branches and landed unharmed. He found himself in considerably deeper woods, enemies on all sides. The bear roared, closing off his escape. "Well," the Marksman said, reloading his weapon. "I've missed hunting."

The Horseman reappeared at the main entrance of the lodge and fired an arrow. It missed and landed in the ground ahead of Victor. The Marksman turned back, a man out of options. "I once asked you, when we were young, if you felt pain for your animals."

"I remember," the Horseman said.

"I've always wanted to know if that was true. Thank you for lining up the test subjects."

The Marksman fired into the Bear's flank and it roared in pain. Apparently he'd been correct about the Horseman's connection to his animals because he wheezed in pain, falling to his knees. A wolf charged at him and Victor cut it down expertly. The Horseman seized again. The animals collectively seemed to ebb outward in preparation to charge. "Let me go or I promise you'll feel the death of every single one."

Darius and Rhys shared a look. They weren't connected to the Horseman. They could always fight, but something was much more dangerous about the Marksman now. He was feral. Death was not a pleasing color on him.

The Marksman turned back, seeing that his path was clear. He bolted. "Throw me your knife!" Darius called to the Horseman.

The Horseman looked skeptical, but did it. Darius caught it by the blade, readjusted and with a mighty heave, hurled it into the Marksman's back shoulder. He roared, but continued running and shooting at the Horseman's animals over his shoulder. His skin began to grow fur and his body began to morph. The Horseman fitted another arrow. As he looked off there was no more Marksman, just the animal roaring and wailing as it charged into the woods. He lowered his bow and looked to the boys.

"You must go," he said looking forlorn as he tended to his wounded animals.

"I'm so sorry we—" Rhys started to say.

"No," the Horseman said. "I do not judge you. We made that man. And his father. Boy, is your mind clear?"

"Yes," Rhys said.

"Then use it," the Horseman said.

Rhys knew what the Horseman was going to ask. He'd been asked quite a few times.

"Kill him, boy. That is the payment you owe."

24

THE DEAD KING'S TENT

NEIL VAPROS

Neil had never been to the circus. Sir Vapros always hated competition. He saw all performers not working in his bars and theaters as heathens and lowlifes. Despite his melancholy and anger at being swept up in the journey heading east, Neil couldn't help maintaining a light interest in what they'd discover beneath the blood red big top tent found in a random clearing outside of Brightbow.

It had been three days, and the Wolf had secured carriages for their little group. He'd been kind enough to give Neil and Bianca their own, but Neil suspected that he was trying to shield himself from Neil's wrath. They traveled without trouble, but sometimes Neil itched for action to break the silence. Bianca had a sixth sense for his hidden emotions, and there was no doubt that she'd noticed his anxiety and anger. He'd been able to blame it on his separation from Rhys, but he knew that wouldn't last forever. Eventually, he'd have to tell her the truth.

"I think Neil, Bianca and I should enter alone," the Wolf said to his men, jolting Neil from his contemplation.

The men groaned, clearly disappointed they wouldn't see a show tonight. "I know," the Wolf said. "But entering the tent means putting ourselves at the mercy of the Dead King and we're far from knowing if he's friend or foe."

The men shuffled a bit, but ultimately accepted. "We'll bring you guys a snack," Bianca said with a wink.

They trudged in the direction of the big top through knee-high grass. Neil smelled rum and syrup in the air. Sprightly music swelled as they grew closer to the shining lights within. "When was the last time you saw something like this?" Neil asked.

"A circus?"

"Celebration."

The Wolf stopped for a moment, taking in the pleasantries. "It's been quite a while."

When they entered the open flap the smell grew stronger, and Neil realized there was something sour about it. His hand curled into a fist. Something wasn't right. The music changed, descending now, in a minor key. "The clowns from this circus killed Quintus right?" Neil asked.

"Yes," the Wolf said.

"So you're saying keep your distance from the clowns with weapons?" Bianca asked.

"As a rule, I'd say *always* keep your distance from clowns with weapons."

Within were dozens of performers milling about, calling to them. Neil saw things he'd seen separately but never in the same place. Fire breathers, ribbon dancers, jugglers, animals in chains. "What's the striped one?" Neil asked, looking to the far side of the tent.

"It's a bear," the Wolf said.

"Bears come with stripes?" Bianca asked.

"Painted ones do."

As they walked, the tent seem to get bigger and more crowded. It certainly hadn't looked this big from the outside. Eventually they reached the center, where a group of female acrobats were contorting in the air, suspended by golden silks. Neil stopped to watch for a moment thinking of the suspended animals at the Tridenti mansion.

"Eyes on the prize, Neil," the Wolf chided.

"Yes, Neil," Bianca said gesturing to her belt of knives. "Eyes on the prize."

"I wasn't..." he paused and sighed. "Never mind."

The Wolf pointed and they saw the back of a man with a long red cloak. "Our man," the Wolf said.

They passed a row of chairs and entered the ring in which the man was standing. He seemed to feel their presence and turned. The entire circus came to a halt. The music stopped, men and women fell silent, roaring beasts disappeared, even the smell seemed to leave the air. "Visitors," the man in the red cloak said.

He was, objectively speaking, a beautiful man, with curled hair down to his shoulders and rigid bone structure. There was something about his voice that made him sound sick or pained. This was the clear indicator of who he really was. Cartwright was famous for his voice. "Greetings. I am not sure how you came to be in our place of revelry, but you are trespassing. I am the Dead Ki—"

"You're John Cartwright," Neil said.

"I..." he paused. "No, I'm not."

"Yes, you are," Neil said. "My sister had one of those painted portraits of you in a locket."

"So did I," Bianca admitted.

"Wait what?" Neil asked.

"Dammit," Cartwright said. "I admit that's a surprise. I'm not nearly as famous out here."

"We're from Altryon," Bianca explained.

"And exactly who the hell are you?"

"We're revolutionaries," Neil said.

"And I'm your pen pal," the Wolf said.

Cartwright's eyes widened. "Oh my, Steven Celerius. I've been so excited to meet you. I had no idea you were coming."

"Desperate times."

Though the interaction seemed amicable, the air remained fraught with tension. A small group of men pushed through the other side of the tent and approached Cartwright from behind. "It's the clowns," Bianca hissed in a whisper.

It was indeed the clowns. They seemed less light-footed than the other attendants in the tent. They fanned out in a semi-circle behind Cartwright, and he glanced over his shoulder at them. "Oh sorry," he said. "I apologize for them and for," he waved his hand in the direction of the frozen members of the circus, "all of this."

"We're not here to hurt you, Cartwright," the Wolf said. "The clowns shouldn't expect any trouble from us."

Cartwright twirled around. "Oh right. I guess they do look like clowns."

The room grew even more silent. "What?" Neil asked.

"They're not clowns," Cartwright said.

"They're wearing makeup," Bianca noted.

"I guess technically they are wearing clown makeup, but they have no formal clown training. They're not funny, is what I'm saying. Clowning is an art. You can't just wake up and *be* a clown."

"I see," Neil said. "So why have you chosen to…"

"Ah yes," Cartwright said. He brought one of the men forward and with the sleeve of his silken robe wiped the makeup from the man's face, revealing a sickly greyish hue. "This man is dead. Or was dead. It's all a little complicated."

Neil thought of Quintus. "No one can die in your presence, is that correct, Cartwright?" the Wolf asked.

"There are exceptions. But basically you have the right idea." He pulled a dagger from somewhere in his coat and stabbed it deep into the man's chest. The man didn't seem to mind. "These particular men have been around the longest and, therefore, have been to death's door quite a few times."

Neil stared at them, wondering how much of their humanity remained. They looked glossy eyed and stiff. "It's also the reason for this tense little moment. No one knows what happens when I die and I must say my friends here are just a little nervous."

"We're not here for a fight," the Wolf reiterated. "We're actually here to see if you're—"

"Interested in a team-up?" Cartwright smiled showing off a glowing, glossy set of teeth. "You want an alliance? You want to be in bed together?"

"Well we…"

"Not the first time I've actually been asked that today!"

Neil was almost certain this was true.

"You see my services are in high demand. Especially with the whole 'conquering death itself' thing." He snapped his fingers and one of his clowns ran off. "You want to crush the Empire, the Empire wants to crush the rebels. Where's a man like me to fall?"

"You've been slaughtering Imperial patrols," the Wolf said. Neil could see his hands curling into fists. There was no doubt that if Cartwright didn't want them to leave they wouldn't.

"True, true," Cartwright mused. "And my last collaboration with the Empire didn't go as planned."

"Little Billy?" Neil asked, remembering the nursery rhyme propaganda distributed by the Empire during his childhood in Altryon.

Cartwright nodded. "It's a satire. I can't believe they published the damn thing." Before he could continue, the clown returned with a familiar figure behind him. "You all know Lieutenant Virgil I assume."

Virgil entered the ring with a measured gait, followed by two Imperial soldiers who looked less than pleased to see the rebel leaders. "Better than most," the Wolf said. "How are you, Virgil?"

Virgil's eyes shifted back and forth, taking in their ominous surroundings. "I've had better assignments."

Neil sometimes forgot that the Wolf had once led Virgil, Carlin, Anthony, and the entire Imperial army. The men seemed cordial with each other. Neil noticed that Virgil completely avoided his gaze, probably wondering if Neil had spilled the truth of his parentage to the rebellion. Neil had not. Neil figured there was a reason Virgil was hiding the fact that he was really a Venator. Virgil had let him live, and Neil suspected there was something deeper at play.

Cartwright clapped his hands. "This is a circus. I think we deserve a show."

Neil let his energy pool in his hands. Was this about to be a fight? He figured the Wolf could make quick work of all three Imperials on his own. "Mr. Virgil comes and gives me a halfhearted plea to join the Empire. Mr. Virgil says he believes in order and believes Lightborns take advantage of normal people. A bold thing to say to a Lightborn, I will admit."

Virgil and Neil made eye contact.

"I see your faces," Cartwright grinned a bit. "I am a Lightborn, yes."

"Of what persuasion?" the Wolf asked.

Cartwright didn't seem to hear him. "My pen pal arrives on the same day asking me to topple this ravenous Empire. I mean, I assume that's what he wants. It's all he can talk about in his letters. How am I to know whom to trust? Where do I belong?"

Cartwright went to a chair farther toward the end of the ring and pulled a cup from the side. A clown went away and came back with a bottle of wine. Cartwright held it up in a toast. He stretched out one arm and one of his other clowns removed a dagger, making a small incision in his arm. Cartwright lowered his arm, letting a drop of blood fall into the drink. "I'm sure you all know about Lightborn blood."

"Know what about it?" Virgil asked.

"It has… consuming properties. It also deteriorates your mind and body, but I don't like a single drink that doesn't." He snapped and performers moved closer, lining the edges of the ring. "Celerius blood makes you fast, Taurlum blood makes you insane, and Vapros blood makes you feel *amazing*."

"What will your blood do?"

Cartwright ignored him again. "Each of you will take a sip of this drink. If your intentions are pure, you will live. If not…" he shrugged.

"And then what will you do with the survivors?" Bianca asked.

"Join them. Provided there are survivors." Cartwright was close to them now, offering the cup around waiting for a brave contender to take it.

Eventually the Wolf reached out and Cartwright chuckled. "Excellent."

The Wolf stood there, armed with the cup and an icy gaze. "Before I drink, please answer my question."

"Which one was that?"

"A Lightborn of what persuasion?"

Cartwright placed his hand on the Wolf's and lifted the cup to the General's mouth. He grinned again. "Of the Saewulf kind."

DEAD KING'S TENT

NEIL VAPROS

"How long until it takes effect?" Neil asked. It had been a few moments and the spiked wine had done nothing to them.

All six had drunk from Cartwright's blood cup, including Virgil's two servants. Neil didn't blame them. It didn't look like they had another choice. The performers surrounded them now, and Neil could see that some of them had wide scars, the kind that most people wouldn't survive.

"John Anima?" Bianca asked after a while.

"Cartwright Anima," Cartwright said. "Mixed things around for my pen name."

"I see," Bianca said. "And how are you...?"

"How do I exist?" he asked. "No idea. Born an orphan. But that's the thing about Lightborns, eh? They get around."

She and Neil had been exchanging glances for quite a bit. Neil didn't consider himself a person with impure intentions, but would this drink really kill him? Or was Cartwright playing games? As Cartwright paced to the Imperial side of the ring to jaunt and taunt, Neil reached his hand toward Bianca's, giving it a squeeze.

She looked at him, and he saw fear reflected in her eyes. "It'll be okay," he said.

She nodded minutely. "We've been through worse."

"Much worse."

"We don't ever say it but—"

"I know," Neil said. "I feel the same way. I always have."

Bianca cast a look over her shoulder. "Do you think this is real?"

"I'm not sure."

"Me neither." Her eyes followed Cartwright. "He seems like the kind of man who would play games with visitors."

"I've also never heard of Lightborn blood having supernatural properties," Neil said. "Although I guess no one's ever tried to drink my blood before."

"Focus on a question," Cartwright called to the group. "It always helps to think of a question that you ask yourself often. It'll remind you what you fight for."

Neil thought of a question: *Do I have to die for Volteria?*

Bianca's eyes flicked over to Neil. She took a deep breath. "It's probably all just a—"

That was the last thing Neil heard before the ground opened up beneath him, swallowing him whole. He fell through swirling darkness.

NEIL LANDED hard in a wooden chair. He looked around and saw a world of flowing wine, morphing and developing into a room around him. Eventually it became chairs and benches and people. Neil felt belligerent.

The swirling red liquid around him became a man. It took Neil a moment to realize that it was Cartwright, or at least Cartwright's doppelganger. He smiled softly at Neil and scratched his chin. "And you killed her? Didn't you?" Cartwright asked.

"Yes," Neil felt himself saying. "I broke her spine."

"You broke her spine," he repeated. "In cold blood. My, my."

Neil looked around. Where was he? Why did he feel no control over his body. He saw another Cartwright, sitting upon a large chair to his right. To his left, was a box filled with Cartwrights. He realized slowly what this was. The Emperor had phased out courts when he took power, but in the old days of the families they'd held public trials for everything. The only question was whose trial was he testifying in?

"Anything else to declare?" the prosecutor Cartwright asked.

"A Taurlum guard," Neil said. "Shot him in the back of the head. Other soldiers too."

"You don't even know how many?" Cartwright asked.

"No."

"He doesn't even know how many," Cartwright said. "And not to mention his terroristic acts in this revolution. He's really started something. Who is this war really for? Can we really say if this senseless killing is for anyone's benefit? What are we really fighting for here? A new reign for the three families?"

The jury murmured in agreement.

"Does Neil Vapros really believe in this cause?"

"Yes," Neil said.

"Really?" Cartwright asked. "Why won't he die for it, then? He'll let others die for the war. I'm sure more killing is to come."

Neil struggled in his seat, but found himself unable to speak and unable to control his own body. "Let me be more direct," Cartwright said. "Why won't you die for the people, Neil?" He ran his tongue along his teeth. "Why will you let so much killing happen?"

"Because I'm selfish," Neil heard himself say.

"I've heard more than enough," Judge Cartwright boomed. "This trial is being called to an immediate verdict. I find the defendant, Neil Vapros—"

Suddenly the world around Neil swirled again, then consumed him. He was tumbling hard.

～

THE EARTH REAPPEARED BELOW NEIL. He gasped, cheeks basted in tears and hair swinging in front of his face. He pushed it back and looked for Bianca. She was beside him, awake and shivering. He wrapped her in a hug. "How was that?"

"Could have been worse."

"What did you see?"

"I fought a large smoke cloud for your body," she said.

Neil paused. "Large smoke cloud. Was it my father?"

"No clue."

"Did you win?" he asked.

"I don't remember."

Neil looked up at the Wolf, who stood on wobbly knees. "You made it."

"You sound surprised." He sounded shaken.

"Where were you?"

"Dancing with my wife. In an extravagant ball."

"Sounds great," Neil said.

"We drowned in a flood of red wine."

"I take it back, then."

Neil lifted his head to see what happened to their competitors. At first, he thought that all of them were dead, but then he realized that Virgil was alive, clutching his knees and sobbing on the ground. Cartwright watched a few feet away. The men behind Virgil were certainly dead. "Have the losers carried away," Cartwright demanded.

"I thought no one could die in your presence," Bianca said.

"Evidently this is the only way," Cartwright explained.

His men did the job lugging the corpses. Neil found that odd to watch, dead men carrying dead men. Cartwright turned back to the rebels. "I guess we have our verdict. How was the trip?"

"Lovely," Neil said.

"Oh really?" Cartwright asked. "Was it?"

"Yes," Bianca said, begrudgingly. "It was wonderful."

"Looks like Virgil thinks so too."

The Lieutenant made his way on shaking legs and stood watching Cartwright, eyes unrelenting and filled with horror. Cartwright nodded to him curtly. "I'm so sorry Mr. Virgil. But at least now you know your intentions are pure." He turned back to the rebels. "As for you all, you've earned my trust and loyalty. I will join you and your cause under one condition."

"Which is?" the Wolf didn't seem thrilled.

"There is a boy. Green skin. He is my responsibility."

"We've met him," Neil said.

"You will help me reacquire this boy."

The Wolf nodded. "This can be done."

"Then I shall help you. It takes us quite a while to pack up, so maybe you could send me a letter? Let me know where I'm needed? We can discuss logistics of your little war and how I fit in." Cartwright didn't seem to find what he was looking for in the Wolf's eyes. "I know it'll take time to gain your trust. If you'd like, I could have Mr. Virgil beheaded? Maybe that would speed things along?"

"No, that won't be necessary," the Wolf said. "If your test is accurate then he's a man with true intentions."

"Yes," Cartwright said.

"If it's all the same to you, maybe I'll stick around your circus for a while," the Wolf suggested. "Help ensure a seamless transition?"

"I'll have the clowns prepare you a cot."

"Just let me walk my comrades out."

The Wolf turned to Bianca and Neil, seeing their skeptical looks, he took them aside. "Calculated risk," he explained. "We've already lost the camp. We won't survive if he wiggles out of this one."

"Fair," Neil said. "He probably expected all of us to die during that trial. Hell, I'm surprised all of *us* made it through the trial."

The Wolf and Neil shared a moment of tense eye contact. The Wolf knew the subtext of that quip. Neil hadn't expected the Wolf to survive. Were his intentions really true? Or was Cartwright's test just one big parlor trick? The Wolf didn't look away, as if to reaffirm the purity of his intentions. He didn't want Neil dead. He wanted the people free.

The Wolf crossed the room and helped steady Virgil on his feet.

The Lieutenant was shaking hard and his stare seemed miles off. "Shall we go, friend?" the Wolf asked cordially, ever the gentleman.

Virgil nodded. The group trudged back through the circus after a cursory goodbye. The performers watched them go. Once outside the tent Neil realized that, like the rebels, Virgil had a small force waiting for him. What should have been a massacre was not. Without their leaders to guide them, the rebels and Imperials sat side by side in a tension heavy ceasefire. Virgil saw his men and began to shake again. The air was silent aside from his rapid breathing.

"What did you see?" Bianca finally asked.

"The world I want," Virgil said. "Carlin's world. Without Lightborns."

"You hate Lightborns?" Neil asked in surprise.

"I don't know," Virgil said. "I hated my father. My brothers. Seeing them do what they do... It made me think Carlin might have a point."

Neil waited to see a look of surprise pass across the Wolf's face, but it didn't. Of course, the Wolf knew. He'd served with Virgil for years. Bianca didn't react either, but she rarely did. "Men taking advantage of other men? Remove those men from power. That's how I was raised. No one takes advantage of the land," Virgil said.

"But..." the Wolf said, nudging him along gently.

"But I made a vow. Two vows actually. One to Anthony and one to the country I love. One to Altryon. One to Anthony." He was shaking again. He grabbed his hair, pulling at his scalp, as if to remove the poisonous discourse. "I vowed never to kill my brothers when I joined the army. And I did that."

"Carlin did that too," the Wolf said.

Neil wondered what the relationship here was. The more the Wolf spoke, the more he recognized the tone. Was Virgil just like him? One of the Wolf's pawns? "I said I could never do it. Told Anthony over and over again. I'd do anything but kill Carlin."

"I understand," the Wolf said. "You believe in him."

"I'm a fool for that. I know his heart has turned black." Virgil had tears sliding down his face. "Carlin killed brothers. I killed brothers. Maybe mine is black too."

"It seems you're on the precipice of a decision." The Wolf had his hand on his sword. Neil hadn't noticed this before. That was his way, support but with self-assurance.

"I cannot keep two vows. Not when they are in conflict. And I must choose one."

Virgil walked toward the direction of his men. "May I ask which one?" the Wolf called.

"I wouldn't know which to tell you. I haven't decided yet."

His red cloak was swallowed by the night, turning it a shade of black. Neil was going to wait until Virgil was too far away to hear them speak. But then he remembered that Virgil was a Venator and it probably didn't matter. "So he's one of us? Man on the inside?"

"No," the Wolf said finitely. "The Empire was his first home. He had nothing. Ran away from the Doctor and found us. He loved Anthony and he loved Carlin. I think seeing one kill the other did something to him. Broke him."

"But Cartwright says his intentions are pure."

"Yes," the Wolf mused, "I suppose you can want the right thing and be conflicted about how to get it."

Neil and Bianca said their goodbyes to the Wolf who walked back towards the big tent. Then they rejoined the rebels in the direction of the Wolf's backup camp. As they sat in the carriage silently, Neil lowered his head into his hands and thought about Virgil and what the Wolf had said about him. Neil knew how he felt, pulled between two impossible outcomes. Die for the Wolf or live for Bianca.

Neil knew the "Trial of Neil Vapros" wouldn't leave his mind anytime soon. It was almost certain where it was going, but he was still disappointed. He would have liked to hear the verdict.

REBEL BASE CAMP

NEIL VAPROS

Neil awoke feeling hot. He and the rebels had reached another of the Wolf's camps hours ago, but something felt odd since he arrived. The air was thick and humming. Everything felt electrified.

This sudden feeling that awoke him escalated that tension. His arms and chest flushed with blood and sweat pooled on his brow.

He stood and abandoned his tent. There were a few men standing guard on the other side of camp. Other than that, the night was silent. Neil felt a lulling so he went down the road away from camp, barefooted. This feeling was familiar to him. Hadn't he felt this sometime before?

He stripped off his shirt. Down the dirt path there was a lake. Neil decided he'd submerge himself. Maybe that would cool his fever. The heat didn't necessarily feel bad. In fact, it made him feel a sense of ease, as if everything was going to be all right.

Neil was knee-deep in the water now. He'd heard this buzzing before hadn't he? It was shortly after getting the letter from Alex. He'd been reading it earlier in the carriage and dug around in his pocket for it. He'd been in such dire straits since its arrival he hadn't had much time to think about Alex or Serena. He read the last passage over.

I'm not sure if this should worry you, but last month Serena vanished from the island with our fastest ship. She still doesn't know about our mother's deception, and I assume she's going somewhere to sulk. Either way, I'd steer clear of giant pirate ships.

Where had she gone? Off on the carefree adventure she'd once promised Neil? Or maybe...

Neil's head cleared all at once. Serena was missing from the Ocean's Jaw. The unrecognizable sound faded from the air, and the chill from the water crawled up his spine. He now recognized the feeling in his chest and the bliss that consumed him. The sounds in the air weren't the melody of Altryon, singing just for him. It was melodic humming from the lips of a Lightborn. Neil hadn't gone to the water by choice; he'd been lured there. He turned to run, but Serena stood at the edge of the pond waiting for him.

Neil lifted his arms to defend himself, but Serena was in the water too, and it amplified her already formidable strength. She swung her fist and his defenses fell. Without making a sound, she clasped her hands around his throat and lifted him into the air. "Mamba." His old name sounded like a curse.

She looked different. When he knew her well, she'd been carefree and unbridled like the ocean breeze. Now her eyes were filled with something new. When people wanted to kill Neil, he often saw anger in their eyes and adrenaline feeding that anger. But Serena was the exception. Her eyes filled with unfiltered pain.

He wanted to say something to cleanse the sadness from her eyes, but he couldn't push any air through his lips. Words were out of the question. "We trusted you, Mamba. We clothed you. We fed you. We gave you something when you had nothing. What did you do? You killed my mother. You lied to us. You betrayed our trust. You left our mother twitching in the sand of our own beach. And then you left."

Neil's thought about igniting his hands and burning Serena away, but he knew it wouldn't work. In the water she was immortal, and it would only serve to make her angrier. "You heard what my mother said at that first banquet. You listened to her speak about how much she loved her family. She spoke about how she'd do anything for her children. I have to do this, Mamba. For my mother. We... I trusted you," she faltered. "I loved you, Mamba."

Neil wanted to cry out that he wasn't the spy, but no words escaped his throat. She tossed him deeper into the lake without taking notice of his weight. He didn't try to swim away. He knew that was foolish and he'd need his energy. "I'm not—" was all he could manage before she barreled into him and dragged him back to the shore by his throat.

Her eyes drifted to the tattoo on his flank. "You marked yourself? You took a trophy?" She dropped him and he collapsed on his hands and knees in the water.

Neil wheezed, "It's not a trophy."

She stared at it. Then the anger came. She lifted him back into the air. "You tattooed a snake onto your body? You chose to honor my mother with a snake? Is it a joke? Is it some stupid joke?" She was sputtering and crying now. Neil shook his head with the little control that he had over his neck.

"It's not a joke?" she demanded.

It took a few moments, but the pain in Serena's eyes was replaced with confusion. She lowered Neil slowly and shook her head. "It's not a trophy," she said to herself.

Neil shook his head with great pain and limited range of movement.

"This tattoo represents my mother..." she murmured. Her grip was loosening, gears clicking away in her mind.

She threw Neil hard into the bank and picked him up again. "Why didn't Alex want to pursue you?" She was speaking to herself. "He wanted to just... let you go."

Her eyes drifted farther off into the lake where the letter was floating on the surface. She released him and lept into the water. She appeared next to him in an instant, scanning it, holding it delicately. He saw her eyes stop on the last paragraph. The one that included *She still doesn't know about our mother's deception...* Serena looked at Neil

145

again. The pain was back, and it made him want to lie to her. He wanted to tell her that she was right, that he'd actually been the spy. He wanted to tell her that her mother had been perfect. Serena covered her mouth. "My mother is the snake." She was still looking at Neil's tattoo. "My mother was the spy."

Serena unraveled into tears. She fell backward into the water, crushed by her new realization. He let her process it without interruption.

Eventually she grabbed him and pulled him to shore. Maybe she remembered how poor of a swimmer he was. She left him there and stood a few feet off, deep in thought.

"Mamba..." she said eventually. "I was going to kill you."

Neil shook his head and tried to speak through his damaged throat. "You wouldn't believe how many of my friends have tried to kill me before." It was all he could think to say.

"You should have told me."

Neil wanted to justify his position. He hadn't told Serena that her mother was willing to sacrifice her for a reason. That wasn't the kind of thing any person needed to hear about a parent. "I... I should have told you."

She leaned into her hands. "That camp... It's yours?"

"It belongs to Volteria."

"Do they allow visitors?"

The Wolf absolutely did not like visitors. Neil stood and rubbed his throat with one hand. "I'm sure they'll make an exception," he said. She helped him up.

With that, he led her back toward his tent at the center of the camp.

27

REBEL BASE CAMP

NEIL VAPROS

"Well?" Neil asked.

"I'm thinking," Serena said, taking a sip from Neil's wineskin.

They'd been in his tent for almost an hour. Neil wanted nothing more than a light, carefree Tridenti conversation, but he always found himself subconsciously steering them toward the greater whirlpool. The rebels were going to take Abington. If they couldn't they'd be too scattered to organize. No matter how much he hated asking Serena for something, he needed the Tridenti now.

She assessed him carefully. "So, Mamba goes away, hits the mainland and becomes this hotheaded revolutionary, huh?" She looked him up and down. "One step on the shore and he forgets how to laugh. Forgets his joy."

Neil smiled. It was fake. "Sometimes you don't get a choice."

"How do you look so much older?" Serena asked.

"Memory came back."

"All of it?"

"As far as I can tell."

"And with those memories," she waved her hand through the air, "weight."

He nodded. There was a tragic dissonance between them. They'd been so close and he'd never felt any struggle to talk to her once. He'd fantasized about hopping on that boat she talked about and never looking back. Following sunset after sunset. But the air between them was now too thick to clear. He'd killed her mother and no matter the reason they'd never be the same. She was an orphan, and he was championing a rebel cause.

"So every single memory?" And just like that she still had a spark of that Tridenti joviality. "Anyone in particular come back to you? Anyone important?"

Neil was about to say when the flap of his tent opened and Bianca entered. Her eyes flicked back and forth between Neil and Serena, then narrowed. "Hi there."

Neil and Serena met eyes. *Yes. This was her.* "Hi," Serena said, jumping off of Neil's desk where she'd been sitting. "I'm Serena. I'm a friend of Mamba's." She realized what she'd said. "Neil's."

"Oh, that's so odd," Bianca said. "Neil's never mentioned any new friends."

"None?"

"Nope."

"Well, he's hard to get along with." Serena winked and Neil wasn't sure how good of an idea that was.

"I'm Bianca."

"Charmed."

The balance was holding. "And what were the two of you discussing?" Bianca asked.

"Mamba… Or… Neil, I guess, was pitching me the revolution."

All sense of jealousy and tension faded. Bianca's eyes came alive. She scanned Serena, taking note of the clothing and the hair. "You wouldn't happen to be…"

"Serena Tridenti," Serena smiled. "My family is a little more famous than it would like to be right now."

Bianca shook her head wildly. "We've been trying to reach your family for months."

"We stopped taking letters. A little more trouble than it's worth."

"Right," Bianca said.

She knew of Neil's time there of course. Neil saw it occur to her that Serena wasn't trying to murder him. "And you're..."

"I'm aware of what really happened," Serena said. "Now."

Neil's face got a little hot.

"Well are you... Do you...?" Bianca said facing Serena again.

Serena was still, her once clear eyes filled with conflict and pain. She had wanted to kill Neil an hour ago. Now she was being convinced into joining a war that her family had sworn to avoid. Her eyes found their way to Neil. Was there enough there? Did she owe him anything at all? Of course not. Right?

"The shore holds strong, right?" Bianca said.

Serena turned.

"That's what I've heard. Your motto is 'The Shore Holds Strong.' I don't know as much about your family as Neil does, but I know you want what's best for this land. The Empire can't rule without oppressing. The people's thirst for freedom is too great." Her voice was clear and strong, almost as melodic as Serena's. "If this war ends and the people aren't free, there won't be a shore to protect. We're well past imprisonment, Serena."

Serena was silent for a moment, then her facade broke into a smile. "All right, Neil. I get it," she laughed. "She's something."

"Is that a yes?" Bianca asked, resolution firm.

"I'll do what I can. Alex is here and there, but he's not exactly good at staying inconspicuous. I'll follow the sunken ships until I find him." She reached her hand to Bianca and they shook hands. "Abington is on the ocean. If we do make it, we'll be at our strongest."

Bianca nodded gratefully. "Thank you."

Serena approached Neil and wrapped him in a hug. "I'll see you soon, Mamba."

She reached the exit to the tent before she turned back. "You know, Bianca, my mother once tried to gain a foothold in this war."

Neil's stomach sank. It was also the day she'd been killed.

"And when she died, I expected my first reaction to be anger and sadness. But it wasn't. It was relief." She looked over at Neil. "It was because I realized she wanted an empire of her own. I knew she didn't just want to topple the Empire. She wanted one of her own and there was no limit to how far she'd go to get it. My mother was not a good person. I know that now. She would have hurt a lot of people."

Bianca looked over at Neil and her eyes passed over the tattoo on his arm.

"We don't want an empire," Bianca said. "We want something for the people. A rule that represents the people."

Serena didn't turn back, and Neil thought he saw a tear. "Then I'll see you both in Abington."

Neil and Bianca sat in silence after her departure. Neil went back and sat on the bed, decompressing.

"You never said she was pretty," Bianca said eventually.

"Well... I hadn't noticed," Neil managed.

Bianca rolled her eyes. "You're the worst."

"I might be the worst, but I also just got the Tridenti to join the war."

"*I* got the Tridenti to join the war," Bianca teased. "You went swimming and had a nightcap." She joined him on the bed.

"Ah yes. Where would I be without you?"

"I don't know," Bianca muttered. "On a pirate ship probably."

She socked him with a pillow. Neil wanted to mention that he'd turned down Serena's offer to travel the world together, but he decided not to. Not every fight had to be won. While he was reasonably confident in their ability to topple the Empire, he was not reasonably confident of his odds in a scrap with Bianca.

He pulled her close and once again prayed he'd never have to leave her.

28

IMPERIAL MILITARY FORTRESS

LILLY CELERIUS

Lilly awoke at the sound of her cell door opening and every muscle in her body contracted. She heard light footsteps coming down the stairs. She hadn't been drained yet. Carlin had been leaving her to rot and starve, eaten alive by her own anxiety. Was this her first draining?

She turned her head slightly, but her vision was blurry. She saw an Imperial guard. Not much else. The man came to her side and took a deep shuddery breath. She groaned. "Just get it over with. None of the 'this is going to hurt me more than it's going to hurt you' nonsense."

"It might," came the reply.

The voice was familiar. Lilly craned her neck to see who it was. "I made a vow to your brother when he took me in. Protect his family if he was unable to do it himself. On the same day, I made a vow to the Empire. Stand by my brothers and serve the Empire."

"Virgil?" Lilly asked, an inevitable drop of fear coloring her words. "What are you...?" Her mouth kept moving, but no sound came out. Her mind sputtered uselessly. Virgil made a vow to protect the Celerius? Since when? He'd been hunting her at Carlin's side for months. Unless...

"I am consumed by this, Lilly. This dichotomy."

"You'd be amazed how often I get this speech," Lilly said.

He nodded. "Carlin can't decide whether or not to kill you." He pulled a knife from his vest. "And neither can I."

She tensed. For a moment she thought he might be her protector, but this was certainly not in line with that theory. "I have to choose, Lilly. Anthony or Carlin. My two brothers. I either kill you, forsaking my vow, or I kill Carlin and betray my country."

"I can tell you what I'm partial to."

She didn't mean it as a joke, but he laughed. It was unexpected for him too. She could see his face, illuminated by the slightest shard of light. His eyes flickered back and forth and he looked like a man pulled apart. "I believed in him. Despite all the cruelty and the abuse, I believed in Carlin. I believed in his world. The one he kept promising. A world where no one could take advantage of anyone. Then I was shown that world... The one I was fighting so hard for... Can I trust a man who wants to free us from Lightborns but uses Lightborn power?"

"I don't know," Lilly said truthfully. She really didn't. She had never imagined men truly believed in Carlin, but evidently Virgil did. Some people really did hate Lightborns. On a certain level she understood that.

Virgil clutched the knife harder and lowered his eyes to her. "I've decided."

He swung the knife quickly. Lilly's last thought before it landed was whether she'd feel it. Virgil was a killer of the utmost precision. When she was younger, she'd seen him butcher animals at the Celerius estate. She'd always been in awe of his speed and humanity in killing. She hoped that she'd simply be gone, just like all those animals.

But Virgil pulled his hand away, and the restraints holding her arm to the table were sliced in two. She looked at him, in confusion and gratitude.

"Run, Lilly."

"Run?"

"Carlin is nearly out of blood. If he gets yours... I don't think anyone could stop him." Virgil sheathed the knife and with a new, iron-clad determination began ascending the stairs. "But if he runs out... I've seen him without it. I don't think he'd survive."

Lilly wanted to argue. Carlin was in the building. They had the drop on him. Would it be so hard for the two of them to kill him?

"I know it's hard," Virgil said. "But something will get him. It'll either be the withdrawals..."

"Or?"

"Or it'll be me."

29

OUTSIDE ABINGTON

HAROLD THORNE

Harold Thorne watched as dozens of men rifled through his cargo brought from the city. Boxes upon boxes of explosives, stuffed to the brim. He'd been outpacing the Wolf at almost every opportunity. Because of this he'd become the Empire's most valuable resource. But now, he was toeing a delicate line. Bigger plays meant bigger risks. He was used to this. Spending money to make money. Sacrificing lives to save lives. Losing ground to gain it. This, however, was his most dangerous decision yet.

The rebels wanted to blow the bridges to keep the Imperial soldiers from entering Abington. So what was there to do except fill Abington to the brim with soldiers and destroy the bridges himself? If the rebels surrounded the village, they'd be met with the most densely packed and fortified force in existence. The rebels needed Abington to take the wall and now Abington would be even harder to conquer than the city of Altryon.

Something stuck in his mind. His prisoner had told him they'd planned to surround the city. Did they really have enough men to do that? How big exactly was the revolution? They were always so spread out and under wraps. A headcount was out of the question.

He watched his men set the explosives as he sat on the grassy earth feeling the cool air blow across his scalp. Was he being outplayed? He was winning this war because he didn't think like a military man, but like an innovator. So why did this feel so risky?

He heard something behind him, and turned to see what could only loosely be described as a human. It shuddered as it arrived and its fur faded. "Marksman," Thorne said, disbelieving. "Left your razor at home, did you?"

"I'm out of time," the Marksman wheezed. "I'm absolutely and completely out of time."

Thorne reached into his jacket and removed a syringe. He'd estimated that this would happen. He dipped it into the Marksman's neck. "A temporary fix. But I have good news." He let the solution take effect as the Marksman collapsed, vomiting again. "I've been going through your father's notes which I inherited after becoming Imperial Strategist. I think I've found notes on how to recreate the real thing."

The Marksman retched again. "He never wrote it down."

"Not the final recipe, but there's enough for me to reverse engineer it."

This was another risky decision. A total lie. He estimated that Victor wouldn't be listening to his heartbeat, not during his forced detox. At the same time, it didn't matter how much the Venator claimed to be emotionless, or above emotion. Victor wanted to live. Desperately. Everyone did. Harold was selling hope. something people *always* bought.

"Please," the Marksman whispered. "I need it."

"Tomorrow the rebels will lay siege to Abington. You're going to stand at the top of the Bank of Abington with the nicest rifle money can buy and earn your life, Victor. One hundred dead rebels. That's all I ask."

Victor stood, streams of drool and bloody vomit on his chin. "I accept."

Leaf approached, taking no account of the business being done between the two men. "We're ready."

"Excellent." Thorne patted the Marksman on the shoulder. "Do it."

Harold Thorne watched as four bridges had their foundations blown and listened as tons of rubble collapsed to the ground. The glowing fire illuminated his face. He basked in it. Thorne loved seeing things razed. You couldn't build a new world on ruins. You needed to make foundations first.

And the blood spilled tomorrow would be the foundation of an Empire, stronger than ever before.

30

REBEL BASE CAMP

HIGHEST HONOR

THE WOLF

The Wolf returned to camp as the sun fell. Everyone rushed to see him and speak with him, but he shooed them away and asked to be brought to Neil's tent. The two drank wine and talked about what might happen in the morning.

Eventually, Neil gained the courage to say what he'd been thinking for days. "You know I'm in, right?"

"I'd hoped."

"If it comes down to it, I'll die for the revolution. For Volteria."

"Was it the drink?" the Wolf asked. "That brought about this revelation?"

"A few things," Neil noted. They sat on either side of a war map. Neil traced a finger over it, imagining he could reshape the landscape with a thought. Like he was anything other than impossibly small. "Every time I've ever tried to find some sort of normalcy I've seen endless bloodshed. Josephine, the Tridenti. I can't imagine Bianca being next. I'm a curse."

"All men with a purpose are."

Neil lifted his arm to show his tattoo. "Burdened with purpose."

"It sticks in the mind, doesn't it? I can't remember where I first heard it. But I think of it always."

Neil knew he wouldn't sleep tonight. The Wolf had admitted that Thorne was the greatest mind he'd ever challenged. In order to win this war they'd have to make some very risky decisions. "What do you expect the other side is doing tonight?" Neil asked.

"I assume Thorne is blowing those bridges."

"And Carlin?"

"Either Carlin's dead or Lilly is." The Wolf's eyes filled with a quiet rage and pain. "Virgil is a precision killer."

"Saewulf?"

"I'm not sure," the Wolf said, and they dropped the topic.

They refined particulars of the plan before the Wolf left. Neil had one last thing to say. "I bet he's as nervous as we are. Saewulf, I mean. I think he wants his new world as badly as we want ours."

The Wolf smiled faintly. "Yes, that makes sense."

Before morning Rhys and Darius arrived and were hastily added to the plan. When the slightest suggestion of the sun arrived, the rebel camp split into two groups, all on the road to freedom.

31

ABINGTON

HIGHEST HONOR

THE WOLF

Harold Thorne clutched his spyglass to his chest and watched the horizon. The Wolf arrived before the sun, riding alone on a small carriage. Nearly the entire Empire went to meet him at the gate. He was brought to the center of town where Saewulf and Thorne awaited him. He wouldn't step foot from his carriage, so the meeting took place in the town square. "I will be negotiating on behalf of the Empire!" Harold called to the Wolf.

The Wolf smiled and stepped down. "And I on behalf of the rebellion."

"What rebellion?" Thorne asked, arrogance leaking through his tone. "It dies when you do, Wolf. And this." He pointed at the carriage. "This is all you have left? This is no war. This is an old man raving in a town square. It's disorderly conduct at worst."

"It's actually enough dynamite to blow this entire city block to pieces. Does the Empire exist without Saewulf?" He looked over Thorne's shoulder and then redirected his gaze into the industrialist's eyes. "Does it exist without you?"

"You don't really expect me to believe that," Thorne said.

"Where's your Venator?" the Wolf asked. "He'll be able to smell the gunpowder. I have no doubt."

Thorne discreetly looked over his shoulder toward the bank. He gritted his teeth. Evidently the Marksman had given him a nod. After all, it was true. There was a significant amount of gunpowder within the carriage. A gift from Cartwright.

Thorne straightened his spine and pivoted. "I'm sure you're waiting for your men to cross those bridges and then blow them. I imagined you found quite the surprise when—"

"No."

"I…" Thorne stopped. "No?"

"No." The Wolf paced away from the carriage and reveled in the panic around him. There were nearly one hundred armed soldiers standing in this square, soaked with sweat and terror. "There are two differences between us, Thorne. One, I am a military man. You are not."

"Seems to have worked out all right for me."

"Two, I never underestimated you. I knew you'd blow those bridges the second you took Mr. Jacobson." He could see Thorne processing. "You must be wondering what advantage I could possibly gain from having Abington fortified beyond my wildest fears. Your entire military base occupies the city I want. This is the smart choice. The innovator makes a smart choice.

Thorne was silent, processing faster now. "But when your entire army leaves the base to protect the village, who protects the base?"

Thorne's face lost every ounce of blood. The Wolf saw his knees quiver. Behind him, Saewulf's eyes grew wide, then filled with rage. "That's no problem. I can send my men—" Thorne started to say.

"Send them where? You don't have any bridges."

Thorne looked back to Saewulf and then back to the Wolf. "I…"

"You see Thorne, the innovator makes the smart choice. But no amount of literature can prepare you for war."

For once, the Wolf could tell that Harold Thorne had *no idea* what to say. That was fine, because the Wolf had quite a lot to say. "Why do you think I want Abington so much? Because it's close to the wall?

Not half as close as the military fortress you've left defenseless. It is attractive to me, simply because it has the largest population. Well, it does now. It's nearly doubled in size in the last five years."

Men around the square began scattering, doing their best to account for what the Wolf was saying. But there was no hope. The ground he stood on was his. "I don't have to infiltrate your village because I already did it, Thorne. I've been doing it daily for the last five years. The rebels don't have to sneak in. They already live here."

The earth shook and the occupants of the square looked off to see a building in flames. The city was destroying itself. "I am not the revolution, Thorne. The revolution is not me *and* the people. It *is* the people. I just tell them where to go. And now, they're surrounding you from every side. They have been for five years."

"Well, you seem to forgot that I have...." Thorne was sputtering, malfunctioning.

Saewulf, having seen enough, lifted Thorne into the air and slammed him into a building. "What if I don't believe you about the contents of your cart?" Saewulf demanded. "What if I snap your neck right here?"

"My men inside the cart blow its contents and turn this block into ash." His eyes flickered over Saewulf's burns. "You remember what a tenth of a pound of gunpowder can do, don't you? Want to see what thousands do?"

Saewulf's eyes glowed, then stopped. They glowed and stopped again. "How do we appease you, Great Destroyer?"

"You retreat," the Wolf said. "You leave this city and head back to your own. You batten down every hatch and you await the storm that comes." Saewulf bit his lip so hard that a drop of blood came from it. "If it helps you decide," the Wolf said, a cannon sounding in the distance, "it sounds like the Tridenti are here. Just in time."

Saewulf looked at the faces of his men. They looked back, desperate for any kind of leadership. He had nothing for them. He picked Harold Thorne from the ground and pulled him close. He smacked him awake and then sneered at the Wolf. "I need a moment to confer with my men."

They spoke in hushed tones. Finally, Saewulf turned back. "You're not afraid I'll crush that carriage like an egg and whatever is inside?"

"You're going to crush a wooden carriage filled with gunpowder? You don't imagine that will create a single spark? Risky. I guess we could see? I've made a bet or two in my day."

Another moment of conversation passed. The Wolf was surprised Thorne had lived this long through such a blunder. He might have lost the whole war for the Empire today. "We will leave," Saewulf announced after a time. "We will return to our city, and when you arrive at those walls we will crush you like ants on a hill."

"I will see you then," the Wolf nodded. "I apologize for any disorderly conduct."

The Wolf could remove his blade in less than a quarter of a second and considered unleashing it in this moment. Not just because killing Saewulf might mean winning the war, but also because something was wrong. The air was fraught with tension as he expected, but not the right kind of tension. This uneasy victory might not hold. However, something told him his sword would do no good.

Saewulf and his men retreated halfway up the street. The psychic turned and with a mighty heave, he ripped the walls off from around the carriage, sending splinters of wood everywhere and exposing the contents of the cart.

Instead of two tons of dynamite, as had been promised, the cart contained a myriad of ornate fireworks and Neil Vapros holding a large fuse. "Now!" the Wolf said.

Neil ignited a fireball in his hand, then in one quick motion, materialized over to the Wolf, grabbed him, and materialized the two of them into an alley out of Saewulf's reach. This had been the plan, as the Wolf had never expected his bluff to work. They darted through the alley until they found their separation spot a few blocks over. "I can't believe that worked as well as it did," Neil huffed.

The Wolf was having just as much trouble believing it. "A lot of it was true."

"Except…"

"The bomb."

Behind them the square ignited into chaos as thousands of pounds of fireworks went off, coloring the sky and filling the air with haze. The Wolf never would have sacrificed an entire city block, but he certainly did need the gunpowder for a convincing lie.

He remembered freeing a group of villagers from some bandits when he was a young soldier and them showing their thanks with a small firework show. He hoped that was how the people of Abington would remember this day. Not as a bloody battle, but as the day the sky cracked open and all the light broke through.

3 2

ABINGTON

HAROLD THORNE

Harold Thorne had made some bad investments in his time, but he had to concede that this was his largest blunder of all. Not only had he put the Empire at risk of losing Abington, but in his eagerness to protect this crucial city, he'd also lost their last remaining base outside the wall.

When optimism faded, Thorne's default mode was the one that kept him in business for decades: damage control.

The fireworks quieted down eventually, and his ears stopped ringing. The air was hard to breathe, let alone see through. He waited for a break in Saewulf's enraged screaming to make an offer. "If I can stop the rebels from taking Abington, do I get to live?" he said between coughs.

Saewulf turned eyes glowing. "Maybe."

Thorne nodded. That was good enough. "I appreciate your leniency."

He didn't really want to die today. Things had been going so well until this moment. He looked over his shoulder and signaled the Marksman. The command could be roughly translated to: *start shooting everyone that isn't in our uniform.* He turned to the platoon at his back. "Start taking hostages. They don't just want to take the city, they want to free the city."

He struggled. What else was he willing to do that no one else was? What could set him apart?

"Saewulf. Remember that conversation we had?"

"About demolishing the village?"

"Yes."

Saewulf spun in an arc, admiring his surroundings. Thorne could see an even larger battle transpiring in the psychic's head. "Either we take it or they do."

In response, Saewulf lifted his arm and roared, bringing down a building and showering the earth with a cloud of debris and dust. Thorne had never seen anything like it. He reminded himself in that moment that he was on the winning side. Any side that had Saewulf was unbeatable. He watched as every villager in sight fled screaming.

"Carlin is still at the base. It might remain ours."

"It better." Saewulf was breathing heavily.

"Leaf!" Thorne called.

The boy was by his side before long, engaging in a sarcastic salute. "Have my men fill this city with gas. Go block-by-block, starting from the center and moving outward. Kill everyone who isn't in our colors."

Saewulf lifted his hand, pulling up a large piece of debris and sending it through a nearby wooden building. "That was the orphanage," Leaf said almost amused.

"Not the worst thing that's happened to that place." Thorne murmured.

As his men began fanning out, destroying Abington piece by piece, he gently reached into his coat and removed a yellowing letter, finished with a wax seal. Thorne wasn't exactly confident in his ability to keep Abington. They'd been several minutes late to the battle, and he didn't need to be a military man to know it meant losing.

He did have one thing left: this little letter. Sure, the Wolf could humiliate, trample, and outsmart him, but he still had this. The Wolf had fireworks, most of the Lightborns, and the heart of a warrior. But at the end of the day, Thorne suspected none of that would change the outcome of this war. Harold Thorne held faith in an investment he'd made long ago and its ability to end all of this foolishness. The Wolf could strike him down with a blade, but Thorne suspected he could destroy everything that mattered to the Wolf with four little sentences of blue ink written in perfect handwriting.

He placed the letter back in his coat pocket and patted it gently. "I'll be okay," he said to no one in particular. "I'll be okay."

ABINGTON

THE MARKSMAN

Nothing had ever been this blurry for the Marksman. Details faded in and out, and every smell of the city violated his nostrils. It had never felt this horrific before. The withdrawal had never stung his mind and his senses so much.

He turned to the stockpile of ammunition behind him. Why was he here?

Death.

It was always death. It followed him like the train of a wedding gown. He loaded his weapon and looked to the streets below. He saw Harold Thorne in perfect detail, signaling him. Begin now.

He looked around. One hundred dead men. That was the bargain, right? He saw a man with a sword charging at an Imperial soldier. He inhaled, sensed the wind, and fired a bullet through the man's skull.

Ninety-nine left.

He spied a group of men sneaking through an alley. They were the rebels, right? They smelled like rebels. He fired through one of them.

Ninety-eight left.

The others ran and he shot them in their backs, bullets coming down like rain chosen just for them. The last one turned and the Marksman saw a glint of fear in his eye as he peered up at the bank tower. He put a hole through that glint.

Eighty-Nine left.

The Marksman looked street by street now, shooting holes through every man with dirt on his face. It was getting harder to see. Whose colors were right? Sweat dripped from his forehead into his eyes and he forgot how to blink it away. He finished off an entire row of men trying to escape into a bar.

Sixty-two left.

The sweat that poured into his eyes slid down his cheeks now. This was closest thing he'd ever had to tears. He reloaded with one arm and let bullets fly with the other. For the first time he saw them as birds with the message of something bigger on the way.

Fifty-eight left.

All these men in red, swarming around like fire ants. He'd crushed fire ants as a kid until he'd lost his power over it. Then he grew to respect them. These were not fire ants. They smelled like men, and he'd never lost anything from killing men. Men *always* had a reason to die.

Ten left.

They looked so confused. He could hear somewhere in his mind Harold Thorne yelling, screaming. Why did they wear red? No one could see them bleed, but they must have been able to smell it right?

One left.

His eyes came down to a person holding up the beams of a school. The person smelled like sweat and salt water. Victor fired a shot. It drew blood, but not enough. The figure ran and Victor smelled their blood. Victor fired again, then dropped his rifle. It fell from the tower. His heart was beating so fast.

That was enough. Was that enough?

In a way he was so jealous of the Vapros boy. The Marksman dearly missed his father's voice. Maybe it wouldn't be so bad to hear it in his head.

"And now you enter the void," the Doctor had said.

Victor could hear his own heart. He had always been able to hear it. Nothing was quite so peculiar as not hearing it as he folded forward and plummeted from the top of the tower.

IMPERIAL MILITARY FORTRESS

VIRGIL

For the first time in his life, Virgil had direction. He'd been a Lightborn hating Lightborns his entire life. Then he'd been a Venator killing Imperials, then an Imperial killing rebels. Every man he ever met pointed him somewhere and asked for blood. And he'd given it. Because no one asks the killing machine how it feels.

He shoved his way through the military base until he reached Carlin's office. Two men stood at the door. "He's not ready to—"

Virgil spilled both of their guts and caught their bodies before they fell. He lowered them to the ground, making sure their armor didn't make a sound against the stone. He then opened the door with urgency. "She's escaped!" Virgil cried.

Carlin was reading at his desk, but he startled upright with his face white. "Hold her off. Lock down the base."

He bolted around the desk and to the back wall of his office. He found his small safe and inserted his key. He grabbed the red vial and popped the cork. Suddenly, he was holding nothing and his face and hands were coated in small specks of red. Carlin froze, trying to understand what had happened. There was an arrow in the wall behind him. He turned to see Virgil already notching another one into his bow.

"Carlin Filus. You are a danger to the one I am sworn to protect. For this, you must die. Make peace."

"Virgil you..."

Virgil lowered his bow, removed the iron mask from his coat and threw it between them. "There is nothing to say."

Carlin stared at it, his breath a low engine, fueling his rage. "You..."

"I," Virgil said.

"I trusted you," Carlin said. "Loved you."

"And I you."

Carlin drew his blade. "So you buy it now? The Wolf's poison? Lightborns are fit to lead us?"

"No," Virgil said, "but they are fit to do good. You will see."

He fired off an arrow and hoped that would be the end of it. But Carlin even without his special potion was still the fastest non-Lightborn he'd met and the arrow missed. Carlin was across the room, but Virgil weaved away from every swing of his blade. Then they were within distance, swinging fists and elbows at each other. Virgil kicked Carlin off and they circled each other, measuring. "So bold, Virgil." Carlin was taunting. "So bold, seeing how many times I've struck you down in sparring."

"You are my superior. Rude to embarrass you in front of your men."

"You embarrass yourself," Carlin spat. His face was entirely red. "By being infirm of purpose."

"You are right." Virgil drew his blade and let Carlin retrieve his. "Infirm of purpose until today."

They clashed again. Virgil won out this one, dealing cuts to Carlin's arms. Carlin swore and hissed loudly. Virgil held off, letting his enemy tire himself with his frantic swings. "Guards!" Carlin tried to howl before Virgil was across the room again to silence him. He deflected Carlin's first swing and slammed his boot heel into Carlin's face, inspiring a spray of blood from his mouth. Carlin tried to swing again, but was disarmed. Virgil struck him again, cracking a tooth. He caught Carlin's head with his hand and slammed it into the wall hard enough to shake trophies and weapons from where they were hung.

Virgil raised his blade for the execution. "Can any of us kill the others?" Carlin, on his knees, spat. "You said that once. Can any of us kill the others? You said you couldn't. And I believed you."

"I won't hesitate," Virgil said.

Carlin glanced at the wall next to Virgil where the arrow that had broken the vial was stuck in the wall. Carlin stood, inch by inch. "You'd kill your brother? After the blood we've spilled together?"

"Hypocrite," Virgil accused.

"Did you kill your men in Brightbow? The men who trusted you? Believed in you? Who entrusted themselves to your care?"

Virgil tightened his grip. "You killed—"

"And then cut yourself? Cut your own flesh in shame?"

"Make peace," Virgil demanded. He swung.

Carlin was gone before the blade reached him. With extraordinary force he ripped the arrow from the wall and put it through Virgil's neck.

Virgil stared at him, blood coating his chest. Carlin ripped the arrow out and put it through Virgil's ribs. "You once told me your father was a doctor," he said. "You don't have to be a medical professional to know that this isn't the kind of wound that gets cured."

Virgil stared at Carlin, confused and numb. "You know the difference between the two of us, Virgil?" Carlin asked. "It's conviction. It's belief. You've had endless opportunities to kill me. In my sleep, when my back was turned, when I was wounded and weak, but you never did. These are not choices I would have made because I don't care who dies with peace. I don't care what is right. You are one of the fastest men I have ever known, but I know hesitation when I see it." He lowered Virgil's body to the ground. "You want me dead. Everyone wants me dead. Everyone wants me humiliated, but none of you understand that opposition strengthens my cause."

Virgil's vision was going dark until a light shone over him. He allowed his face to release from a grimace of pain into a sigh of acceptance. "Lilly Celerius is free. And she is running to your end. All your ghosts are coming home, Carlin. All of your ghosts are coming home." Virgil found Carlin's eyes. Then he slumped back into Carlin's arms, accepting his end. There was a reason Virgil asked men to make peace before he killed them. Virgil could imagine nothing worse than dying stuck in a duality. Virgil had lived ripped apart by every man who wanted to own him.

But when Virgil died, he died with conviction.

ABINGTON

NEIL VAPROS

Neil went to the pier first, throwing fireballs through entire squadrons of men on the way. One of them tried to swing at him, but he was shot from somewhere up above. Neil decided not to think where it had come from.

He reached the pier and the docks creaked under his heavy footfalls. The ship was here. The Tridenti leapt from its deck into the shallow waters, armed with rusted swords and whatever they could find around the ship. Neil saw Alex clutching a spear and wrapping a net around his free arm. "Alex!"

Alex turned and his determined stare broke into a grin. "Mamba!"

"Thanks for showing up."

"Thanks for the invite," Alex said. "But why am I just now hearing about this? You should know me well enough to know I'm always down for a siege."

"You're absolutely right. My apologies."

This was the easy flowing banter that he half expected when he saw Serena for the first time again, but Alex had always been a little more low stakes. "Where do you need us?"

"If any ships show up—"

"Sink them. Got it."

"And if they try to retreat on their ships?"

"Sink them."

"You got it," Neil said.

A squadron of soldiers appeared at the end of the cobblestone street. Neil threw a fireball, scattering them. Neil always tried to turn off his brain when he fought, especially in dense battles like these. Even though he'd wanted to be an assassin as a child, he simply wasn't a warrior and couldn't stand the thought of the damage he might do.

A soldier ran at him at full speed and Neil launched a fireball into his chest. The man collapsed, skidding across the cobblestone. Another soldier tried to flank him, but he found Alex's spear buried deep in his chest before he could do any damage. Neil glanced back and saw that Alex and Serena were behind him, ready to advance.

They fought together and felt the connection forged months ago returning. Neil found that he didn't need to speak. He could simply do what he planned and his friends would fall behind him.

They cleared the entire street of enemies, and Neil turned to face them. He didn't know what to say. They were all breathing heavily. "Is that all of them?" Alex asked.

Suddenly, the ground shook and cracked. Neil felt a surge of anxiety. Was this Saewulf? How could they hope to ever defeat someone with such raw power? Could Saewulf really split the earth at will?

A building a few feet over began to rumble, and Neil saw what was about to happen. "Alex, Serena it's..." The building's supports were cracking. Worse, Neil could hear people inside. Even some cries from children. "What do we...?"

"Get the people out," Serena said as she lunged over, positioning herself at the base of the building, pressing on it. "I'll hold things together." Neil was amazed by her strength, but remembered that she was still damp from the ocean. Water was lending her strength.

Alex and Neil broke through the doors and helped the swarms of people running out, mostly children. Neil realized they must have been taking shelter here. He couldn't imagine they expected entire buildings to fall today. Neil heard footsteps in the street and realized soldiers were coming for Serena. She was left defenseless, holding the building together.

Neil charged out and threw a few fireballs. Serena began to sing in a low hum. The soldiers around Neil slowed, confused. The building's supports failed and Serena ducked under, holding it up. Her song was softer now and those around her were stirring. Neil watched as ash and dust poured from the walls and onto her body. Neil realized with horror that the water on her body was turning to mud and her strength was fading. The children exited into the street, looking around dumbstruck.

A shot rang out through the air, Neil didn't know from where, and Serena cried out. She looked to Neil and he ran to her side. "Go," he said. "Get to the water."

He grabbed what remained of the building and she bolted toward the ocean. He watched as she went, limping at first, eventually making it to a sprint. He saw her leap into the air. And his heart leapt too.

Then he heard the second shot and saw her go limp a second before plunging into the bay.

ABINGTON

HIGHEST HONOR

THE WOLF

The Wolf entered what was left of a bar near the more populated district of town. This had been his choice for a rendezvous point before Saewulf had decided to pull down buildings left and right. He pushed over a fallen beam and entered the decrepit ruin through the doorless threshold.

The ground was stained with dust and pools of blood. The Wolf found a small squadron of his men, dead. He lifted his hands, stretching energy throughout the ruin, attempting to detect a culprit.

Suddenly, he felt his back split and fell to the ground, gasping and wheezing. He could see a rebel man lying a few feet away with a playing card buried in his forehead.

"I hope you know it wasn't an easy decision," Barlow Venator said as he threw a card to the back of the Wolf's head, dangerously close to his spinal chord. The Wolf sprang up and leapt over the bar, catching two more cards on the way. "But Venator aren't made for war. We're not the warrior types. We get a plot of land and we protect it. Mine's Arkney, and I was promised its independence if I cut off your head." Barlow paced the bar, looking for an opening to throw a card through. "Harold Thorne might be a worm, but the fellow sure knows how to make a deal."

"I've got a plot of land too." The Wolf threw a bottle from behind the bar. "It's just slightly bigger than yours."

He removed the cards and felt his skin healing over. As a younger man, that happened much quicker. He groaned in pain and palmed another bottle. He could see Barlow trying to flank him, but noted a weak patch of wall and darted through it into the streets. Barlow tried to follow him through, but the Wolf chucked his bottle, deterring his would-be assassin for a moment.

He bolted through the decomposing city with his Celerius speed, halving a few Imperials as he went. This was a controlled retreat. He was sure his odds against Barlow were good. He just needed to shift things a little more in his favor.

He expanded his mind and felt the cards as they sliced through the air behind him. He deflected some with his sword and dodged the others. However, one well-placed card caught his wrist and he lost his sword. He mentally mapped out the street ahead and tried to decide where to stage a last stand. He couldn't sneak up on a Venator, even Barlow. He'd have to trade the element of surprise for a stronger fortification.

He shoved his way into a small restaurant, knowing what was in the back room. The Wolf kicked open the door to the kitchen, then to the room behind it. He flipped over the game table with a small groan and palmed entire handfuls of cards. Barlow came through the door, lining the walls with a neat row of steel-tipped playing cards. The Wolf launched himself from behind the table, tackling Barlow and bringing him to the ground. Barlow swung, and the Wolf took it on the chin. He tore the Dealer's holster from his hip, littering the ground with cards. Then he rolled into a standing position.

Barlow palmed a handful of cards. "This your tactic Wolf? You going to…"

His fingers slid over the cards, sensing the weight of them. For the first time he acknowledged his surroundings. He was in an underground casino. Since the Wolf had flipped the gaming table, the ground was littered with cards, not all of the steel-tipped variety. "Well..." Barlow said, trying to discern which cards were the right ones. "Damn."

The Wolf charged, swinging mercilessly. The first cards Barlow threw were paper and bounced impotently off the Wolf's chest. The Wolf slaughtered him in the ensuing fist fight. Once Barlow finally did find one of his steel-tipped cards, he was too punch drunk to use it. The Wolf slammed the Dealer's head into the wall, scattering a collection of chips. Barlow tried to lift his head, but the Wolf delivered a solid kick, eliciting a spurt of blood.

Barlow pulled a knife, but the Wolf delivered a cry, the Howl as his men knew it. Barlow collapsed, seizing in pain and clutching his ears.

"I can't imagine how much that hurts, Barlow. Especially with your hearing. I trained with the Venator for years. By your side."

"I remember," Barlow said, exposing his bloody teeth.

"You had your own ways of interpreting everything. Tinkering with your vows. Rigging the game. I respected you always, but I never thought you were right."

"Oh yeah?"

Barlow tried to stand. The Wolf stopped him. "Yes. You always wanted to get away with something, so you never thought about learning. You never learned to 'know the terrain.'" The Wolf lifted an arm, gesturing at the room around him. "You see everything and nothing."

"You're a little too focused on teaching," Barlow said with a light chuckle. "And not so focused on doing what really has to be done."

The Wolf realized he hadn't sensed the area around him in a while, but he realized too late. The front of the restaurant exploded, and Saewulf entered. How was he here? The Wolf had been running through town. Maybe he'd been spotted.

The Wolf took one more look at Barlow, who grinned ear to ear. "What's the matter? Didn't keep an ear to the ground? You don't know the terrain?"

The Wolf considered leaning in to snap Barlow's neck, but knew that would cost precious seconds. He bolted, sending his body through a stained glass window on the opposite wall, lining his body with small cuts and gashes.

His feet hit the road and he barreled into the nearest alley, taking a moment to catch his breath. He disarmed the first soldier he encountered and rearmed himself. Within the next few moments he was back in the fray, reorganizing troops and killing Imperials.

The tide turned and eventually Imperials began retreating. The Wolf wasn't sure if they were ordered to or if they were just smart enough to know this wasn't going to go their way.

Somehow the Wolf was winning Abington. If all went according to plan, maybe he'd take the military base too. Victory was hardly ever in sight for him. He hated thinking of it, just in case it would never be. But today he allowed himself a thought. *What if we win?*

Even when the smoke faded and the Imperial military retreated to Altryon, the Wolf couldn't shake the sight of Barlow grinning at him. He always thought he was on the winning side, the right side, because the Venator supported him. At least the ones he respected did. But Barlow's betrayal unsettled him deeply. Was he really too weak to do what had to be done? He could have snapped Barlow's neck, but it mattered too much to scold him first.

Sometimes the Wolf felt like an all-powerful hand, tracing a bloody trail across a map. Sometimes he felt so small and so weak, unable to truly shape a single thing. He'd won this battle today, but he now had to carry a heavy doubt.

He returned to his rare hope, the one he allowed himself to have in this moment. *What if we win?*

ABINGTON

NEIL VAPROS

Neil sat in the water, knees in the sand, water up to his chest, holding Serena's arm as she drifted back and forth in the pull of the waves. He kept hoping to see the wounds heal and the blood fade from the water. Something in him knew it wouldn't. She was dead before she hit the water.

He couldn't possibly calculate the amount of blood on his hands and how long it would take for him to feel this wouldn't kill him too. He'd asked her to come here. He'd done this. For the first time, he saw her resemblance to her mother.

Alex came to lie in the water with him and the tragic nature of the occasion was lost on neither of them. They'd sat in silence over Alex's mother's body too.

Eventually, Alex stood. Neil looked up at him, in awe of his resolve once again. "You're not crying."

"It'll all come at some point," Alex said, "but seeing all this..." He pointed at the smoldering village behind him. "There's a lot of perspective in it."

"Alex..." Neil stared down at Serena's lifeless body. "I'm a curse."

"You also happen to be one of the greatest friends I've ever had." Alex lifted his hand, and Neil realized maybe there were tears he was hiding for Neil's sake. "The Tridenti don't have guilt."

"How?" Neil begged.

"We spend our entire lives on the sea. The sea consumes everything it touches. We know that it grants us strength on the condition that we return to it. I don't fear it, and Serena didn't either. It's a Tridenti's purpose."

"Don't you understand?" Neil was sweating, his body rejecting itself. "I asked her to come here. I—"

"War is war, Neil. How many people do you think the Empire kills per year?"

"Thousands," Neil said with hesitation.

He'd seen thousands just in this war, but he'd heard of worse. Ordinary people slaughtered and robbed with no opportunity to claim justice.

"I will grieve her, Neil. Believe me I will." Alex looked off to the sea. "But there are a lot of kids walking around right now who wouldn't be if not for her sacrifice. That's a hell of a thing to take solace in."

Then he did something that Neil couldn't even fathom. He smiled. "You know," he said, "I keep having these dreams. This glowing man comes to me and, in a way, he sounds like everyone I've ever lost."

Neil tried not to let his jaw drop. How many people was the Man with the Golden Light visiting? "He told me about a Lightborn forged in fire."

"Who is going to die for the new nation?"

Alex's eyebrows lifted. "Yes. You're still here, Neil. Fighting. You walk into this fight every day knowing that one of them is going to be the last. It's not your fault for asking Serena to do the same. I love her, and I know you do too. I don't blame you for trying to help people."

Neil stood, face still red with shame. Alex bent down and lifted his sister over his shoulder. Neil walked out as far as he could with Alex until the water reached his neck. Alex turned back and nodded at

Neil, a universe of complex emotion in his eyes. "Watch this. I regret that you didn't see it happen to my mother."

He placed Serena on the surface of the water and her fingertips began to glow with golden energy. It consumed her arms and eventually covered her, lighting nearly all of the water in the bay. In another moment she was fading, becoming all of the light in the ocean. Alex couldn't help but let slow tears slide down his face. "The Tridenti don't fear death, Neil. Why would we? It's beautiful. All there is to fear is a life without meaning."

Just like that he was gone into the water, leaving Neil to bathe in the light. Neil drifted back to the shore eventually. He imagined the Wolf was going insane searching him out. He looked to the crumbled remains of the building Serena had held up. How many people were alive because of her?

Neil went to the town square where big smoke clouds billowed. No one else was here, but Neil didn't mind. He stood in the center of the clouds, letting them envelop him. He let his hands pass through them, making long streaks. Thinking of Serena, he made a decision about his future.

Neil Vapros was going to die. But before he did, he wanted to feel everything.

PART II

"We must cultivate our garden."

-Voltaire

IMPERIAL PALACE

HAROLD THORNE

"Do you remember that speech I gave you about power?" Thorne asked.

Thorne had no more legs to stand on. He'd monologued his way out of capturing Neil Vapros. He'd lost Abington and the base. Under his advisement, the Empire had been forced to retreat back within their walls. Not to mention the Marksman's psychotic break. He'd killed as many Imperials as he did rebels. Whereas any other man would pack up in the middle of the night, Thorne had built far too much in this city to leave it.

The Emperor sat back, assessing. At least it looked like he might be assessing. His eyes were cloudy and vacant. "Turn men against each other? That was the gist wasn't it?"

Thorne bobbed his head back and forth. "We are essentially left with a simple problem." He paced around the war room, passing by Carlin's chair and doing his best not to make eye contact with Saewulf. It made him feel safe to see Carlin here. He was the only other man who had more military blunders under his belt. "You have a force trying to crush you outside the wall and a force trying to crush you inside the wall. Ideally, they'd coordinate. However, we are blessed with a city that is airtight and a seamlessly running propaganda machine."

"You want to do what? Turn the rebels inside the city against the rebels outside the city?" Carlin asked.

"You're smarter than you look," Thorne said with a grin.

He regretted saying that. Carlin didn't react. Reports had come in. Carlin's second in command had tried to murder him after freeing Lilly Celerius. To add insult to injury, Carlin was immediately forced to flee as the rebels overwhelmed the base. Thorne considered himself one of the greatest living minds. Even he couldn't calculate how many slaps in the face this equaled. Instead of fuming and screaming, as Thorne had expected, Carlin became reserved and intense.

"I say we do this: starve out the people until they're rabid, and tell them it's because the 'savages' are starving us out."

"A lot of people will die," Saewulf said.

"More fuel to the fire," Thorne mused with a nod. "We'll of course have to lend some extra protection to the nobles to make sure we don't end up with a class war, but if by chance that wall does come down, the rebels will be met with other rebels. Maybe our two problems solve each other."

"That would not be easy to pull off," the Emperor boomed. Thorne nodded, while stealing a few glances at Saewulf. The psychic looked like he was deep in thought, and Thorne wondered where all that brainpower was going. "It also implies that you expect that wall to come down."

"I'm being cautious," Thorne retorted. "That wall seems impenetrable, but a lot of things seemed impossible before this year."

The Emperor stood without a sound. Thorne wondered if Saewulf had helped him up. He moved so fluidly. "Your suggestions are intriguing," the Emperor declared. "However—"

Thorne was slammed into the table by an invisible force. He seized, air vacating from his lungs. "You do little to earn your life. You lost Abington and our base and, on top of that, you invested your faith in the Marksman, who killed about fifty of my men."

"I didn't know." Thorne's mouth was gaping open and closed like a fish. "I didn't know he'd—"

"Strategists strategize," the Emperor said. "You failed to predict the outcome of your relationship with the Venator and you failed to predict this very encounter. Did you really think we'd allow you to live?" Thorne tried to speak, but he felt the air around him running out. "Carlin, draw your sword and behead this disappointment." Carlin stood and drew his sword, letting the ring of the steel against its sheathe echo throughout the room. Thorne fought with all his might to reach into his coat pocket. "What's he going for?"

"A gun?" Carlin suggested.

"That'd be foolish."

Thorne finally got one finger into his pocket. With a mighty groan he removed the letter and let it flutter to the ground. Thorne saw Carlin and the Emperor look at each other, "Should I...?" Carlin asked.

The Emperor shrugged. "I suppose. Maybe it's his will."

Carlin grabbed the letter from the floor and turned it over in his hand. "I've seen this wax seal before."

"And?" The Emperor's voice was impatient.

"I don't remember, but it's definitely familiar." Carlin cracked the seal and unfolded the letter, giving it a cursory glance. "It's an old letter to the Wolf from..." His expression changed. He looked at Thorne in disbelief. All at once his malformed lips broke apart to let his jaw drop. "Is this real?" he demanded.

Thorne did his best to nod.

"Free him," Carlin said to Saewulf. Saewulf lifted his head, seemingly upset about being ordered around, but there was a desperate urgency in Carlin's voice. He waved his arm and Thorne wheezed. "This is..." Carlin shook his head, and then laughed almost silently. "I can't even believe this."

The letter was snatched from Carlin's hand and floated into Saewulf's. He read it over and his eyes widened as well. Saewulf lifted Thorne from the floor and slammed him against the wall. "Explain."

Thorne was dropped and he straightened his coat as he stood. "I make investments," he said. "That is my job." He placed a hand against the wall, trying to keep from vomiting.

The Emperor's hand found the letter and pulled it to his face. He lowered it quizzically. "You actually…"

"I did. She came to work in one of my shops years ago. She was beautiful and charming and well educated and I decided she was unfit for floor work. She ran books for me for a time until she grew careless. She trusted me enough to reveal her true identity, and I realized what she could mean one day."

"You kidnapped her?" Carlin asked.

"I put her under house arrest," Thorne said. "I knew the Wolf would be a problem one day and figured she could end up being a valuable bargaining chip. I made an investment."

"Quite an investment," the Emperor said.

"It's paid off far better than I ever imagined," Thorne admitted. "That being said, allow me to cash in my final chip." He stood taller now. This had actually worked. He had them hooked. "Let me live and she's yours. You really want to end this war before it goes any farther? Offer the Wolf the thing he's been fighting for all along. Maybe this is actually about freedom and honor, but a large part of me suspects that this is about revenge."

"You may be the boldest man I have ever met," Saewulf said. It was the most he had said for the entire meeting. "You waited this long?"

"It's my last ditch," Thorne said. "In exchange for my return to your good graces, I will create a rabid force of rebels to kill your savages. I will also give her to you. The woman who started the war. Katherine Celerius." He paused for emphasis. "The Wolf's wife."

39

NEAR THE WALLS OF ALTRYON

NEIL VAPROS

"Do you know the worst thing about your house?" Bianca asked Neil this question about half a mile from the wall beside a twisted tree in the middle of a clearing. She'd told him it was a special spot but then refused to tell him why.

"I don't have a house," Neil said. "I live in a tent, just like everyone else you know."

She swatted at his face. "Your old house, moron. The bunker."

"What was it?" They were entangled underneath the tree. Neil felt like they'd been talking forever, lost in the ebbs and flows.

"There were no windows. I couldn't knock to ask you to come out and run away with me."

"Might have been for the best. My father was—"

"A prick."

"...not exactly fond of you."

Bianca shrugged, a sly smirk sneaking onto her face. Bianca got it. She always had. "Remember that time I met him in the market?"

Neil did. She'd run up to their family when they were just shy of thirteen and stuck a hand out to Sir Vapros. "I'm Bianca," she'd piped.

"He called me a thug."

"And you cried and ran away."

She twirled a piece of grass between her fingers. "Luckily my little sidekick, Neil Vapros, showed up to tell me I was the 'prettiest thug he'd ever seen.'"

"I was always slick." Neil elbowed her playfully.

"Yet you never made a move sooner."

"Along with being the prettiest thug I've ever seen, you're also the scariest."

Her smile was as sharp and shiny as her blades. "Sweet talker."

A small light appeared in the distance. "It's starting," Bianca whispered.

Another small light appeared, followed by two more hovering in a sporadic aerial waltz. Neil watched, perplexed and enchanted. Soon there were dozens involved in a seamless harmony, lighting the space around them. Neil looked back at Bianca and saw the lights reflected in her eyes.

"What are they?"

"There are a lot of names for them. Fireflies being the most common."

Neil had never seen anything like them. He saw one particularly brave bug flying higher than the others, sparking and sputtering as it reached canopy heights. What a brave little bug. What allowed it to fly so much higher?

"You know, I never found anything so beautiful as I did when I saw it through your eyes," Bianca said. "From alleys to hovels in the slums you made everything beautiful."

"I grew up underground."

"You grew up rich, " Bianca said. "And you *still* loved every corner of my neighborhood."

Neil took her hand. "It was your home."

With the swirling lights around them he could sense she was broaching a question. With her hair illuminated by the moonlight Neil knew what she meant. There was nothing like having someone know your past and appreciate it "I'd like to see this whole world with you, Neil."

"I'd like to see it with you too."

"Is that a promise? Everyone wants a piece of you, Neil. I can never tell how much of you I have."

He wanted to protest, but stopped midway through forming a sentence. She was right. Of course, she was right. Even now how much could he promise her? Deities were walking around prophesizing his death. What was the difference between a false promise and a hopeful one? "Can I have one of your knives?"

Her eyes narrowed, but eventually she handed it to him. He held it in his hand until it grew hot. She leaned back from him. "What are you doing?"

He didn't answer. He let the metal grow soft and pliable in his hand, smoothing out the sharpest parts. Then he pulled it in half and shaped the two pieces into circles around his ring and smallest finger. They were red hot, but cooled into dark iron circles, which he produced in an open palm.

"Are they still hot?"

"I can't tell," Neil admitted.

She reached out delicately and took the smallest one, lifted it to the light, and watched the fireflies through it. "Is this a...?"

"Promise? Proposal?" Neil asked. "Yes. Whatever you want it to be. If we make it through, we'll go see the world."

She leaned in and kissed him. When she finally pulled away he knew she was looking at the same lights reflected in his eyes. His gaze passed over her shoulder, just in time to see that brave, highflying firefly swept into the eager maw of a raven gliding silently through the night.

40

IMPERIAL PALACE

HAROLD THORNE

The Emperor's cloak danced in the wind. Thorne noted that it made him look like something other than a man. Something much bigger. Seeing the Emperor standing on his balcony addressing the people with the hood pulled over his face reminded Thorne of an image he'd seen, but couldn't remember.

The Emperor cleared his throat, and it echoed supernaturally. Another one of Saewulf's powers, Thorne assumed. "Citizens of Altryon."

Thorne watched as people far and wide gazed up with confusion and fear. Thorne scanned the crowd for the slightest suggestion of admiration, but found none. "My only true task as your Emperor is to guide you all into a brighter tomorrow." His voice rang clear. Thorne wondered if they saw him as he did, a mythic figure. "I am tasked with the sacred burden of protecting each and every one of you from those who would seek to take advantage of you. I stand before you, a man ashamed."

A chill went through the crowd, and Thorne tried not to grin. "Hundreds of years ago, savages stormed this city and slaughtered its people. Our people. This very city is raised from bloody soil, courtesy of our ancestors and those feral men. Now it seems they've returned."

A murmur broke out across the crowd. Thorne saw children bursting into tears. "Yes, it is true," the Emperor said. "The savages are back for the same thing they've always come for. Blood. However, in their absence we did not grow feeble and weak. We fortified and dug our feet in, growing strong in that blood-soaked soil. Our roots lie so deep, who could ever tell where they end? I speak to you today in the name of transparency and honesty. I am not going to crush these savages alone. Some tasks are too great for singular men. This is where I have failed."

He outstretched his arms and the cloak billowed around him. Was Saewulf doing that? Or had the wind taken it? "I am merely a man, but I do lead the strongest and most resilient people this world has ever known. I have grown this nation. That is where I have succeeded. I lead Altryon. And Altryon is all of us. Those savages are coming, and I understand your fear. But Altryon is built on the tradition of killing savages. Our walls are for them, not for us."

There were cries from the crowds. Some people cheering, some upset. Thorne couldn't tell who outnumbered whom. "We put up those walls not to say we are weak, but to show we are strong. If the savages breach our gates, we will fight until their blood wets our soil again."

He lifted a fist into the air and earned a cheer. Then he turned and walked back into his palace. Thorne and Saewulf followed. "How was that?" he asked, clearly self-satisfied.

"Inspirational," Thorne said. "Pitch perfect. And now..."

"Carlin sent the letter," the Emperor said.

"Good," Thorne said, body flooding with adrenaline. "Leaf will assist in the ambush."

"Excellent." The Emperor glided to his chair and sat, still not removing his hood. "You are dismissed."

Thorne stole one last look at the Emperor before he left. What did the man remind him of? What figure?

In the hallway he caught a glimpse of the Empress, which made him quite a lucky man. She'd been shielded from the public eye for weeks. "Empress!" Thorne called.

She turned and eyed him. "Thorne."

He'd seen her from a distance once before and had even heard her speak. He sensed something eerie and off about her now. She didn't strike him as empty eyed like the Emperor; she just came off as a little odd. "Is everything... satisfactory?"

"Everything is how it should be."

He could see the heavy layer of makeup on her face. It was so thick that her features hardly shifted as she spoke. "Does the Emperor remind you of anything in that big cloak of his?"

"He reminds me of my husband. Good day."

That certainly wasn't it. Thorne spent the rest of the day milling about and wondering. It struck him hours later as he walked through the city in the direction of his residence. As a child he'd had a book with a painted cover. He remembered it now, adorned with a cloaked figure. He thought of the Emperor, with his sunken cheekbones, billowing cloak, and booming voice. He reminded Thorne of that scythe-wielding figure from the cover of his book. He reminded Thorne of death itself.

A FOREST IN ALTRYON

HIGHEST HONOR

LILLY CELERIUS

Lilly came upon the carriage on the second day of her journey. She'd been wandering down a dirt path in the direction of the mammoth walls in the distance. She'd bribed a supplier to bring her into Altryon in his cart. But she'd have to make it to a small farm outside Shipwreck Bay by morning to reach the rendezvous point. It had been a tough decision, where to run to after her escape. Virgil had rescued her at the military base outside Abington, but died doing it. That sacrifice inspired her to follow his final plea. "Run," he said.

But where to? She'd considered burying herself in the woods somewhere, but Imperials were everywhere. She decided to try to get inside the impenetrable walls of Altryon. After all, it was the one place no one would be looking for her. It would be a hassle, but if denying Carlin her blood could kill him, it was worth it.

She encountered a slight problem on her journey through the wilderness. Though she was a strong and formidable warrior, Lilly had little survival knowledge. Her hunting experience was non-existent and she couldn't even imagine skinning and cooking an animal. She'd thought about eating berries at the end of the first day, but remembered seeing a man at the rebel camp choke to death with purple skin because of something he picked off of a tree near Abington.

On the second day she was starved and could hear her stomach roaring, insatiably. Finally, enter the carriage. It was giant, and seemed to glow from within. A man sat at the front, guiding the horses. He had long reddish hair and he smiled at her as he pulled his carriage to a stop. "Hello!" he called.

There was something about his voice that caught her off guard. She'd never heard anything like it before. She took a step closer. He did look familiar. "Are you...?"

"No," he said.

"Cartwright," she said. "John Cartwright."

"My brand recognition is far better than I thought, I will say."

She heard something crack and her eyes fell on his hands. "You want one?" He tossed her a peanut and she freed it from its shell. It did little to soothe her and she found herself simply wanting more. "I'm actually on the way to see your uncle."

She eyed him a little more carefully now. "How do you know who I am?"

"You know who I am, which means you're from the city. Also, your buttons are made of gold."

Lilly glanced down at her coat. "You helping to bring down the wall?"

"We're certainly going to try." He cracked another peanut and threw it to her. "Seems you won't be there."

"No." She inhaled the peanut. "Helping the rebels in another way."

"How's that?"

"Killing the Imperial General," she said instinctively. "Or... staying out of his clutches."

"Oh my." Cartwright stepped down from his spot at the top of the carriage. "Revenge killing. What an interesting thing."

"He's killed everyone I love. Death is the bare minimum of what he deserves." She took a step back as he approached. She'd read his poetry, same as everyone else in Altryon, but she really didn't want to be near *anyone* she didn't have a strong read on. "What do you know about killing?"

"More than anyone else." His confidence was resolute. "No one can die in my presence. You've heard that, yes?" She nodded. "Well I spend all my time with dead men and women, and men who think they're about to die but don't, and men who kill other men only to see them live."

"Fascinating." She tried to follow the conversation, but could only focus on her hunger.

He tossed her the full bag of peanuts. She removed one, refusing to take her cautious eyes off of him. "May I tell you a story?" Cartwright asked. "You can eat 'til I'm done."

"Deal." That one was a no brainer.

"I never really knew the extent of my power until it became a pattern." Cartwright went to pet the horses, and Lilly realized that they were covered in scars. "Men would drop around me and then miraculously live again. What a charmed and happy life I lived until I realized I was the one who did it. That's when I set out traveling, hoping my true parentage would never be discovered. I have no idea who my father was, but apparently there are more Animas running around than we as a society originally thought."

She eyed his hair. It was red like Saewulf's. This did nothing to help her feeling of unease.

"I came to a town where I met a woman by the name of Joan and she told me I could stay in her humble home for as many days as I wrote her poetry. Joan was pregnant, but had sent the father packing long ago. Evidently he had a mean streak." His eyes fell when he said that. "I left for a few days. When I returned, I found Joan on her last breath. I arrived in her final moments and because of this she did not die, though she wanted to. I asked who did it and she refused to say. I had my own little theory of course."

"The father?" Lilly asked.

"Right. I stayed with her until the baby came, but the delivery was complicated. We called the village doctor, hoping he could be trusted. In the end, he exposed us for what we were: an undead mother and the man who couldn't help but pervert nature. They tied us down and brought the child to a fire, well beyond where my power could protect it. They put the baby in the center of the flames and left him to burn to death. I heard the child crying all night."

Lilly had forgotten to eat she was so stunned. "All night?"

"The child was pulled from the fire in the morning and when the ash was cleared away his skin was green. They left it in the square to starve and it did not. Soon they started revering it. Fearing it." He shook his head. "It was such a little thing. It didn't know anything."

"What happened to it?"

"It grew. Eventually we were released, Joan and I, but they refused to let us near the unkillable child born from a dead woman. We watched it grow from afar. Joan grew cold, of course, and treated me as a curse. I accepted that. Upon the boy's fifth birthday, I left the village. Moving on once more."

The air was thick around Cartwright. She understood how he'd made a living telling stories. Time seemed to pause for them. "I always thought the child was a walking corpse. It never spoke, never looked anyone in the eye, never made a noise. It just wandered. Once I left I realized the truth. The green skinned boy was not being silent, he was waiting."

"Waiting for what?" Lilly felt goosebumps up her spine.

"For me to leave." Cartwright continued to absently pet the horses. "And once I did, he poisoned the entire village, including his mother."

Lilly stared at him. "And they all…"

"Every single one."

The air was silent. Even the bugs hushed to hear the end of Cartwright's story. "The boy then went place to place, doing the two things he was really quite good at, killing and evading me. I heard he tracked down his father and put an end to him. Terrible business really."

"And what does this have to do with me?" Lilly asked after letting the full weight of the story befall her.

"The boy is my responsibility. I created him," Cartwright said. "He consumes my waking thoughts. He took Joan from me, the woman I loved." Cartwright took a step toward her and took a peanut from the bag. "I know for a fact that I must put an end to the boy, however, I know that when it happens I will never feel satisfied or any better."

Lilly didn't like that answer. "How do you know?"

"Because I know a lot about killing." Cartwright ascended his carriage once more. "You can keep the bag. You look hungry."

He spurred the horses and they lurched forward. "I can see in your eyes, the temptation." Cartwright said. "The need to kill Carlin fills your every breath. Not just because you hate him, but also because you think it'll bring an end to your grief. But once he dies you will know the true horror: killing never made anyone feel any better. It's a void that is never filled. A never ending well. And on that fateful day, when you finally get what you want, you'll have to ask yourself the hardest question of all: were you staying alive because you wanted to kill Carlin or because you truly find joy in living?"

He rolled away, his men waving through the windows of the carriage. In the light from within, she saw all the scars and wondered how many she'd have if hers didn't heal.

REBEL BASE CAMP

NEIL VAPROS

Neil didn't consider himself an overly perceptive person. However, when the Wolf brushed by him and claimed he was going for a "walk," something in Neil's brain stung. This was the reason he was digging through the Wolf's tent in the middle of the night. He was slightly surprised that no one outside tried to stop him, but then he remembered that the leader was actively building a revolution on his role as the Phoenix. Why wouldn't people let him go wherever he wanted?

The pressure had been getting worse in the days since the siege, with the word "Phoenix" being passed around. Neil was almost certain the rumors came from the Wolf. Probably giving his followers some false hope to hold onto as the stress of the upcoming battle loomed. He couldn't imagine they viewed him as he viewed himself: a hunk of flesh on the sacrificial alter.

He found the letter without much difficulty. It was next to the unfinished glass of wine. He unfolded it carefully and examined its contents. It was to the Wolf from someone he hadn't seen in a long time. She spoke of hidden codes and old memories. Neil's eyes narrowed and he grew anxious as the letter went on. Could this possibly be a letter from…?

Neil read faster until his eyes fell on the name written below, Katherine, and the note scrawled in black as a small postscript. *Come alone to your old camp, or lose her again.* That particular note was signed from the General himself, Carlin Filus.

Neil didn't wait to comb through the letter with any scrutiny. It didn't matter if it was a forgery or not. The Wolf believed it was real, which meant the revolution and all of its leadership was in grave danger. Neil got to the edge of camp and his hands ignited, propelling him into the air. He soared above the camp until he saw the Wolf galloping along one of the dirt roads, his white horse partially obscured by the trees.

Neil followed, drenched in sweat from the effort and landed in the road, cutting off the Wolf's path. The horse he rode definitely didn't enjoy being ambushed by a flying man engulfed with flames and reared back neighing in fear. The Wolf calmed it. "Neil. Move."

"Think of the people, Wolf. You don't know that it's real."

The Wolf had a desperation in his eyes Neil had never seen before. Gone was the calm and collected general. "It's real." He shook his head. "I don't expect you to understand. But that's my wife."

Without warning the Wolf spurred his horse into a gallop, brushing past Neil and barreling into the woods. Neil had expected this and was flying again before the Wolf was out of sight. He attempted a more aggressive approach for his next encounter, barreling into the Wolf and ripping him from the horse's back. He heard a bone crack, but wasn't so worried about that. He heard it realign just as fast. He saw the Wolf struggle to resist drawing his sword as he stood. Neil couldn't imagine what the man was feeling. "I do understand." Neil was gasping for air now, exhausted from his flight. "I do know."

"You can't possibly," the Wolf growled.

"I do," Neil countered. "Bianca and I are engaged."

The Wolf stood a little straighter, guard falling as he began to comprehend the subtext of the conversation. "When?" he asked finally.

"Tonight. An hour or so ago." Neil held up his hand, showing the makeshift ring. "You asked me to die for this. You asked me to die for this revolution knowing I had someone I loved who wanted to be with me too. You said you would give *anything*."

"I would."

"Then walk back to your tent," Neil demanded. "Because if you walk into their clutches you're not coming back. You will die in the ashes of our last camp."

"I made it out of Abington."

"That was your trap, Wolf. This is theirs. I saw the look in Thorne's eyes. And in Saewulf's. No matter how much you say you're not the revolution, a lot of people believe you are."

"What do you suggest I do, Neil? Let her die? Let her die again? I started this war because of her. It was always for her."

"I'll go." The words left Neil's mouth before he fully comprehended what he was saying.

"You'll go?"

"They're expecting you, right? I can't imagine they've prepared for me."

"Neil, I can't risk—"

"Maybe this is it," Neil said. "Maybe this is me fulfilling the prophecy. Maybe I die to keep you alive."

"I couldn't ask you to do that."

"It's not for you," Neil said. He pointed over the Wolf's head at the rebel base looming behind in the distance. "It's for them."

He took a while to finally respond. "I don't know, Neil."

"Is there any other way to stop you?" Neil asked.

"No."

"Then I'm going," Neil said.

The Wolf glanced over Neil's shoulder at the base. "Want to bring a friend?"

"Yeah," Neil said, "I might even bring a few."

~

NEIL APPROACHED from the sky and was sure that those on the ground saw a flash of flame as he landed in the field near the camp. "That's far enough!" he heard Carlin yell.

This was not ideal in the slightest. Standing in the center of camp were Carlin Filus, the green skinned boy, Barlow Venator, and an entire squadron of armed men. "You're not who we expected," Carlin snarled.

Neil hadn't expected all of them either. Barlow Venator was the most concerning of the bunch. However, he did have an amber colored bottle in his hand. Maybe his senses were dulled enough to not know what Neil in mind.

"Change of plans," Neil called back. "The Wolf is done doing in-person meetings."

"Then I suppose he's also done hoping for a reunion with his wife." Carlin countered.

Neil could sense the tension. They assumed they'd be dealing with the Wolf so they'd probably concentrated all of their traps and firepower near the main path. Neil made the calculated choice to fly to the other end of the camp. Even without advanced hearing, he could tell they were trying to recalibrate. "I don't strike your fancy even a little?" Neil called. "Saewulf playing hard to get?"

Pull them in. That's all he needed to do. He needed cracks in their defenses just big enough to slip through. He sensed the soldiers moving in his direction.

"No, you'll do quite nicely," Carlin said. "I just wish there was someone to bring the news of Katherine Celerius's death back to your base."

Leaf pulled a canister from his belt. Carlin waved his hand, rejecting that idea. Neil remembered that the gas was flammable. Neil lit a fireball in his hand. Could he kill them all with one perfectly placed ball of flame? Could he cripple the Empire's military right here and now?

Carlin seemed to wonder the same thing and snapped his fingers.

There was a visible moment of confusion as if his men were asking if he was sure. He snapped again and they went to the other side of camp and hauled back a hostage, arms bound and a bag over her head. "Try anything and I will remove her head," Carlin pledged.

"In time?" Neil asked. "I've heard you're not as fast as you once were."

Carlin inhaled slowly and exhaled. The rumors of his speed and how he'd achieved it were getting around, and Neil could see a deep shame behind his eyes. Neil's eyes flicked over to Leaf's belt again. "I can't think of a good reason not to turn you all to ash."

"Because she'll die too," Carlin said.

"I don't know her," Neil said. "I don't even know if that's really her."

"So you didn't come here to bargain or to rescue her, eh?" Carlin was coming alive now. Getting a little more heated. "You expect me to believe that?"

"He doesn't have it in him," Barlow Venator accused.

"Seems like the right decision to me," Neil said.

For a split second Neil considered what he was saying. Blow the belt and create unfathomable discourse within the Empire. How many lives would that save? In that moment, while performing his blood based arithmetic, Neil understood the Wolf and everything he'd done. He decided to pivot.

"Remove the bag." Neil demanded. "The Wolf isn't making any decisions until he knows whether or not it's really her."

Carlin seemed to consider that. "He should know not to play games."

"Sure, but he's not an idiot."

"And what if we kill you right here right now and keep our hostage?"

"You think I can't take you?" Stalling was not easy and Neil could feel the tentative peace crumbling. "A slow old General, a drunk traitor and a..." He paused. "What are you, Leaf?"

"Bored," Leaf called.

"Got it," Neil said.

Carlin released the hilt of his sword and pulled the bag from the woman's head. He removed the gag. "Tell him who you are."

"I'm no one!" the woman cried.

Neil examined her. He'd never seen her before but the Wolf had given him a basic description. Strawberry blonde hair. Thin frame. It was hard to see but her eyes might have even been the hazel he'd described. "Satisfied?" Carlin asked.

"We'll be in touch." Neil still had no earthly idea whether or not it was Katherine Celerius, but he figured he'd upset the apple cart enough. In a burst of flame, he shot into the air, soaring high above, hoping he'd held them off for long enough.

OUTSIDE THE OLD REBEL CAMP

RHYS VAPROS

Katherine Celerius was returned to the cart bound and gagged, the hood back in place. Barlow Venator agreed to ride with her. They'd come with three carriages filled to the brim with men, and it was clear that everyone was disappointed. The Wolf had made the smart choice, something that hadn't been expected. Hadn't he started this entire war after hearing of his wife's death? Hadn't his passion and rage kick-started his desire to dismantle the Empire?

Barlow dragged her into the back of the carriage and signaled to the driver. The carriage lurched back and forth. He took this ride as an opportunity to pop the cork on his drink. "That was disappointing," he mumbled to himself.

"Looking for another go at the Wolf?" one of the soldiers asked.

"Yeah, I woulda won this one." There was a notch scratched into the bottle, presumably how far he could go without losing powers. Barlow drank right past it. "Woulda put all fifty-two cards in him this time."

Barlow pulled out his cards and began shuffling. Despite his current state of inebriation, the cards moved fluidly in his hands, trained by decades of muscle memory. "You boys ever played Arkney shuffle? I guess where you're from it's called Backtrack."

"Never played," one of the soldiers said.

"It's pretty complicated," Barlow admitted. "It has to do with making sacrifices. You sacrifice your cards and their cards until you each only have one card left. Fun part is the cards stay face down for most of the game and you have to bluff. You've gotta look into the other guy's eyes and tell him your card is worth more or less than his. It's a lot about lying and a lot about hoping that you're making the right calls and decisions."

"Gamble a lot?" the soldier asked.

"All the time." Barlow continued shuffling. "Too much."

The carriage was silent aside from the sound of the wheels bouncing and the cards sliding over and below each other. "You gambled when you switched sides, didn't you?"

The soldier across from Barlow was talking a lot. Barlow's eyes narrowed. That comment seemed like a slight. "I guess I did. What's it to you?"

"You ever have doubts?" the soldier asked. "Ever wonder if you picked the wrong side and can't go back?"

"I did what I did for Arkney," Barlow said. "Not for your people."

Bianca removed the helmet, exposing her feminine features and ashen hair. "Arkney is our people."

Barlow tried to throw his cards, but his drunken fingers fumbled and Bianca got off the first throw, burying a knife deep in his chest. He tried to remove it. Once he managed it, she followed up with another. He tried to lift his bottle to throw it, but the soldier next to him grabbed his arm.

Rhys removed his helmet too and Barlow groaned, defeated. "You know I have played Backtrack. It's pretty popular in Altryon." Bianca leaned in and twisted the knife. "You know the most important unspoken rule about Backtrack? Despite the name of the game, it's never smart to go back on your word. Once you make a decision, you stick to it. In my experience, the ones who make commitments win.

The ones who don't…" She eyed his wound. "Well… They end up with nothing."

"I… It's…" Barlow looked so confused. "Arkney must be free."

"They'll all be free," Bianca said. "Shame you won't live to see that."

Bianca kicked open the back door of the carriage. Rhys grabbed her arm and the arm of the bound hostage. "Should have known when to cash out," Bianca said, delivering a final knife into the left side of Barlow's chest.

Rhys teleported Bianca and the hostage to the side of the road and the second half of their plan kicked in. Darius emerged from the bushes. With a mighty cry, he plowed into the side of the carriage, upending it on its side. He pushed until it reached the edge of a ravine, then sent it over the edge. It rolled and rolled, ending as a heap of bloody planks of wood at the bottom.

"I never really liked that guy," Darius mumbled.

They panted, searching the road for the other carriages. They were nowhere to be seen. Rhys suspected this was because they didn't want to be followed.

Neil found his friends eventually, landing by their perch at the side of the road. "Did it work?"

Bianca gestured toward the ravine. "He's dead."

"How'd you know they'd send her with Barlow?" Neil asked. "How'd you know which carriage?"

"It was a guess," Rhys admitted. "I knew they wouldn't send her with Carlin. He's got too many personal emotions tied up with the Celerius. I also figured they wouldn't send her with Leaf because who knows what's up with that guy."

"Agreed." Neil put an arm around Bianca and gave her a little squeeze.

"Barlow already fought the Wolf and won, so I figured they'd bet on him again."

"Well," Neil said. "Good guess."

They all shared a look, as they turned to the woman lying on the ground next to them. Bianca lifted the hood cautiously, revealing the woman's face. She removed the cloth gag and cut her binds. The woman stood up, and her posture gave her away. This was the kind of woman the Wolf would marry. She regarded them. "Hello," she said. "I'd ask what all that business was about, but I think I've gathered enough."

"Yeah?" Darius asked. "Care to tell us what's going on?"

"The fact that you're alive is... surprising," Rhys explained. "It's wonderful, but your death was widely reported."

"Yes, I assume it was," she said. "I've been living in the attic of an industrialist for years now, under lock and key."

"Harold Thorne?" Bianca asked.

Katherine nodded. "So they're using me to catch the Wolf, yes? Cripple him with his heart?"

"Yes," Neil said.

She regarded the road coolly. She didn't cry and didn't seem the slightest bit shaken or scared. Rhys wondered how much she'd been through to keep calm in the midst of a kidnapping. "So he did it? Joined the people?"

"Yes," Rhys said.

"That's good," she said. "His guilt was killing him."

She dusted herself off and regarded the road around her. "Well, time to return, I suppose." In her voice was a profound sadness. Rhys suspected he'd need time and wisdom before fully appreciating its layers.

"Return where?" Neil asked.

"To death, young man."

She began walking down the road and Neil followed. "Wait!" he demanded. "The Wolf he... He's been waiting so long. He... he needs you."

"No." She continued walking resolutely. "Steven needs to free the people out here." She didn't turn back to face Neil, but stopped and her eyes scanned the expanses of the land. "When we were married, he spoke of it always. The horrors he saw. I supported his decision to confront the Empire, knowing it could kill him. Knowing it could kill us both. I did it because Steven was given an extraordinary opportunity to change things and help those without power.

Rhys could see Neil shaking. What was this about? "I expect my death taught him that his decisions had consequences. I also expect that it taught him that there was no going back. The only way out for him was forward. I will not soften his conviction. Not now. I was dead all along."

"But what about—"

"What about what?" she asked. "I have been shut away, and stripped of my agency, but I refuse to be a pawn. The Empire will not use me, and neither will the rebels. This makes sense to me."

"I..." Rhys could see Neil struggling to speak. "I understand," he finally managed.

"Life is about what you love or who you love," she said. "When all this is over, I'll find him. Until then... dead once more." She ambled down the road in the direction of Brightbow, lights visible in the distance. Rhys thought about escorting her, but she didn't seem like the type to allow him. "It's nice to see that you're all working together," she said. "I always found the feud to be quite a foolish thing."

Then she disappeared, and they watched her go. The group shared a silence as they reflected on what had happened and what they should do. They walked back to the base at half-pace.

When they returned, they found the Wolf. And then Neil told him a lie. Neil told a crushing lie because he knew thousands of lives depended on it. Katherine Celerius was dead. When the Wolf received the news, Rhys saw something in him die as well. But not the lust for war. Rhys was sure that would never die.

44

REBEL BASE CAMP

NEIL VAPROS

Neil tried not to be ashamed of the lies they told the Wolf. He'd told lies himself right to Neil's face. On today of all days Neil expected the Wolf's melancholy to be at bay. After all, today they were going to try to bring down the wall.

Neil entered the full strategy room. Bianca, Rhys, Cartwright, Darius, and one of the Jacobson's (Neil could never tell which) sat around the table bickering. "You don't think you should come through the forest?" Rhys was asking. "May I ask why?"

"I don't like forests," Cartwright said. "They're filled with dirt and disease, creatures and creepy things of every single sort. What could be more terrifying than that?"

"Says the guy who walks around with a small army of undead clowns," Darius muttered.

"All right, noted," Cartwright said. "Fine, I'll take the forest, but the rebels are paying for a new pair of boots."

"I'm sure we can swing it," Bianca said.

The door opened and the Wolf entered. "How are we doing?" He had a little more light in his eyes, but Neil knew he'd suffered a heavy toll.

"Well," Bianca said, "ironing out details."

"James," the Wolf said, reminding Neil of which brother it was, "are you confident in your siege?"

"Oh yes, sir. I was just explaining that I'm going to have to flank from the south since I can't bring the cannons through the forest." He lowered his voice quite a bit for the next part. "Or my trebuchet."

"What?" the Wolf asked.

"What?" James asked.

"Did you say trebuchet?" The Wolf looked incredulous. "It's back in Abington, isn't it?"

"I enlisted some help to have it brought here."

"Wait…" Darius said. "You mean the catapult? You said the Wolf asked for that. I pushed it for two days."

"It's not a catapult." James blew out a breath in frustration.

The Wolf rubbed the bridge of his nose. "Start with the cannons. If that doesn't work, feel free to test out your cata—"

"It's not a catapult!"

"Cartwright," the Wolf interrupted. "Still confident that you can bring down a big enough section of the wall for us to fit through?"

"How thick is the wall?"

"Incredibly."

"We'll see if fate decides to humble me then."

Everyone glanced at him, desperate for any assurance. Cartwright wasn't exactly well liked among the rebels. Sure, he was eloquent and pretty, but he didn't have the heart of a warrior. "Darius, I'd like you and Rhys with James," the Wolf said. "Bianca with Neil, Cartwright, and me."

Neil and Rhys glanced at each other. They hadn't liked being separated before. Neil could tell neither of them was enthusiastic about it this time either. "That all right?" the Wolf asked as if it were a genuine question.

"That's fine," Rhys said.

He really did look like he'd improved since seeing the Grand

Master. He'd had his hair cut back short and the deep-set bags beneath his eyes had vanished over the course of the last few weeks. "Where to once we're inside the city?" the Wolf asked. "I admit I don't have the connections I used to there."

Bianca unrolled a map and placed it over their schematic of the wall. "There's a bar in the Nightlife district that should work," she said. "It hosts quite a bit of revolutionary activity and it's half underground with quite a few exits, if it comes to a fight."

"The Hideaway," Neil said, pointing it out to Rhys.

Rhys smiled. "I wonder if Alfred is still there."

Neil remembered the night he and Rhys had been accosted by a religious zealot in the Nightlife district and forced to duck into the Hideaway. Alfred was the first person under Vapros employment to ever openly question the feud. Neil had originally found that upsetting, but now he saw the old man as the only one with a strong enough moral compass to say what was right. "Neil, any idea how we can get in contact with Robert Tanner?" the Wolf asked.

"I had a contact in the slums before we escaped," Neil said. "I'm sure if he's still alive he can track him down." Something occurred to Neil. "If he's alive."

"That's true," the Wolf said. "Like it or not, we have no idea what's been taking place inside those walls or what they think of us."

"We're the savages," Bianca said.

The Wolf nodded, contemplating. "I suppose not everyone will see us as saviors, here to free them from starvation and the Empire's crushing grasp. I suppose we might enter those walls to meet a city of people who wish our demise. Either way, we must stand resolute in our beliefs." His hand was shaking a bit. Neil wondered if he was the only one who noticed. "The Empire has leeched these people of their rights and their power and, most importantly, of their voices. When those walls come down, we return the power to the people."

Neil thought of the Man with the Golden Light and how his voice always appeared in a chorus. Nothing to him was ever more powerful than the echoes of that harmony. "At the end of today we will either be one step closer to the Emperor's throne or one step farther beneath his boot. Either way, my beliefs are the same. Dismissed," said the Wolf.

He left the room and the others dispersed slowly until it was just Neil and Cartwright staring at the map. "Quite frightening," Cartwright said. "Today's endeavor."

"Yes," Neil agreed.

"Do you like logic puzzles?" Cartwright asked. Neil stared at him. "Me too." Cartwright put a hand on Neil's shoulder. "I stand next to a boy who must die for the revolution."

Neil felt a sour taste in his mouth.

"Yet no one can die in my presence. If we take the wall together, how is that possible?"

"It means we both live, right?" Neil asked.

"Or they kill me and then kill you," Cartwright said. "Seems much more likely. Although I'm not sure it's possible."

"Your death?"

"Right," Cartwright said. "You see, I have never died before. Have you?"

"No."

Cartwright smiled, the lights glinting off of his immaculate teeth. "Don't worry. I hear it's okay." He traced a finger over the map, examining it one last time. "I hear it's really not so bad."

45

THE MARKETS OF ALTRYON

LILLY CELERIUS

Lilly felt a little ashamed. Outside the wall she'd told people she was "raised in Altryon." She thought that was true, until today. She bounced aimlessly around the markets, trying desperately to find the street corner she lived on as a fugitive. Over a decade of memories in Altryon and she couldn't navigate one of its most popular districts. She was sure Neil Vapros wouldn't have this problem.

Although Neil was a Vapros, lurking in alleys and sauntering through the streets was their thing. Until her days as an outlaw, she'd rarely travelled anywhere without her fortified carriage. Even when she was a fugitive she'd often send out her remaining loyal guards rather than make a public appearance. At first she'd thought that was clever, staying hidden, but now she wondered if she was just too posh to be among the people.

The mission today was to find her old apartment. She'd hidden quite a bit of gold and weaponry under the floorboards. There was no doubt the place was occupied by now, but she figured she could bribe or rob whoever lived there now. She'd feel bad about it, if it came to robbing, but she needed money to stay hidden. Being under the Emperor's nose wasn't exactly the safest thing.

Finally, she found the corner. She remembered it was above a bakery, and the smell of freshly baked rolls brought her to the right place. She entered discreetly and shuffled to the staircase cramped into the corner of the store.

She ascended the steps slowly and approached the door. Testing it, she found it wasn't locked. So far so good. Maybe no one was home. She crept in, holding the door as it swung inward, careful of its archaic hinges.

The place looked abandoned enough. At least the living space. She couldn't be sure of the two bedrooms. Lilly went to the corner of the room and found the false floorboard she and her men had installed. She lifted it to find it exactly how they'd left it. She was palming a few handfuls of gold when she heard the creek.

She swiveled around and there she was: a small girl, staring with eyes full of terror. Evidently she'd been in one of the bedrooms. Lilly quickly lifted a finger to her lips. "Please—" she began.

The girl screamed. The other bedroom door opened and a man appeared. Why did he have a sword?

Lilly palmed her blade and rose from her knees. What could she possibly say? Neil would probably have a quip in mind. Something about working for the landlord, but that wasn't really her style. "I'm just here for—"

She noticed the seal on the hilt of the sword. She wasn't just robbing anyone. "You're an Imperial soldier," she realized aloud.

"And you're Lilly Celerius." His voice was grave and desperate.

Her fingers curled around the hilt of her blade. She could take one man, no problem.

His eyes shifted to his daughter. "Please..." he whispered. "Don't hurt her."

Right. The daughter. Lilly turned her head slowly taking in the scene. What could she do? She couldn't kill this man in front of his daughter. But if she let him live...

"I was never here," she said quickly emptying the contents hidden in the floor and filling the bag she'd pilfered in the markets for this endeavor.

He nodded. "Of course."

It was a lie. She knew it was a lie. Carlin would make him a noble. All he'd have to do was tell him that Lilly Celerius was in Altryon, within his clutches.

She lowered her blade. She knew it would cost her life, but what could she do? Cut him down in front of his child? She sheathed her blade and left slowly, filled with rage and shame.

In the streets, she remembered Cartwright and his lessons on killing. It occurred to her that she'd never made this choice before. She'd never chosen mercy. How many orphans in Altryon were orphans because of her? With haste, she barreled through the streets so fast she doubted anyone could see her. She became a blur.

Where wouldn't Carlin look?

It struck her suddenly, and she leaned forward picking up in speed.

Lilly was going home.

46

THE WALL

RHYS VAPROS

The fields outside of the walls looked far different now than they had on Rhys's first night outside the city. On his first night, there had been morning dew, illuminated by the full moon. Today the fields were littered with bodies and arrows.

They were into hour six of the siege. All of them were soaked through with sweat. For the first time ever, Rhys wore metal armor as he sat in the trench tending to their cannon. They'd struck the walls six times and barely made a dent. The Empire's cannons were in short supply and didn't fire as far as the modified ones the Jacobsons had built. At the moment, they seemed safe enough and out of range. Rhys couldn't shake his unease. He'd seen Harold Thorne navigating the walls with his green-skinned boy, and those two were known for making unorthodox decisions. "What do you think they do now?" Rhys asked.

James Jacobson was his only confidant here. Darius had run to intercept arrows for some men gathering supplies. "I think they open their gates and send out men to fight us," James said.

"Really?" Rhys pondered the idea. "Quite dangerous, opening their gates isn't it?"

"Perhaps," James said. "But if we try to charge we'll run right into range of their archers and guns. Also, who knows what kind of traps Thorne has laid on the inside."

Rhys nodded thoughtfully. "Are the cannons underperforming? In your estimation?" He really enjoyed talking to James. Finally, someone who was thrilled to discuss strategy. He hadn't made this connection before because of concerns about dealing with his mental stowaway.

"No," James said. "This is exactly how I assumed they'd perform. We don't even really need to bring the wall down. We just need to be loud enough to draw their attention."

"So that Cartwright can make a hole in the wall?"

"Indeed."

"But if we do bring down the wall?"

"Huge bonus," James said.

A noise split the sky, and Rhys poked his head over the top of the trench. "They're opening the gates."

It was true. "Then we're almost certainty going to die," James said.

"Really?" Rhys asked.

James looked like he was doing calculations in his head. "Not if they take prisoners, I suppose."

Rhys watched as organized squadrons of military men marched from the gates in their direction, rifles at the ready. Rhys scanned the battlefield for any advantage. He saw cracks in the walls, but little else. How long did they have before their men crossed the field? It was clear that having divided manpower, there was no way to come out on top in a head-on shootout. "Could anything make them retreat?" Rhys asked.

"If the walls come down," James said. "They'll have to regroup."

Rhys twisted around to view the terrain behind them. Was there anything they could do? He saw Darius returning, a spec against the vast hillside. Then his eyes fell on the trebuchet and his brain did some involuntary addition. "I have an idea," Rhys said. "I have a *really* bad idea."

The soldiers were almost upon them. James threw a homemade bomb out into the crowd, staggering them for a moment. A soldier made it to the edge of the trench. Before he could turn his gun on them, Darius was there, crushing him with his oversized hammer. "How do you work the trebuchet?" Rhys called through the sound of gunfire.

"There's a lever," James screamed, "Don't stand behind it when it fires or it'll-"

That's when things became too loud for Rhys to hear. He materialized out of the trench and behind Darius. They'd taken down the first unit, but more were on the way. "Darius do you trust me?" Rhys asked.

"I don't like that question," he said between heavy breaths.

"Taurlum can only be killed when their skin is punctured right?"

"I think."

"Can blunt force trauma kill you?"

"Rhys, I don't know the meaning of the word."

"Okay good."

"No, Rhys. I literally don't know the meaning of the word."

"Oh," Rhys said.

Suddenly the trench beside them erupted into flames. Rhys noted the giant wagon, outfitted with a cannon, rolling toward them. Seated atop the monstrosity was a man in a gas mask. Rhys could guess who it was. "Thorne is here. Please trust me. I think this is the only way."

"I trust you," Darius said.

Rhys caught Darius by the hand and pulled him toward the trebuchet. James Jacobson followed at their heels, avoiding the crumbling earth around them. Thorne exited his carriage and began firing a revolver into anyone in his range. "Why are we...?" Darius asked, but Rhys had no time for explanations.

"You've got to curl inward, like a cannonball," Rhys said. "Arms over your head, locked tight. You're wearing armor plus with your skin I think..." Rhys trailed off, making last minute calculations.

"I..." Darius realized what Rhys was suggesting. "Are you insane? You tiny madman. You're going to kill me."

"I think it'll work. I really do."

Darius shook his head rapidly. "It'll kill me."

"You took hits from Nikolai. His size and weight? That's the equivalent of getting hit by a cannonball."

"You're asking me to *be* the cannonball," Darius yelled.

"I know," Rhys said. "I know. I don't know what else to do."

Darius looked up at the trebuchet. "This is insane."

"If we don't force a retreat we die," Rhys said. "All of these people die..."

Darius looked off at the men being slaughtered around him. "I—"

"Don't move." They heard the voice behind them.

They turned to see the man in the gas mask holding his revolver to James Jacobson's temple. "Step away from the catapult or the boy dies," Thorne hissed.

"It's not a—" James started to say.

Thorne removed his gas mask with his free hand and laughed. "What were you going to do? Fire yourselves at the wall?" He eyed Darius for a moment and noted their expressions. "Wait... You really were...?"

"We're a little desperate," Rhys admitted.

He could see James sizing up Darius, then looking back to the trebuchet. "It might work," James said, so quietly that almost no one heard him.

"Step away or I paint the grass with this kid's less than average sized brain," Thorne said.

"Do it," James said. He sounded serious.

"Your brother was the same way," Thorne said, ferocity in his eyes. "He didn't fear death either when I offered it to him."

"That's because he knows that as long as one of us lives our name lives on," James said.

He ducked suddenly, and Thorne wasn't fast enough to fire a shot. Rhys materialized over and tried to wrestle the gun away, but Thorne kicked him off. James took off running toward the trebuchet. Thorne fired two bullets into his back. Rhys realized with a start that Darius was on one end, bracing himself. "Darius—"

"I trust you little buddy," Darius said.

Thorne's gun clicked, out of bullets, and he charged over, vying for control of the lever with James. "You think you can take down this wall with a ridiculous cata—"

"It's a trebuchet!" James hissed gripping the lever with the last of his strength. "There's a difference. A trebuchet swings back."

Rhys heard the lever swing and a mighty crack. He looked off to see Darius gone, flying into the distance. The arm of the trebuchet swung back. With a deafening noise, it came down, crushing the skull of the smartest man in Altryon. Thorne's headless body stood for a moment, shoulder dressed with accolades of his own brain matter. Then he fell, nothing anymore.

Rhys ran to James, but saw that the arm of the trebuchet had killed him too. Rhys took a weighty breath and looked off, hoping this was worth it.

He saw new cracks appearing in the wall. With a sudden rumble, a wall that had stood for hundreds of years began to crumble. Rebels all around cheered, and men of the Empire dropped their jaws, gasping for air. Rhys felt a wave as the debris hit the ground and dust filled the air. What now?

For the first time in his life, Rhys cried out to rally the troops. One bold and glorious command. "CHARGE!"

And the rebels did.

Rhys went through the breach, stunned there were no men to greet him. Where were all the Imperials? He realized the truth as he saw them fleeing through the streets. They were running to the palace. What was left of this city was now a battleground. The endgame was here.

Rhys had no time to be concerned about that though. He followed the wreckage and the destroyed buildings until he found Darius, lying facedown in a street. Rhys flipped him and tried to feel for a pulse, though it was difficult through his iron skin. "Please be alive, Darius. Please," he breathed.

"My favorite bar is on this street," Darius groaned, as a thick spool of blood streamed from his mouth. "How did that work? That shouldn't have worked."

"I don't know," Rhys admitted. "We were out of ideas."

Men were running past them, deeper into the city, looking for places to put down roots. "I can't believe I did it," Darius said.

"I know." Rhys breathed in the air, and it felt a little thicker than it had when he'd lived here. Must have been all the dust and debris. "You're the most important cannonball in all of history."

A pack of Imperials surrounded them, sword and guns drawn. Rhys raised his arms slowly. "Rhys Vapros. Darius Taurlum. You're under arrest."

"For?" Rhys asked.

"For... being Lightborn scum," the soldier decided.

Darius lifted his body painfully and grinned at them. "Might want to add destruction of property to the list."

THE WALL

NEIL VAPROS

Every day since Neil had escaped the city of Altryon, he'd envisioned going back, walking through the gates with people cheering him. For some reason he never saw this conflict ending in so much bloodshed, but here they were. On the field of battle, taking back that city where Neil was born. Neil had always thought he'd reenter the city to a warm welcome. He didn't, however, at any point imagine he'd return to the city with John Cartwright and an entire army of human shields with clown makeup.

They went through the forest and trekked the fifty open feet to an unguarded section of the wall where Cartwright could work his magic. His men surrounded them on every side, ready to soak up any stray bullets and arrows. Neil huddled behind one of the taller men. "What happens if they see us?" Neil asked.

The Wolf opted for a long dark coat to hide his identity, yet retained a small blue streak of war paint. "If they know it's us, I imagine they'll turn their cannons and blow us to pieces. But I'm sure James has them well distracted."

Neil grimaced. If the Empire knew he and the Wolf were in

shooting distance, they wouldn't last a minute. Cartwright reached the wall and extended his fingers, placing his hands against the stone. "What happens now?" Bianca asked. One of the clowns shushed her. "You're lucky you're already dead," she said to him.

Cartwright inhaled deeply. Then exhaled slowly. The wall began to shake. Grains of sand fell as Cartwright pressed forward. He stopped after a few moments. "What's happening?" Neil asked.

"Anima move things with their minds," Cartwright said. "I'm trying to move the material inside the wall."

Eventually he was moving through the wall, making a tunnel roughly his height in diameter. After ten minutes, the ground was littered with sand and pebble-sized stones. Cartwright was drenched with sweat. His crimson coat turned a deep maroon from the work. This made Neil fear Saewulf all the more. He bet that Saewulf could bring the whole wall down with one hand.

Eventually Cartwright broke through to open air and collapsed to his knees. "Unbelievable," Neil said.

"I know," the Wolf said. "We're in."

Suddenly, Cartwright was seized from the other side of the wall and many things happened at once. The clowns rushed through, desperate to protect their savior. In their urgency to get through, the tunnel was jammed. "Wolf, I—" Neil began to say.

"Go!" the Wolf begged.

Neil let his energy flow into his hands and shot into the sky, flying high over the wall. He'd never flown like this before and for a moment he thought that his entire body might be on fire. He soared and landed on the other side. A few of the clowns were through and already viciously attacking a group of men.

Once Neil landed, he drew the attention of everyone in the street and someone called out, "Men! Stop!"

Neil looked to the voice and saw none other than Robert Tanner with a blade to Cartwright's neck. "Neil?" he asked.

The air was still. "Robert. I told you I was coming back."

Robert was still wearing the green coat Victoria had bought him, even though it was stained and faded beyond recognition. "You can fly?" Robert stared at him as if he was a figment of his imagination.

"Sort of," Neil said.

"And you're running around with a bunch of clowns?"

"Sort of," Neil said. "What's happening?"

The remainder of the clowns came through the tunnel, followed by the Wolf and Bianca. Robert eyed them. "Bianca Blackmore?" He looked deeply confused. "Savages are coming to Altryon. Everyone in town's been saying it."

"That's us, boy," the Wolf said. "Pleased to meet you."

Robert sheathed his weapon. "You are?"

Neil knew this confusion. It was the confusion of everyone who'd ever lived in this city under a blanket of lies and deception. "You don't look... how I imagined." Robert shook his head. "All the propaganda. We don't know what's real."

Neil reached his hand out and Robert took it. "We're real, Robert. And we're taking this city back. Together."

Robert's men watched them, skepticism their common language. "They won't hurt us? Your men?" Robert asked.

"We don't intend to hurt any of the innocent," the Wolf said. "We intend to free them from this corrupt Empire's rule."

Robert was about to say something, but a sound cracked the tension. The entire amalgamation of people turned to watch as the wall crumbled, miles off. Neil gasped. Dust filled the air, and everyone stepped back, fearing how far the debris would travel. When it was over, Robert looked to Neil, eyes filled with confusion, hope, and fear. "I..." He tried desperately to control his tongue. "What's out there?" he finally managed to say.

"So much, Robert," Neil said. "So much."

48

THE HIDEAWAY

NEIL VAPROS

In the Hideaway, a grime covered bar in the Nightlife district, two rebellions became one. Robert and his men from the slums were perched on the bar and gathered at tables as the Wolf and his small pack of insiders entered. Cartwright brought the clowns to fortify a makeshift safe house, so it left only Neil and Bianca to accompany the Wolf.

It was strange being back here, a place Neil had once known so well. Everything in the city looked different. It was clear that without the families to run their businesses things had collapsed. Neil bet things would change much more before this war was over. All that remained to finish this revolution was the deaths of the Emperor and Saewulf.

Altryon was a war zone now, but one thing in the Hideaway remained the same. "Mr. Vapros," Alfred the bartender said. "Come for the usual?"

"Come for the city actually," Neil said.

"So no ale?"

"No, I'll still have an ale."

Alfred smiled. "I've really missed you, sir. This place has missed your people."

"Well, their people are back," Robert announced to the bar. "And they're going to help us take this city back. The Empire is in its final days." His men gave a rowdy cheer, and Neil remembered when he had once controlled this room in a similar way. "With our combined force, that palace will become a killing ground. Thorne, the Emperor, Saewulf." Robert hissed Saewulf's name, "They'll all be dead."

"Who replaces them?" someone called.

"We do," Robert said. "The people do."

Neil sensed a feeling of unease. What was happening? "That okay with you, Vapros?" someone called.

"Yes," Neil said. "Of course. Why wouldn't it be?"

Bianca shifted inward a slight bit. "You ruled these people too once," she said too quietly to be heard.

It finally clicked for Neil. These people were afraid of the Lightborns and with very good reason. How were they to know they weren't trading Saewulf, an oppressive Lightborn, for a few others wearing different colors? "We didn't come to—"

"Take back your throne?" a bearded man asked.

"This city can't take any more of the feud," another voice said.

"Do you know who that is?" Neil pointed to the Wolf. "That's Steven Celerius. I count less than ten close friends in this world. I can assure you, a large number of them are Taurlum and Celerius."

Neil looked to the Wolf who was standing back, watching patiently. Neil knew what he was doing. The more he spoke about his faith in the revolution, the more it became his own. "Look, I understand your point of view," Neil said. "We Lightborns have earned little of your trust over the years. I concede I've been away for a while. I don't know the true state of things."

"Exactly," someone called.

"The Lightborns are not here to rule over you... We're here for..." Neil paused. What were they here for? It had once been so easy to make speeches. "I'm not religious. I never have been. Despite all these powers, I never truly believed the legend of where they came from. The Man with the Golden Light. A fairy tale."

The bar was dead silent. Neil glanced over. The Wolf looked *very* intrigued. "But I have seen him quite a bit recently. In my dreams." Neil made eye contact as he scanned to room. "I don't know what they are. Prophecy or just that. Dreams."

Robert was wide eyed, and Neil wondered why. "The only thing I can be certain of is the sound. The voice of the Man with the Golden Light. It sounds like…" Neil had trouble with this particular part. "It sounds like thousands of voices. Maybe more. Speaking all together as one."

He held his hand out and a small fire appeared. "I don't know where this really came from, and I don't know if I truly believe. But I do know that my perception of a God has the voice of the people. All the people."

Neil let that weigh on him. He had decided to die if the cause needed him but this was the first time the meaning of his action settled on him. "The voice of the people is the voice of God. Saewulf and the Emperor chose not to hear that voice. We're not here to lead you. We're here for one reason and one reason only. We're here to tear down their gates and bring that voice screaming through their halls. Deafen them with it."

"The voice of the people is the voice of God." Neil looked over, and saw Robert's eyes filled with passion. "The voice of the people is the voice of God." Robert said it again, louder this time.

He chanted until the bar joined in, reciting it to each other until the volume of their voices became deafening. When it finally ceased, Alfred knocked on the bar. "I think he's earned that ale, eh?"

Now the Wolf and his people were accepted with open arms. "I've never been more attracted to you," Bianca told Neil under her breath.

"Do we drink with the rebels?" Neil asked.

"I think it's our only choice," the Wolf said. He cornered Neil before he went to the bar. "That was a good speech."

"Thank you," Neil said.

"No, Neil it was… It was really quite good. It's almost

unimaginable that on the day the walls fell, the most inspiring moment of my day happened in a seedy Vapros bar. Thank you for everything."

"You're welcome," Neil said. He meant it.

They stood and planned at the bar for hours. The Wolf paced back and forth, sharing his knowledge of Imperial code and reaping the benefits of the rebel's tight-knit network of soldiers. After the sun set and they lit a few candles, Robert approached Neil. "May I speak to you?" he asked.

"Sure," Neil said.

He walked Neil to the window and peered out, watching to see if anyone on the street lingered. "Was that all true? Everything about the Man with the Golden Light?"

"Yes," Neil said.

"Then you're really him?"

"What?" Neil asked.

"I see him too, Neil." Robert ran a hand over his green coat. "He told me something about six months ago. I had no idea who it could be until you came down from the sky like that, engulfed in fire."

Neil's stomach dropped. He knew where this was going.

"One Lightborn, forged in fire, dying to bring about the new nation." Robert's eyes were misty. "It's you, Neil. You're the Phoenix."

49

THE HIDEAWAY

NEIL VAPROS

The candles burned low, as the rebels planned through the night. The strategy was simple in theory. The Wolf would infiltrate the masses. The rebels would move from house to house until they surrounded the palace. They would lay siege to it. One large and ever-looming problem remained. How would they kill Saewulf? How could they even get close to him?

A lot of people looked to Neil for that. He'd gone toe to toe with him once, but things felt different now. Saewulf was stronger. Neil didn't know how, but there was no denying it.

"When do we attack?" Robert asked.

"As soon as possible," the Wolf said. "The longer we wait, the longer they have to fortify."

"Could we move in two days?" Robert asked. "That's more than enough time for me to mobilize."

"Yes," the Wolf said. He suddenly gripped the table. "I'm sorry. It's just now hitting me…"

"I know," Robert said. "We could end it. We could end it all."

Neil hadn't said much to Robert regarding the prophecy, just that he believed it was true. He'd collected another person he couldn't let down. Neil was surprised by how much Robert had come into his own. Gone was the boy he'd known. He'd aged five years in the mere one that Neil had been away.

"We should move to a more inconspicuous place for final preparations," the Wolf said.

"What?" Robert asked. "Why?"

"There are people who live above this bar. I can feel them," the Wolf said.

Robert paled, as did the rest of his men.

"What is it?" Bianca whispered.

"The apartment above the bar is empty," Robert said. "Feel anything else?"

The Wolf was still. "How busy is the Nightlife district these days?"

"It's abandoned."

"Then we're surrounded," the Wolf said. "Any way out?"

"Door to the sewers is in the cellar," Alfred said.

Neil had once seen a statue garden, and it looked suspiciously like the inside of this bar right now. Any sudden movement could betray their unease. How had they been found?

"Spy in your midst?" Bianca asked.

Robert shook his head. "We would have been caught a long time ago."

"Cartwright sell us out?" Neil suggested.

The Wolf shook his head. "He's not the type."

A memory stirred in Neil's subconscious. "It's me," Neil realized aloud. "My room in the Vapros bunker. It's filled with coasters from this place."

"They knew you'd come to your favorite bar," Bianca said.

"Where can we go that they won't expect?" the Wolf asked. Urgency was mounting in his voice. "Somewhere defensible."

"Celerius estate," Neil said.

Everyone in the room looked at him. "Neil, that's—"

"No, that'll work," the Wolf said. "Closer to the palace, easily defensible, and we'd have to be insane to go there. It'll work."

"Then to the sewers," Robert said. "One by one. Starting with those closest."

The rebels filtered out at a snail's pace. Robert moved to the bar just as slowly. "Pour some drinks," he said to Alfred.

"How many?"

"All of them."

Alfred nodded and began pouring the alcohol onto the bar, covering every inch. "I'll need you, Neil."

Neil nodded. Robert's idea was a good one. Take some Imperials with them. Even so it was hard for him to imagine roasting his favorite bar. Neil turned to see that it was mostly empty now. "They're preparing weapons," the Wolf said, arm extended. "They're going to breach any second."

"To the cellar then," Robert demanded.

Bianca looked to Neil. "Go," he said. "I promise it'll be all right."

She didn't look convinced, but went with the Wolf. Only Robert, Neil and Alfred remained. The boards above began to rattle, hard. Robert's hands curled into fists and something seemed to possess him. "Saewulf."

"Robert we can't win. Not here."

"Why not?" Robert asked. "He has to come through that door. This might be our best chance at a fight on our terms."

"I..." Neil realized that Robert might be right. "Alfred, you want to go?"

"Trek miles through the sewers with these knees?" He grabbed a rifle from beneath the bar. "I'm a little old for that."

Robert pulled a long dagger and a revolver from his coat. "When Saewulf gets to the center of the bar, light it up."

"Then what?" Neil asked.

"We take our revenge."

The whole bar shook now. Where would Saewulf come from? Certainly not the front door? Neil pooled his energy in his hands. Was it all going to end here?

The ceiling exploded and Saewulf dropped into the bar glowing with dark energy. Neil threw a fireball by instinct, but with a wave of

Saewulf's hand it deteriorated. "Vapros," he said. "Having one last drink?"

"Having quite a few," Neil said.

He threw his next fireball at the ground. The drinks ignited, sending the bar into a state of inferno. Saewulf moved his arms blindly, just in time to sway the bullet trained at his head courtesy of Alfred. The old man tried to reload. Saewulf put him through the wall.

"Saewulf!" came an inhuman roar. Robert vaulted off one of the tables, desperate to put his dagger through Saewulf's eye. Saewulf caught him in mid-air, where he hung uselessly.

"Do I know you?" Saewulf asked. "This feels personal."

"Do you even remember her?"

Saewulf eyed him, cautiously putting his body between them. "Do I remember…? Victoria Vapros?"

Robert seized wildly at the sound of her name. "That makes you Robert then. You know she mentioned you in the end." Robert's eyes widened. "Yes, I remember. She was a martyr. One more dying for a better world."

Robert forced his revolver in Saewulf's direction and began firing. One bullet ricocheted off the floor and stuck Saewulf's leg. He howled and dropped Robert, who swung with the dagger. Saewulf lifted his arm and flung Robert across the room. Neil threw another fireball. This one made contact, sending Saewulf into the bar, where he lay dazed. Robert lifted his gun again. "You die for a better world!" he screamed and fired the remaining shots.

Saewulf, realizing he was in danger, slammed his hand into the bar and brought the entire roof down. Neil leapt into the back room, narrowly escaping the debris. Luckily for Neil, he didn't mind a little smoke and heat. He went back, found Robert, and dragged him through to the sewer before the Imperial soldiers could get to him.

Neil didn't stop running until he was sure they'd have a moment's rest. Robert groaned, half awake, body in shock. His face had been badly burned, and Neil didn't want to wipe away the ash in fear of what he might see. "Is it bad?" Robert wheezed.

Neil stared at him. "I don't know, I…"

"Do I look like him?" Robert was shaking. He pulled himself toward the water, trying to see his reflection. "The burns… do I look like him, Neil?"

"No," Neil said. "You look far better. We have to get to the—"

"He came right to us. Right to me. And I couldn't kill him."

"Keep it together, Robert," Neil demanded. "He's probably trying to crush all of the Lightborns before we can get to the palace."

Robert lifted his burned head with a start and turned over to look at Neil. "Wait… If he's here that means…"

"That means what?" Neil asked.

"No one is protecting the Emperor." Robert was breathing heavily. "No one who could stop you."

"What?" Neil tried to follow Robert's train of thought.

"Neil, you need to get to the palace. You need to end this today. On this morning, you can kill him and end this rule."

Neil realized the full gravity of that. "I…"

"Run, Neil," Robert said. "End this. Saewulf's probably already on the way back. You have to beat him there."

Neil stood with his friend for a moment, then his feet carried him toward any exit he could find. He made his way to the street and oriented himself. He saw the palace in the distance and flew, leaving a stream of fire as he went to end the war.

CELERIUS ESTATE

LILLY CELERIUS

It had been quite a while since Lilly had been in the Celerius estate. She viewed it differently now. She used to see the weapons on the walls as evidence of achievement. These were weapons that had been tempered in blood and hard won.

Now she saw them as a grave warning. Power invites competition and envy and greed. The Celerius had not fought to be great, as she had originally suspected. They fought to stay alive. First the savages, then the Feud, and now the Empire. From the moment they'd been blessed with power, it had become their curse. Now she and the Wolf were the only ones left.

She went room to room, starting on the bottom floor. It was completely empty, like a ruin. As she walked, she draped her hands over everything. Such opulence and wealth. Was this what everyone wanted so badly? Had the Celerius ever deserved it in the first place?

She found her room and combed through it. She approached the mirror at the other side of the room. There was a trepidation in her step. Why was she so afraid to look?

She realized when she sat down. She had been so beautiful then.

This was where she sat when her hair was long and her makeup was from the finest boutiques in the city. She expected to see herself as something hideous now. A muddy rebel rat.

When she saw herself reflected in the mirror, with her hair short and choppy, with skin worn darker by the sun and the dirt, she realized she never loved the look of herself more. There was some grit to her that she'd never seen before. She noticed the scar from Carlin's blazing sword and wondered how many imperfections she left on him. When was the last time she'd seen a mirror?

She now identified far more with the weapons than the portraits or the porcelain on the walls behind her. She pulled her fist back and put it through the mirror. That was enough of that.

She extended her hands, feeling the extent of the Celerius estate. What was she looking for? Her senses passed over Thomas's room, then Edward's, then her parent's. She thought of how much she'd lost. Her mind traveled back to the little girl in the apartment and her Imperial father. She felt pride that she hadn't made the little girl like she was. Alone in the world.

She sensed Anthony's room. Larger than the others. He hadn't asked for it, but it had been given to him. Now she realized it was much bigger than she realized. She stiffened. Far in the back of his room, she could feel a smaller room. A closet? No, that couldn't be it. His closet was on the other side of the wing.

She moved quicker now, steadying her nerves. It was probably nothing. She reached Anthony's room and went where she felt the spare room. Where there should have been a door, she found a painting. Definitely suspicious.

She'd seen the painting before, but wasn't it formerly in the living room? This had been done by one her father's favorite painters. She didn't remember the man's name, but she remembered the name of the painting: *Man Kills the Storm.*

It was a depiction of thirty of so small figures with swords pointing upward. Why was this here? When had it been moved? What was it hiding? She removed the painting and, as expected, she found a door.

It was locked, but Lilly knew her brother well enough to guess the combination on the first try. The date of Anthony's ascension to general. She thought of the swords on the walls again. Maybe if he'd stayed out of the military he'd still be alive. Power invites conflict. Her eyes flickered to the painting and she wondered what had come first. The men with swords drawn or the storm.

She opened Anthony's secret room. The door groaned. It was small, but littered with documents, books, and weapons. What was this place? It was too dark to see, so she went out and fumbled for a candle.

As the light crept up the walls, she gasped. Covering them were papers and sketches, the largest being of a face she knew. Why had Anthony drawn Saewulf? She looked closer at the papers and realized that he'd been tracking the psychic's comings and goings, filling page after page with speculations and observations. Had Anthony known what Saewulf was? What he was capable of?

Her eyes fell on Anthony's desk, which was adorned with a lone wooden box. She opened it and found herself confused by its contents. There was a scrap of paper underneath and she read it frantically.

She'd always wondered why Anthony had gone down so easily. Why he'd rolled over so Carlin could kill him. In recent days, she'd wondered if Virgil had been his ace in the hole. A protector for his family. But maybe he'd prepared something else. Something to fight off Saewulf.

She piled his books underneath her arms and grabbed the box, bringing them out of the hidden room and into the light. As she did, she realized why Anthony had chosen that painting to cover his secret room. *Man Kills the Storm.*

As she began to rip open the books and pore over her brother's handwriting she learned the truth. The rebels were the *man*. The people were the *man*.

And Saewulf was the *storm*.

IMPERIAL PALACE

NEIL VAPROS

Neil exploded through the windows of the throne room, sending glass everywhere. The floor to ceiling doors were thrown open. Guards charged at him, but Neil filled the room with fire and sent them scattering. He pulled out his knife and scanned the room, veins alight with adrenaline. He decided he wouldn't say anything. He was done with speeches and ideas. He was killing the Emperor.

He saw the man on his throne, and Neil materialized into striking distance. With all his loss and rage, he drove his knife into the Emperor's chest.

He waited for the cry, the look of surprise, and the end of it all.

The Emperor gave him nothing. He cocked his head, confused.

Neil pulled the knife out and put it back in. The Emperor still gave him nothing. Neil took a step back, reeling. Was he already dead? Had someone gotten here before him? The Emperor's eyes were wide open. "Confused?"

Suddenly, Neil was ripped from the throne and pressed into the ground. "Playing with the puppet, Neil?"

Neil's mind raced. What was happening?

Saewulf spun him around, lifted him, and slammed him back down. "I wonder if he felt it. I imagine he didn't. He hasn't been very responsive of late."

Neil tried to fight, but Saewulf was more powerful than ever. "This is the best kept secret in the realm, so I expect your discretion."

"I…" Neil tried to summon fire. He couldn't. "What's happening?"

"The Emperor and I used to play a good deal of chess together. He always figured the most important person in chess was the king, because he was simple. In reality, you know the most important person in chess? It's the man moving the pieces."

Neil gazed up at the Emperor's lifeless form. "You… You're controlling him?"

"I am him. Have been for a while," Saewulf said. "A trick I picked up from a Venator called the Horseman. He never thought to use it on a person."

"You're…" Neil couldn't comprehend what was happening. Everything had been Saewulf. For how long had the entire country been taking orders from him? "People would have—"

"Noticed? Stopped me?" Saewulf demanded. "No one loved him. Not even the Empress. Especially not the Empress. All I had to do to convince her was tell her the beatings would stop."

"You're a tyrant. You've killed so many. All in another man's name."

Saewulf pressed Neil harder into the ground. Neil's knees cracked against the polished floor. "You still don't understand," Saewulf accused. He walked around so Neil could see him. Tears slid down his face. "This is still the feud. It's always been the feud." For emphasis, he tossed the Emperor's body across the room. "The Wolf's inner circle, Lightborns. It's *all* Lightborns. Mine too, besides the puppet. This war is Lightborns and men who want to be Lightborns. Even Carlin is drinking Celerius blood." He shook and the ground cracked. "You really think it's not in our nature to abuse these gifts? Or to be abused?"

"You can't just slaughter us." Neil spoke whatever words came into his mind. He didn't have the strength for anything else. "This power is a burden. But it can be used for good. If we give the power to the people and we—"

"You're allowed to think that!" Saewulf roared. His lower jaw shook. "You grew up buying drinks for nobles in the center of this town's greed and avarice. I grew up in a silver mine. I slaved away for men who didn't care if I lived or died. I slaved away for men who didn't care if my sister lived or died. What can you tell me about burdens, Neil? What can you tell me about abuse of power? Righteousness?"

"You're a Lightborn who was taken advantage of by other Lightborns. And now you take advantage of others. How are you different? You're exterminating people. Normal people are dying for this. My sister died for this. At your hand."

Saewulf turned away and Neil saw the deep conflict in him. How to change the world without being the thing he hated? "I did kill your sister. And part of me thought I would really enjoy it. I did in the moment. But I didn't lie to Robert. I remember everything. It's the nights when I have to weigh their souls against the souls of those who will be safe in a world free of Lightborns."

"How's that going?" Neil could feel every ounce of his blood pounding away in his cheeks. "That balancing act?"

"Everything always comes up red," Saewulf said. "And that is why you are unfit to lecture me about burdens." He removed something from the pocket in his coat. He held it into the light and it gleamed. "I freed myself not with my extraordinary gifts, but with a shard of silver and a hatred for those who would water fields with the blood of those weaker than them. And now I carry the weaker into the new world. I carry the weight of everyone fleeing from you and your people."

Saewulf raised one hand. The Emperor's body floated back into the throne. Neil felt his knees come up from the ground slightly and used this opportunity to materialize out of Saewulf's hold. In the same motion he drew his knife, swinging at Saewulf. Something was wrong. Neil struck slower than he ever had, and Saewulf was able to bob out of the way. The psychic grabbed his hands with incredible strength. Neil's fingers cracked and bruised. With one halfhearted kick, he sent Neil clear across the room. "How are you...?"

"This strong?" Saewulf asked. "You don't know how badly I want to tell you, Neil, but I'm tired of your lectures." He pulled Neil back and lifted him so they were eye to eye. "I'm not going to argue with a man who can't change my mind. I made my resolutions long ago."

With a mighty grunt, he hurled Neil into the wall. Before Neil could attempt to materialize, Saewulf's power seized him again. "I don't need you to gape in awe at my plans or my power. I need you to die, Neil."

Neil felt his vision fading.

"Altryon needs to you die."

CELERIUS ESTATE

THE WOLF

The last time the Wolf had seen the Celerius estate in person, armed men ripped him out of it in the middle of the night. He considered fighting then, but he'd been younger and part of him still trusted that the judicial system would protect him. This was an important lesson learned over the years. Systems only protect people who benefit them, and the Wolf had long ago exhausted his worth.

Now he pushed the door open slowly. He could feel the insides of the house. It seemed abandoned, aside from one figure in the main dining room. He could wager a guess as to who it was. Or maybe it was a hope.

Just in case, he'd made Bianca and the other revolutionaries hide in the stables. He wasn't going to risk having his numbers thinned before their final stand. He also didn't want to startle Lilly with an entire unit of revolutionaries.

Lilly vanished after Virgil's death. The Wolf was willing to bet that she ran to avoid Carlin's clutches. Coming here was certainly a bold decision, although he'd made it as well.

When he entered the dining room, Lilly was standing there, swords drawn and teeth bared.

"Uncle?" she asked, her voice a whisper of disbelief.

"Hello, my dear."

She ran into the Wolf's arms and cried. He found himself overwhelmed.

When they finally parted she studied his face. "What's wrong?" she asked.

"Being here is a little odd, is all," he mused. "My dreams have been getting worse and all of them seem to take place in this house."

"They're just dreams," Lilly said.

"In my experience, dreams are never just dreams. They're always the forecast of something bigger coming. Premonitions."

She regarded him uneasily, then turned back to the table. "I found something. Notes Anthony was taking on Saewulf."

"Anything useful?"

"Anthony believed Saewulf was somehow controlling the Emperor. He was utterly convinced that if Saewulf was killed before he could influence the Emperor, then we would avoid extermination."

The Wolf found a bottle of wine and decided they'd share a drink from it. It had been so long since he'd had such luxuries. He found a corkscrew and popped it open. "I think he was right. That doesn't do us much good now."

"There's more," Lilly said. "He knew Saewulf was an Anima and was looking for ways to kill him."

The Wolf lowered the bottle. "Did he find any?"

"He thought so."

She showed him the box. The Wolf approached and opened it. "We're supposed to kill a man who can level cities with a bracelet?"

She turned it over in her hand. "I can't find a description of what it does. But evidently it was invented by the Imperial Doctor."

The Wolf examined it closely. There were hooks on the inside. He went over to the pile of books and flipped through, looking for any possible mention of the cuff. "Something doesn't add up," he muttered. "Saewulf is powerful. But he can be killed. Look what that grenade did to him. Why would we need this?"

"That was a long time ago," Lilly said. "Something tells me he's stronger now."

The Wolf heard someone running through the hallway. Then the door was thrown open. "Someone's coming over the hill," Bianca said.

The Wolf nodded. "Return to the stables. There's a tunnel underneath the bench in the fourth stall. It'll take you deep into town."

"I'll tell Robert and his men."

She charged back through the door. The Wolf turned to Lilly. "Go."

"Go where?"

The Wolf gently laid a hand on her shoulder. "First, bring that box to Neil Vapros. He's the only one who can finish this."

"Okay," Lilly said. "You think he'll know what the bracelet does?"

"We can only hope. Second, do not let Carlin get to you. I've known many Celerius, but none as strong as you. I fear with your blood he'd be nearly unstoppable."

He could see her eyes filling with conflict. "What if he does find me?" she asked.

"Then you must kill him," the Wolf said forcefully. "You must show him that he is no true Celerius. Now go."

"You're not coming?"

"I'll be behind you."

He could tell she knew he was lying. Lilly put her hand on the side of his face. "I love you," she said. "I don't think any of us ever said that enough."

"I love you too."

"You'll see the new nation," she promised him.

"From somewhere, I'm sure."

And then his family left the estate. On the run again.

Moments later, the doors opened again. "We're out of time," Bianca said. "I guess they figured out our plan."

The Wolf feared this would happen. It was hard to move an entire force of people through a city without turning heads. "We could only stay under their noses for so long."

Bianca gestured frantically. "Come on."

The Wolf drew his sword and shook his head. "I'm smart enough to know that what's in the box Lilly found ends the war. As does the help of the young woman who holds it. I can't risk anyone getting their hands on either. Go, Bianca. I will slow them down."

He saw the complicated emotions battling on Bianca's face. "You can't, these people they—"

"These people have outgrown me."

"That's ridiculous."

"I once asked Neil if he knew what I would sacrifice for my cause. He assumed all I would give was his life."

"What?" Bianca asked.

"I don't respect hypocrites. I wouldn't deserve respect if I didn't live by my principals. To ask Neil to forfeit his life is to put my own on that same chopping block." She was silent. Begging him to go on. He regretted never making her a part of Neil's decision.

"This is what I want, Bianca," the Wolf said. "This year has been long for you. I imagine it has even almost broken you a few times. Understand that I have lived this life for decades now, and I am so tired of running."

"I could do it," she said. "I could hold them off. If Carlin gets your blood—"

"You think you could hold back Carlin? Or Saewulf?"

"I could try."

"That is why you've been an incredible right hand, Bianca. You're selfless."

The door behind them shook. Bianca took one last long look at the Wolf. "Before I go, I need you to know. Your wife, she's—"

"Alive? I know." A slow sad smile fell over the Wolf's face. "I read that letter, the one Carlin had sent to me. I know you found her and I know what she decided to do. She's far stronger than I am."

"Thank you for your service," she said eventually.

Her face was a mask of guilt. The Wolf wished she didn't feel that way. He would have done the same thing. The Wolf nodded to her, releasing her and she was gone.

Carlin came through the door flanked by dozens of men. He licked his malformed lips. He'd hungered for the Wolf's death for so many years and now he was finally close enough to taste it. Leaf entered last, filling out their pack of villains. His green skin gleamed even in the shadows.

The Wolf waved his sword in a salute. Bianca, Lilly, and the rebels didn't need much time, but the Wolf would give them every second he could. "Steven Celerius," Carlin said. His voice rang throughout the hall. "You're not the Celerius I expected to find here."

"No?"

"No," Carlin admitted. "I was looking for Lilly. I was scouring the farthest corners of the realm when I got notice that she was here in Altryon, right under my nose. Smart."

"So you figured she'd come here."

"Yes. The place I'd least expect her."

"Well I hate to disappoint you." The Wolf sized up Carlin who was sweating hard. How much blood did he have left? Was he still powerful enough to win this fight without it? He counted the men. There were easily thirty.

"So much running... So many battles... So many speeches... and it all ends here, in your own living room," Carlin said. "It ends two rooms away from where I killed Thomas."

The Wolf gripped his sword and tried to remain strong. This wasn't over yet. When he gained the courage to speak, his voice boomed like cannon fire. "I have always been pursued by darkness, Carlin. Day and night, birth until death. It has never ceased, never rested and never shown a lapse in strength. But neither have I." He saw Carlin's confidence tarnish. "You're not the first servant of evil to catch me."

Carlin lifted his blade. "Well, I'm the last."

Carlin was across the room in a blink, waving his broadsword and screaming. The Wolf dodged swing after swing. Carlin's men charged behind blades drawn. The Wolf tried to calm his panicked mind, to swing around and strike Carlin, but every single blow was parried or deflected. The Wolf felt fear rise in his chest. How had

Carlin grown this strong? How strong would he be with Lilly's blood?

Smoke filled the room. This was Leaf's contribution. The Wolf blocked another swing and retreated a few feet, breathing heavily.

"I can see why you lived this long. You've grown faster in your old age."

"And louder," the Wolf said. He dug his feet in, channeled his energy, let out a cry. He used the Howl rarely and only in times of great danger, but this qualified.

Men all around the room buckled to their knees, holding their ears and screaming back.

Carlin cut it short, closing the distance between them, and swinging his blade against the Wolf's arm, leaving a deep gash through the arteries. The Wolf kicked him off and sped to the other side of the room, cutting down any man who dared to come within five feet. He panted hard.

The Wolf twisted his blade. What would give Lilly more time to escape? Running, or standing his ground?

He killed two more men before Carlin came back for more. The Wolf took another cut to his side, then one to his leg. Men filed in on either side, lashing out desperately. A shower of swords upon him, the Wolf fought on, trying his best to summon another scream.

Eventually, a blade found its way through his back. He swung in a wide arc, scattering his attackers, even Carlin. He examined his surroundings, but there was a heavy pounding in his brain. What could he do?

He fought on, as always.

He breathed, assessed, then cut flesh. This had always been his method as a swordsman. Breath, assess, cut flesh. Before long he was alone with Carlin. The rest of his enemies lay on the floor in pieces. The blade was still in his back and the cuts on his limbs took their sweet time healing.

Carlin didn't wait. He swung wildly, over and over again until finally the Wolf looked down and realized that the broadsword was buried in his chest.

In a terrifying instant, he felt his body stop. There was no buzzing of activity as his skin rushed to repair itself. This was it and he knew. Carlin pushed and pinned him against the wall.

"One final Celerius relic." Sweat poured from Carlin's face. "Hung upon the wall for all to see."

The Wolf didn't have time to pontificate on Carlin's insults. He thought suddenly of that fortune teller years ago who told him there was a pack of ghosts following him everywhere. Seeing Carlin, knee deep in dead men, with Leaf standing in the corner, made him glad to be escaping this. To finally be joining those ghosts.

"It's a shame you'll never get to see the new nation," Carlin hissed. "From the ashes of an era of Lightborns, Saewulf and I will bring a new age into the light."

The Wolf's vision clouded. It took every last bit of strength he had to speak. "Step into the light and you will perish, Carlin."

"And why's that?"

The Wolf succumbed to the pull beckoning him onward. "Because that's what darkness does. It dies in light."

And then Carlin was alone in a room of dead men.

53

IMPERIAL PRISON

RHYS VAPROS

Rhys and Darius had been in prison for two days. In the Empire's only act of generosity, they'd put their cells next to each other. Rhys was confined to a painful mask so Darius kept the mainly one-sided conversation going.

For hours in the dark, Darius shared stories he made up or had heard before. Rhys was impressed with his friend's previously hidden creative talent.

This was all they could do besides whisper in hushed confusion about what they had learned. All the Lightborns were alive. Darius had glimpsed his sister Cassandra, and Rhys had seen a cousin while they were being forced in.

Rhys knew they'd mainly been captured instead of killed all those years ago. Why hadn't Saewulf executed them yet? He wanted a future free of Lightborns, didn't he?

Saewulf brought the answer on what Rhys calculated was the second day.

"Gentlemen," Saewulf said. "Enjoying your stay?"

"Actually I'd like to check out," Darius muttered.

Saewulf knelt, staring at Rhys with intent through the bars. "I hear you're an intellectual."

"Sure," Rhys said.

"Well everything is about to make a lot more sense, I'm afraid."

He reached through the bars and put a hand on Rhys's head. Rhys felt tired. Very tired. He felt energy ripped from him and into his hands. "Your sacrifice is appreciated," Saewulf said.

Rhys groaned in pain and discomfort after it was done. Saewulf went to Darius's cell where Rhys heard him doing the same. Rhys had been deeply weakened and could only hear fragments through a throbbing in his head. What had Saewulf done to him?

Eventually his ears stopped ringing and he listened for Darius. "Darius? Are you okay?"

"What the hell?" Darius sounded like his mouth was numb. "What was that?"

"I don't know," Rhys said. "But I feel…"

"Weaker?"

Rhys didn't answer. He felt *much* weaker though.

Saewulf came back again, hours later. He knelt down in front of Rhys once more. "This is more than I usually do it," he admitted. "I need it. This is all coming to an end."

"Need what?" Rhys asked.

Saewulf kept pulling until Rhys lost his ability to think. Was this to keep them dormant? Did he want them too weak to escape?

Rhys heard Darius's voice faintly. "You're farming us," he heard Darius call to Saewulf. "You're farming us for energy."

Rhys could faintly see Saewulf's face, but it remained collected.

"That's why all the Lightborns are alive," Darius continued. "You're using them to grow stronger."

"Figured that one out all by yourself?" Saewulf asked.

"There was a Vapros who could do that," Darius said. "Eric Vapros. About a hundred years ago."

Saewulf finally looked thrown, or troubled, Rhys couldn't tell. "And how do you know that?"

"It's in a book I read," Darius said.

"You can read?" Saewulf asked.

"Yeah," Darius said. "Now."

Saewulf turned on his heels, finished with the conversation it seemed. "Hey," Darius called after him, "wanna know how he died? Eric Vapros?"

"Yes," Saewulf said.

"Yeah," Darius said. "I bet you do."

Saewulf left, glowing faintly in dark energy.

After a few moments, Rhys found his head clearing. *"And what exactly was that?"*

Rhys couldn't help it. He screamed. Wasn't he supposed to be free of this? He'd shut the Doctor away, hadn't he? "Rhys, are you okay?" he heard Darius say. He didn't answer.

"How am I hearing you?" Rhys asked.

"You're weak right now," the Doctor said. *"Weak enough to let a whisper or two slip through the cracks."*

"I can shut you away again." Rhys felt his mind aching as he tried to crush the Doctor's voice.

"You shouldn't do that," the Doctor said. *"Not if you want a way out."*

Rhys stopped and let his mind go soft. *"What do you mean?"*

"Your friend moves metal with his mind. I can make use of that."

Rhys shook his head before remembering he couldn't be seen. *"He's not strong enough to break our chains. We tried yesterday."*

"And he's not strong enough to move the tumblers in a lock?"

Rhys paused, knowing the danger of the voice in his head. Could he really listen to this monster? How many slippery steps could he take before plunging into ultimate darkness?

"I'm reasonable, and you've proven yourself the master of your own mind. I ask for one thing and one thing only," the Doctor said.

"What's that?"

"A debt. A favor. Just one."

Rhys didn't like the idea of this. He knew what this really was. It wasn't an olive branch. It was a temptation. If he said yes to this, what would stop him the next time?

"What's the favor?"

"It's very simple," the Doctor said. "I want you to abandon that precious moral code of yours, just once. We'll decide how and when."

"Rhys, are you okay?" he heard Darius say again.

"I'll do it," Rhys said.

"There are five tumblers in the lock. He must move the third one first. Push until he hears a click."

"Darius, you have to listen to me."

"Okay."

Rhys relayed the instructions until Darius understood. Then they heard it together. Click.

"What now?" Darius asked.

"Are you ready for more?" Rhys gulped. Did he have a choice?

"Rhys, what now?"

"Yes," Rhys said. "I'm ready."

54

ALTRYON'S TOWN SQUARE

NEIL VAPROS

Neil Vapros was brought to the town square at noon. He expected his execution to be a private event, as it would be more secure, but Saewulf had invited the entire city. This was his endgame after all. Neil's death was supposed to inspire a sense of dread in all who tried to fight.

Neil realized on the ride over that this was the largest difference between the Empire and the rebels. The Empire wanted him to die for dread and the rebels wanted him to die for hope. It was hard for Neil to weigh the scales of right and wrong on this one.

Even more surprising was the fact that the Emperor was reportedly going to be in attendance. Neil couldn't fathom how that was going to work. Was there any of the Emperor left? Or was he completely brain dead? Would those knife wounds to the chest do nothing? Was Saewulf simply carting around a corpse?

The doors to the carriage opened and Saewulf lifted Neil into the street. Neil's arms had been locked into thick, heat resistant containers and no matter how hard he tried to summon fire, it didn't work. "Today is our day, Neil. Today you bring about New Altryon. I can't possibly thank you enough for your sacrifice."

Neil looked around at the crowds starting to gather in the distance. It looked like everyone in Altryon was coming to see his execution. There was a platform in the square surrounded by guards armed to the teeth. There was an executioner on the stage brandishing a large axe. Neil wondered if this was how they actually planned to do it. Would Saewulf really let someone else end this?

Neil was pulled to his knees and from afar he heard the Emperor's voice. "Citizens of Altryon. Today we bring an end to our nation's violent era of confusion and mistrust. Today we rightfully take the life of one of Altryon's most violent terrorists. Neil Vapros."

The crowd screamed. Neil realized those in attendance had split opinions on him. Some cheered for his death, some for his freedom. No matter what, there was no chance of him going anywhere. There looked to be fifty archers lining the buildings. Anyone trying to stop this would surely end up pin cushioned.

"I shall be forgoing etiquette today and allowing my faithful servant, Saewulf, to take the life of this treasonous youth. After all, Neil Vapros was responsible for the hateful crime that cost him his face."

Neil glanced at the executioner who nodded understandably. Saewulf stepped onto the stage and extended his arm. Neil felt the air being pulled from him. He looked into the eyes of the people around him, watching as they screamed or cheered. He felt grateful for the screaming ones. How brave they must have been to express their dissent in front of someone like Saewulf.

Neil felt darkness swirling around him and he let it take him. He felt everything go black and his head fell forward. Within the darkness, he felt a stream of golden light reaching for him, yet something kept them at bay. Neil tried to reach for them, but they left him. If he was supposed to move on, why couldn't he?

Then Neil remembered Cartwright.

His eyes sprang open and the crowd gasped. Saewulf turned. "You...?"

Across the stage, the executioner put his fingers to his lips and whistled. Half the crowd, the cheering part, stopped and charged the stage, throwing their bodies against the soldiers, desperate to take a chunk out of Saewulf. He stepped back, horrified and confused.

Cartwright removed his mask. "You don't know me," he called. "But I think we share an ancestor."

Saewulf reached out to throttle Cartwright, but the force never reached him. Cartwright grinned. "Sorry, friend, but that's hard to use on someone who knows how the trick works."

Saewulf looked back to the crowd and saw that his men were almost completely overwhelmed by Cartwright's undead followers. He attempted to use his force to kill Neil again, but quickly realized that no one could truly die here. Neil saw him grit his teeth through the missing gaps of his cheek. "I can't kill you, but I can make you wish you were dead."

Something large leapt from the crowd and landed between Saewulf and Neil. The man removed his coat, showing his golden mane. "Eric Vapros," Darius said to Saewulf. "The one with your same power... He was ripped apart by the people. I know you were just dying to know."

Saewulf tried to turn, but Neil saw Lilly Celerius at the edge of the stage, blocking his way. Darius pulled the axe from Cartwright's hands and split Neil's chains. Neil pulled his arms from the restraints. There was nothing like the power he felt here. All his friends, joined together against their common foe. "You can't take my life here either," Saewulf said, desperation creeping into his voice.

"We'll settle for your reign," Lilly said.

Saewulf realized he was outnumbered and lowered his hands, making the entire stage shake. "You delay it, Vapros. But you know it must come," he yelled. "You know who's foretold it!"

He lifted himself into the air and joined the massive swarm of arriving soldiers. Neil threw a fireball, but missed Saewulf by a mere foot. Neil turned and looked at Cartwright, "I..."

"Worship me?" Cartwright asked. "Thank you. Join the club. Be free, Vapros."

Neil twirled, looking thankfully at Darius and Lilly. "Thank you," he said, voice overflowing with gratitude. How could it be that these were his closest friends? A year ago, he'd been part of a pack of assassins clamoring for their deaths. He could tell they were thinking the same thing. "Is it true?" Neil asked his companions. "Is the Wolf dead?"

Lilly looked down for a moment, then lifted her head. "Yes. And it's up to us to make certain he didn't die in vain."

"But if Carlin has his blood…"

"I know," Lilly said.

She removed a small box from her coat and handed it to Neil. There was a moment of confusion. but suddenly everything made sense. He removed the cuff from the box and placed it in his side pocket.

"Do you know what this is?" Lilly asked.

"Yes."

Rhys appeared on the stage and Neil grabbed him, checking for wounds or evidence of his capture. "Are you okay?"

"I'm okay," Rhys said. "Things are worse than we thought though. Saewulf has been farming power from the Lightborns."

"What?" Neil asked.

"That's why they're not dead," Rhys continued. "And that's why Saewulf's been getting so much stronger."

"How do you know this?" Neil asked. "Where have you been?"

"We broke out of prison half an hour ago," Darius said.

Bianca and Robert broke through the crowd onto the stage. Neil caught Bianca in a tight hug. Would this be his last chance to hold her? He pushed that thought away. Technically he had been killed. Cartwright had just intervened. Maybe the debt that was required had been filled. "You had me worried there," Bianca said.

"You know me," Neil said. "I always come back."

Robert looked to his pack of undead warriors pushing forward. "We've exposed ourselves. This must happen now." His face looked far better than it had the day before. The burn even suited him a bit.

"What must happen now?" Neil asked.

"We've caught them off guard. It's time for our final push," Robert said. "No matter what happens, today is the final day of the revolution."

Neil looked to the crowd. It was true. The undead were forcing back the Imperial soldiers. Robert's men had appeared as well, wielding their makeshift amalgamation of weapons. Neil saw guns, broken chairs, and rusty swords, as the mob advanced on the gates of the palace. Neil couldn't stop watching. The people tore through the gates by the sheer force of their own will.

"What needs to happen to end this?" Darius asked. He rocked back and forth and Neil empathized with his anxiety. They'd never been this close.

"Lilly, go after Carlin," Bianca commanded.

Neil saw a shadow of doubt cross Lilly's face. "I…"

"He has the Wolf's blood," Bianca said. "You're the only one who can."

Lilly looked conflicted and Neil wondered why. Wasn't Carlin's death the only thing she'd ever wanted?

"Darius, Rhys, Neil take the front gates," Bianca said.

"Neil can't," Lilly said.

Everyone looked at her, Neil included. "Neil has to go after Saewulf," Lilly explained. "He's the only one that can end this."

"So it's happening," Robert said. "The prophecy."

Neil's hands began shaking, but they slowed. He had to keep it together for all of them. "What prophecy?" Bianca asked.

"I love you," Neil said.

"Neil, what prophecy?" Rhys asked.

Everyone stared at him now. Darius, Lilly, Cartwright, Robert, Rhys, and Bianca, begged an answer. Neil didn't know what to say. "Just a dream," he said. "It's all just dreams."

"Neil goes after Saewulf," Robert said. "The rest of us will join the foot soldiers."

Neil nodded. He grabbed Bianca and pulled her into a deep kiss. Her fear was palpable. "What prophecy?" she asked in a near silent breath when they parted.

"I'm so lucky," Neil said, "for every moment I ever got to spend with you, so lucky."

Neil stepped back and smiled at Rhys. "Be good brother. Be brave."

He ignited his hands and flew off toward the palace, where everything would end.

Bianca turned back to Robert as Neil became a speck. She grabbed him by his coat, threatening to rip it in half. "Robert," she demanded, jaw clenched and teary eyed. "What prophecy?"

IMPERIAL PALACE

CARLIN FILUS

Carlin burst into the throne room. His father and Saewulf were together. "What's happening?"

"It didn't go as planned," the Emperor said. "They're besieging our gates."

"Well..." Carlin couldn't accept this might be the end. "What does this mean?"

"It means we must fight to the death for our rule," the Emperor said. "It means we must end this with no mercy. All the rebels are in one place. We can crush them here."

Carlin eyed his father and saw that something was very different. "What do I do?"

"You're the General. Lead your men," Saewulf said. "Have you used the Wolf's blood?"

Carlin removed a vial from his pocket. He swallowed its contents, then braced himself for the change. His body shook and his forehead quivered. This was a stronger batch than he'd tried before. He groaned as he sank to his knees. "The Celerius will be coming for you," the Emperor said.

"I've planned for that," Carlin said.

"Good," Saewulf and the Emperor said at the same time.

Carlin regarded the interaction suspiciously. What was so different? Why did everything feel so odd? His brain hadn't worked right since he started drinking this blood mixture.

Carlin looked to Saewulf, then back to the Emperor. "My head hurts so much."

"It's okay," Saewulf said. "Focus on the girl. Lilly Celerius. She took everything from you. She took Virgil."

Carlin's hands tightened into balls. Had she taken Virgil? Or had Carlin lost him. "Go my son," the Emperor said. "I'm proud of you."

What had his father said? Proud of him? A slow realization dawned, and the last year started to make a lot more sense. Carlin found his adrenaline and rage mixed with sorrow and horror. He wanted to use the rage to cut right through the psychic, but he just found himself tired.

"How long?" he asked looking deep into Saewulf's eyes. "How long have you been controlling him?"

Saewulf looked ready to lie, but Carlin saw him make a calculation. "A long time."

"Is there any of him left?"

"I don't know. Does this change anything?"

"I don't...." Carlin drew his blade. He'd always been fighting to earn his father's love, hadn't he? What had all this been for? "I thought this was for him."

"And it wasn't?"

"I don't know."

"Kill the Celerius, Carlin," Saewulf said. "Kill her and you'll remember how strong those beliefs of yours are. If we don't crush those Lightborns, you know what they'll do?"

"They'll rule us," Carlin said.

"Yes."

Saewulf stopped puppeting the Emperor and he lay in the chair, with all the life of a ragdoll. Carlin looked at Saewulf. Wasn't this also a Lightborn leading them? He shook his head, trying to shake out the confusion and doubt. "I'm going," Carlin said.

He charged through the doors and went down the hall. His traps were set in the main entryway. As he waited for the Celerius to come, he heard his father's voice in his head over and over again. *"I'm proud of you."*

It wasn't real, but if he didn't think too hard he could pretend. Carlin had learned at a young age that if he believed in anything hard enough it became true.

IMPERIAL PALACE

LILLY CELERIUS

Carlin left the door open for Lilly and she sped right in. He stood at the top of the stairs, face wet with sweat, knuckles white from the strain of clutching his broadsword so hard. "Lilly Celerius."

She let her blade carve a path in the air. "Carlin."

He descended the steps slowly. "Did you ever think you were wrong Lilly? Wrong to pick the side you picked?"

"No," Lilly said.

"It might surprise you to know that I have." He got to the bottom of the stairs where they circled each other. "But walk this far and it becomes clear that there is no going back. There's no doubt this deep into the mire."

"I don't really care what you feel, Carlin."

That was a lie. She wanted him to feel her sword through his chest. She dashed forward and swung, only to be parried. He kicked her away and took advantage of his superior sword length. He flung his arm down, punishing her defenses. She stepped back. He grinned. "Weakness." He pointed at her throat with the sword. "Years of fighting and still weaker than I am."

He swept in and cut a deep dash in her chest. This one was slow to heal. She evaded his next swing and leaned in, drawing a line across his face. Blood poured from his lips and he gasped, stepping back. Before she could finish, Carlin sped up the stairs and through an open doorway. She followed, heart pounding in her chest. She had done it. She'd put a mark on him. He wasn't that much faster than he'd been. She had a chance.

She went through the threshold and found him waiting for her on the other side. She knew she'd made a mistake the second she felt her boots hit the carpet and heard sloshing. Carlin dropped the match he was holding. The room burst into flames, including the ground underneath her. She tried to swat it off, but the damage was done. Her arms singed and sizzled. She collapsed on the other side of the hall, away from the flames, gasping for air. Had this maniac really set the palace on fire?

Carlin saw blood now and rushed through the flames to her downed body, kicking brutally and bruising her singed skin. He pulled another bottle from his coat and held it into the light for her to see. "Your uncle's blood flows through my veins. I can't imagine how he'd feel right now. I can't imagine how any of them would feel, knowing how I used their power."

"Spill your own blood," Lilly hissed. "You've spilled more than enough of ours."

He brought his sword down, but she evaded, closing the distance between them, clawing and biting like an animal. He tried to maneuver his sword around to kill her, but she was in close now. He swung with his free hand, bruising her eye, but she persisted. Eventually he kicked her back toward the flames.

She stood despite the pain, felt her skin trying to heal itself to no avail. Lilly dragged herself back to put her sword through his chest, but he was too quick. He deflected the blow. On his next swing, he cut her deeply.

She lost her nerve and ran, finding herself back at the main staircase. He followed her, swinging so hard that he left deep wedges in the floor behind her. She kept climbing, desperate to escape. He followed, roaring with anger and exhaustion. He caught her near the top floor in front of a stained glass window. "You've run so far and evaded me for so long. Anthony, Thomas, Steven, all dead at my hand."

He lifted his sword. "I am everything you are. I've said it before, but now I believe it. I am everything the Celerius are."

"You're not. You lack the honor."

"Honor again. It's always honor. Don't patronize me by speaking of honor. I am *everything* you are."

Her eyes fell on his lip and the deep gash in it. Something occurred to her. He was missing more than honor. Lilly dropped her sword and with a cry tackled him, sending them both into the stained-glass window. It half fractured. "No!" he hissed and begged as he swung his fist at her. "You can't, it's...." he wheezed. "This isn't how it was supposed to happen. It's not right."

She slammed her head forward, splitting his nose. With blood on both of their faces, she spoke softly to him. "Don't worry. You'll survive. After all, you're everything that I am."

She pushed forward and sent them both falling into the open air. Carlin's cry became a bloody gurgle. Lilly didn't scream at all. She felt free. When they collided with the ground, Lilly heard most of Carlin's bones break. Most of hers too. But there was a difference between Carlin and her. Her bones would heal.

Once she could stand, Lilly looked down. He gurgled once more, furious at her. She lifted her sword and separated his treacherous head from his shoulders. It rolled off into the grass, still adorned with his signature scowl.

Lilly waited for something to happen, for the burdens on her soul to lesson. She waited for closure, for all that unfinished business to come to completion. Instead she found herself looking at a headless body, a bodiless head of no significance. All she'd wanted for the past year did absolutely nothing for her.

Soldiers gathered, seeing their General killed. They didn't draw on her. She was glad for that. She'd lost her taste for killing. Tears poured from her eyes suddenly and she took off running. To where, she didn't know.

IMPERIAL PALACE

RHYS VAPROS

Rhys stared around in awe. This was really happening. The people were tearing down the palace gates, ripping through the soldiers that dared try and stop them. This was it. Volteria was here.

A voice sounded in Rhys's head.

"I want my favor now."

Rhys tried to shrug it off, but his legs became hard to move. He stopped running with the crowd. Darius noticed. "Come on, buddy. We're almost through this."

"Now?" Rhys asked.

"Now," the Doctor demanded. *"I figure this is the perfect time."*

Rhys frantically tried to clear his head.

"My request is simple. I want you to take a life."

Darius's eyes widened. "He's back?" Darius asked.

"You're surrounded by war, this is the perfect time," the Doctor hissed.

"Why that?" Rhys begged.

"Because it will teach you compromise," the Doctor said.

Rhys imagined the Doctor's tendrils becoming larger, filling his head.

"If we're going to share this head, you're going to need to learn a thing or two about compromise. What better way than to make you compromise your one rule? What better way than making you realize that sometimes worthy sacrifices need to be made? It can be anyone."

A soldier charged toward their position, but one swing from Darius and he went flying into the distance. "Rhys, what can I do? What do you need?"

"If you don't, I'll grow into you like a worm in an apple. I'll kill you from within. This one thing is all that I ask."

Rhys frantically looked to Darius. "I need your help."

"Anything," Darius said.

"Kill me."

"No," Darius said without hesitation.

Rhys shook his head hard. "Darius, he's back and the Grand Master is dead. What else do we do? What else can be done?"

Men swarmed on either side and Rhys hoped he would just be trampled under the crowd.

Darius watched as Rhys struggled against the poison in his brain. "Please do it," Rhys said. "It's the only way."

Darius sighed deeply. He lifted his head high. Rhys could see him fighting with himself.

"We're not supposed to do this, because it gives people brain damage," Darius said. "But I think that's the least of your worries little buddy."

"What?" Rhys asked.

Darius punched him, knocking him out cold with ease.

"Go to sleep," Darius grumbled, throwing his friend over his shoulder. "We'll sort this out in the morning."

Rhys's unconscious body began flailing and materialized out of Darius's arms. "What the—"

Rhys's took off running down the street, completely consumed by the Doctor's influence. Darius ran at full speed after it.

Somewhere in his mind, Rhys fought hard for control, but knew it wasn't coming. He wasn't in charge anymore and feared he would never be again until he gave the Doctor what he wanted.

IMPERIAL PALACE

NEIL VAPROS

Neil found himself back in the throne room. It was empty, save for the Emperor's corpse, lying in the throne. Neil approached it with trepidation and placed a finger to his alabaster neck. To his surprise, he found the faintest suggestion of a heartbeat. "You in there?" Neil asked.

The Emperor responded with a groan so slight Neil thought he might have imagined it.

"Sorry about your place," Neil said. "I have no idea how much of this is your fault."

Another slight groan.

"Any chance you know where Saewulf is?" The Emperor's pupils flicked upward. "The roof?"

The Emperor was silent.

There was a ladder system to the roof, but Neil had no need for such things and flew to the hatch, opening it quietly. He stepped onto the top of the palace. He could see everything from up here—his old home, the slums, the wall, and the vast landscapes beyond it. And standing above everything: Saewulf, his arms aloft.

Neil realized with horror that he was tearing up entire streets around the palace, crushing rebels where they stood.

"Saewulf!" Neil called.

Saewulf turned and Neil saw that once again he was crying. "Do you know what you've done?" Maybe it was clear to him that he wasn't winning this war. His hands were glowing and contorting in new ways. "You've ruined everything. You've opened the door for more death, more abuse."

"I know you believe you're right, Saewulf. But the people have decided and they don't want your world."

"Then why come to me? Here to die for New Altryon all the same?"

"No," Neil said. "Here to die for Volteria."

His hands ignited.

The battle began in an instant. Neil channeled so much fire that it ignited the majority of his arms. He felt himself becoming the fire around him as he launched projectiles at Saewulf. Saewulf responded with unchecked power, the dark energy around him turning to tendrils that slammed into the roof, cracking it and showering dust. Saewulf proved to be far more powerful and the shadows caught Neil, swirling around to swallow him whole. "I…."

"Shut up!" Saewulf roared. "Shut up and die for your country!"

Suddenly a blade appeared, sticking out of Saewulf's chest. The tendrils vanished as Saewulf pulled the dagger free, wheezing in pain. Neil saw Bianca, standing tall with another blade at the ready.

"What are you doing here?"

"See that ring on your finger?" she asked, not taking her eyes off of their adversary. "It means that you don't go anywhere. And if you do, you take me with you."

"To death?"

"Anywhere."

Neil examined her, the woman he loved, far braver than he. For the millionth time, he envied her resolve. This was Volteria. People like her were Volteria.

Saewulf stood upright again, chest stained with blood. With

horror Neil saw the wound sealing itself, remembering that he'd been leeching power from other Lightborns. Was he really too powerful to kill? Saewulf was seething. "You don't understand how truly powerful I am. The things I can do."

He extended his arms and Neil was thrown to the opposite side of the roof. "Controlling that old man has split my focus but now... Now I don't even have to touch you to kill you, Vapros."

"Bianca!" Neil called, hoping for anything to save him.

The tendrils wrapped and flowed over him, burying him. Neil felt time slowing around him. He stopped seeing Saewulf and even Bianca. All he saw was darkness.

IT TOOK a moment for Neil to realize that he wasn't dead. He looked around, still surrounded by darkness. A single spark of light appeared a few feet off. It grew into the shape of a man.

Neil's body, or what was left of it, filled with adrenaline. "It's you," Neil said.

He hadn't been visited in so long. Not since beginning to believe the prophecy was about him. But here he was again, in that space somewhere between reality and shimmering light.

"Neil," said the Man with the Golden Light, a shimmering chorus.

"It's been a while," he said. He took a long time before managing to ask his next question. "Was that it? Did I just die for the new nation?"

The Man with the Golden Light approached, getting closer to Neil than ever before. "No, Neil Vapros. That wasn't it."

"So... Why am I here?"

"I am here to offer you a choice, Neil. Go back or stay."

"Live or die, you mean?"

"Go back or stay."

"I wasn't aware that was how destiny worked."

"It's not."

Neil's brain began stalling. "Why do I get a choice?"

"I have often given gifts to those I thought might be worthy. I deem you worthy of a choice. Wake up, continue to fight for Volteria, or finally rest. An end to the killing and death and pain that has plagued you."

Neil found that he could stand. He admired the light surrounding the deity. "Are you what I think you are?"

"Am I?" There was a flicker and in the light of the man he saw a familiar face. Jonathan, Lilly's servant. Then another flicker and he saw Victoria, then Jennifer, then Josephine, then Serena, then the Wolf. Finally, a face he'd only seen in sketches and paintings. His mother's. "Am I the summation of all human life?"

"I was going to compare it to a soup, but your description is much better."

"You spoke truly," the Man with the Golden Light said. "The voice of the people is the voice of God."

Neil sat with this information for a moment and thought about the offer. "To be with you is to be with them? My sisters? My mother?"

"Yes."

"Why do I get to choose? I didn't think destiny worked that way."

"It doesn't."

"I'm..." Neil realized something aloud. "I'm not the Phoenix, am I?"

"No."

"Then... I'm going back," Neil said.

The Man with the Golden Light nodded and reached out, pointer finger outstretched. He placed it in the center of Neil's forehead, and the light spread, covering him in his entirety. "We will be waiting," the chorus sang as Neil became enveloped in light.

FIRE STREAMED from Neil's mouth and eyes. The blackness cleared from his vision. More fire than ever before escaped from his hands. He wobbled to his knees.

Across the roof his adversary stood over Bianca's body, hands blazing.

"Saewulf!" Neil screamed weakly as he desperately tried to rise.

Saewulf's eyes widened and the dark color faded from them. "Don't touch her. She's not a Lightborn."

Saewulf stared at him. "How are you alive?" he screamed in fury.

Neil shrugged weakly. "Friends in high places, I guess."

Saewulf charged. Neil met him. They collided and the force of it sent cracks along the roof. Eventually, Neil was thrown from the roof and toppled through the air. Luckily, he caught himself with a burst of flame before he hit the ground.

Saewulf landed, descending slowly, still glowing.

"So foolish of me. How could I think that I could kill you from afar?" He snatched Neil up in his invisible grasp and drew him closer.

Neil's heart pumped rapidly. It was now or never. He would only have a single chance at this. "We are so similar," Saewulf said. "Bound together on this path. Your death at my hands was always meant to be more intimate. Like your sister's."

Neil floated closer and closer until Saewulf was near enough to grasp him. "One of us was always meant to kill the other Neil," he whispered. "It couldn't be grenades or blades or God given gifts. It had to be like this."

He wrapped his hand around Neil's neck. Saewulf's fingernails were close to drawing blood. "No gifts?" Neil asked. Saewulf stared at him quizzically. "Couldn't agree more." Neil reached into the pack at his side and removed the cuff Lilly had given him. He knew its effects well from wearing one on the Tridenti's island. Neil just hoped that the Imperial Doctor's craftsmanship was enough to contain Saewulf's powers. He wrapped the cuff around Saewulf's wrist. The hooks dug into his skin.

Saewulf snarled and dropped Neil. He waved his hand as if to push Neil away, but found it had no effect. He stared at his hands and tried again. Nothing. Neil threw a fireball and blasted Saewulf across the cobblestones. "What did you do to me?" Saewulf roared.

"I made you the way you want our world to be," Neil said. "Ordinary."

Saewulf back peddled and stared at his hands. Neil could see him trying to form thoughts and plans, but he was coming up empty.

Saewulf whipped his head back and forth in furious denial. He hated Lightborns with every ounce of his soul, but not being one even for a moment left him helpless.

"You think this thing can hold me?" Saewulf roared, clawing at the cuff.

The veins on his arm began to glow, and Neil realized the cuff wouldn't hold. He had to do this now. Neil lifted his knife from his belt.

Suddenly, there was a noise.

Saewulf's expression of fury turned to one of pain and confusion. He took a step forward. As he did, he revealed the small figure behind him.

It was Rhys.

Neil's brother held a knife soaked in Saewulf's blood. Saewulf turned, aghast. "What did you do?"

"I compromised," Rhys said, eyes full of shame.

Neil materialized over to his brother and the tyrant. Had this really just happened? Had Rhys stabbed Saewulf? "I'm sorry, Saewulf," Neil said, and found he meant it. "But this had to happen."

Neil followed Rhys's strike with another, this one coming so smoothly it felt guided by the wind. He put the blade between Saewulf's ribs. His third and fourth rib.

Darkness began seeping out of Saewulf's wound and he groaned in agony. Something told Neil it was all the power he'd taken from the captured Lightborns. "You..." Neil saw the disappointment and anger in his eyes as he struggled to speak. "I was..." Blood dripped from his mouth and dribbled down his malformed chin. "No one's..."

"I know," Neil said. "You were so much more than that. "

Saewulf glared at him, questioning him.

"You were the Phoenix," Neil said.

Saewulf looked confused for a moment and then it registered, the way it had for Neil. He was going to create the new nation, but not by killing Neil. He'd die for it. He united the Lightborns and ended the feud, whether he wanted to or not. Because of him, things were changing and a new nation was forming. The anger and hatred changed and something came over him. Neil wanted to believe it was peace.

They heard the sound of the gate breaking down behind them. Darius was there, leading a hundred rebels. Saewulf turned to face them. Neil couldn't help but wonder what he was thinking. These were the people Saewulf thought he was fighting for, but they didn't look upon him as a savior. They looked on him as a plague.

The people charged, consuming Saewulf with blades and fury.

Neil admired his brother. "You...?"

Rhys shook his head. "I can't...I can't talk about it now."

"That's okay," Neil said. "We'll figure it out later."

Darius approached. "Rhys?"

"Can you take care of him?" Neil asked. "I have to find Bianca."

Darius nodded.

"I'll be right back, Rhys," Neil said. "It'll be okay."

Neil's eyes fell over their shoulders at the carnage behind them. Saewulf was certainly dead and the rebels held his corpse aloft. Neil turned away. Even that didn't seem right.

He summoned a burst of flame and found his way back to the roof. He had Bianca in his arms almost immediately. She looked up at him as she woke. "How did you come back?" she whispered.

"See this ring on my finger?" Neil asked. "It means I don't go anywhere."

She buried her head in his chest and he scooped her up. He took a single moment to gaze across the Industrial City. The fires of revolution burned high. There had been so much sacrifice. Parts of the city would no doubt have to be rebuilt and the rest of the wall would surely have to come down. Neil turned away from the city, Bianca in his arms, and felt his heart swell with hope. Down below, the people pulled a new nation from the ashes of the old. Despite what had been lost and the sacrifices made, the fight for something better was beautiful to him.

VOLTERIA

NEIL VAPROS

Rhys Vapros had two requests. Number one was that no one could know he'd put the first blade in Saewulf. Neil could see an unknowable shame in his brother's eyes.

Second was that he be locked away somewhere. Neil fought him on the second, but something in his eyes told him that Rhys meant it. "I must conquer this," Rhys insisted.

So they bestowed Rhys with the Lightborn cuff, taken from Saewulf's body, as they convened in the throne room, trying to make sense of their new nation.

The Emperor was dead. His eyes had fallen on Saewulf's body and he'd muttered one final statement before he passed. "Those are my boots, Saewulf."

The rebels crowded around his throne, talking of what was next and what was to be done. The people outside danced and drank and cheered in the streets. In the room that night they became Volteria.

Lilly was gone. Everyone swore they didn't know where. Some worried, but Neil didn't. Lilly hadn't seemed like the governing kind, and she'd gotten what she came for. Neil wondered if killing Carlin had done anything for her.

Near their final deliberating hour, Neil decided he had to go down to the dungeons. He had to see his father. They'd agreed everyone would be let out, but it hadn't happened yet. Neil had an inkling of an idea why. There was no way of knowing how many below were of the old world and whether they would have a place in the new one.

Neil left the talks during a particularly heated moment and walked through the palace in pursuit of the dungeon. He turned a corner. At the other end of the hallway was Leaf, the green-skinned boy.

Most of the Imperials had been taken into custody and stripped of their weapons, but here was Leaf, just waiting in the hallways. There was a book clutched in his hands and an indecipherable look in his eyes. Neil was unsure what to do, until Cartwright appeared behind him. "Ah," he said. "Young one. It's been so long."

Leaf looked almost like the Emperor had, lifeless. Neil wondered if Thorne had been a sort of Saewulf to him. Leaf extended the book slowly and Cartwright took it. He flipped it over in his hands a few times and smirked. "What is it?" Neil asked.

"Lullabies," Cartwright said.

"Little Billy?" Neil asked.

"No, better ones." Cartwright said. "Ones that actually work."

He flipped through the pages and found one covered with writings and doodles. Neil could see that the lullaby was called *Three Fathers*. "This your favorite?" Cartwright asked.

Leaf nodded.

"You rewrote the last line," Cartwright noted.

"I had three fathers, and none of them birthed me. All of them loved me and all of them hurt me." For once Neil heard a skip of rhythm in Leaf's voice.

"May I borrow your knife, Neal?" Cartwright said.

Neil passed it along.

Cartwright placed his hand on the back of Leaf's head and closed his eyes.

The knife floated out of Cartwright's hand and found its way into

Leaf's chest. The boy collapsed and Cartwright caught him. Neil saw a deep sadness in his eyes. "Is he dead for sure?" he asked.

"I don't know," Cartwright admitted. "He does this sometimes. Pretends. Something tells me it's not over. That I'll carry this burden forever."

"So you'll...?"

"Lock him away somewhere," Cartwright said. "You know, Neil. I know a lot about killing. But not so much about death."

"I know a lot about death."

"Yes," Cartwright said. "We should be friends." He walked back in the direction of the throne room. "After all, the world is about to get a lot more boring."

Neil knew it would take time to grapple with what he'd just seen. Cartwright's last words hung in his mind. The world *was* going to get a lot more boring. Neil was happy for that. It's all he'd wanted for so long. A boring life with Bianca.

The door to the dungeon opened and light streamed down the darkened staircase. Neil descended carefully, step by step. Something weighed on his heart; an incredible anxiety consumed him. He'd been waiting for this moment for a long time. *Right?* This was all he'd been able to think about... *Right?*

It didn't take long to find his father's cell. Neil knew the tattoos by sight. His father had been deprived of a shirt in his prison, and his trophies were on full display, plastered across his skin. His arms were chained to either wall of the cell and his legs dragged on the floor. He looked up when Neil entered. The mask covering his nose and mouth explained why he wasn't able to escape. Limited oxygen meant limited power. "Neil?" His voice came through the mask like a hiss.

Neil wrapped his fingers around the bars. "Father..." He didn't know exactly what to say. "Are you all right?"

"How are you here?" He bore his weight on his legs and stared at Neil.

"The Empire has fallen," Neil said. "We brought it down. Saewulf, Carlin, the Emperor... They're all dead."

Neil heard the disbelief in his father's voice. "You did this? You, my son, did this?"

"I did... With the help of the other families."

That's what he'd been afraid to say. He realized it as the words left his mouth. He awaited a lecture or a lashing, but Sir Vapros laughed. "Oh my..." He laughed once more. "You really are such a better man than I ever gave you credit for."

Neil's heart swelled. His father wasn't angry. Could this be pride? Had Neil finally achieved what he'd always wanted? His father's acceptance was at arm's reach. Neil slipped the dungeon key into the lock.

"What do you plan to do with them now?" Sir Vapros asked. Excitement filled his voice.

Neil was about to turn the key, but that bothered him. The wording was wrong. "What?" he asked, trying not to seem phased.

"Not even I would have thought to use the other Lightborns as my foot soldiers. I never thought it could be done. They've always been hard to manipulate."

Neil couldn't breathe. He felt like maybe his oxygen was also restricted. "What do I plan to do with them...?" Neil repeated.

"I mean, now that we're in power. How do we stop them from seizing it? Let me out, Neil. We've got to get this just right. It'll take a lot of planning."

Neil's hand shook and the key rattled in the lock. "Father... The feud is over... The Empire is gone... There's no more fight to win."

"Are the Taurlum and Celerius still alive?"

"Yes, but—"

"Then there is still a fight."

Neil wanted to crumple up inside. "The feud is dead, Father."

His father looked at him, a chasm of misunderstanding between them. "The feud dies when they do." His voice boomed in his mask and throughout the dungeon.

Neil pulled the key out of the lock. He thought of Mama Tridenti and her plan to destroy the Empire at the expense of her children.

"Jennifer and Victoria… They didn't make it," Neil said. "They were killed by the Empire."

Sir Vapros's eyes were sharp, measuring now. "I would weep for them, but it looks like you've already avenged them."

Neil was baffled. His father's eyes didn't show an ounce of regret or grief. He was calculating. Plotting. "I have two questions for you," Neil said.

"Can it wait?" Sir Vapros groaned. "I've been in here for no short while."

"Jennifer was once assigned to kill a Celerius boy. Edward."

"I remember."

"Did you know?"

One of Sir Vapros's eyebrows began to rise. "Know what?"

"Did you know?" Neil repeated more harshly this time.

Sir Vapros leaned forward and his chains rattled. "Did I know my daughter was spending her nights with the Celerius scum? Did I know she was fraternizing with the enemy? Did I know she was spitting on the one cause that we hold dear in this family? Yes, Neil. I knew. I knew she had a frilly little crush on that pathetic boy. So I chose to make her learn a lesson. I chose to make her stronger."

"You told her the Celerius were planning her assassination."

"How are you still so naïve? You look older, but you are still so young. I told her what she needed to hear to realize her potential."

Neil felt fire in his chest. He felt dizzy. For his entire life he'd taken his father's words as law. They were right. They were unquestionable. Now when he heard them, they sounded abhorrent and poisoned with hatred. "She loved him."

"She should have loved her family more."

Neil palmed the key and stared into his father's eyes. He wanted to know the truth of this next question. "Would you ever stop fighting? Would you ever live side by side with the other Lightborns?"

Sir Vapros glanced down at Neil's hand. Maybe he recognized that this answer was the key to his freedom. "I will only stop when they are dead. Never before that." He was consistent. And that was all.

Neil let the heat build in his hand. This key wasn't like the other

Imperial keys. It wouldn't fit multiple locks. It had been made especially for this cell. Neil's hand grew hotter and hotter until Sir Vapros noticed. Neil held up the deformed key and dropped it on the floor. He crushed what remained under his boot. He tried to seem brave or fierce. But it just reminded him of the times when he felt powerless in front of his father. He remembered every failure, every beating.

"What a surprise…" Sir Vapros roared as Neil walked away. "How foolish I was to believe in you for even a moment. How foolish I was to believe that you could possibly be anything more than a failure. You came all this way just to disappoint me one last time."

"If disappointing you means ending the feud, then I'm happy to do it. I'll do it every single day until my end."

Neil was walking up the steps now. "You can't hope to protect Altryon, Neil. You're not strong enough. You'll never be strong enough."

Neil's hand rested on the door to the dungeon. "You're right. I could never hope to be strong enough to protect Volteria." He paused, knowing this would hurt his father. "That's why I won't do it alone. Goodbye Father."

He closed the door and grief clawed at him. He pushed it away. There was a new world forming outside. Men like Sir Vapros would only serve to topple it. Neil knew very well that hate is a poor foundation.

The last thing Neil did that day was take Saewulf's corpse outside into the light and place his hand on the back on his neck. He channeled his energy into his old enemy and Saewulf dissolved, slowly, then all at once. His ashes floated away on the wind, indistinguishable from those of the city.

Indistinguishable from those of the old world.

EPILOGUE

People always ask me why we came back. I'm never quick with an answer. The library at Abington was the birthplace of indescribable horrors, but all of Volteria is built on blood-soaked soil. There's no person of my age who doesn't remember the struggle for freedom. I do like that about our new people. The creation of Volteria made them textured. It's a people who believe in right and wrong. I haven't seen much action since, and I don't miss it as much as I thought I would.

I filled the Doctor's coliseum below the library with the rarest books in Volteria. It's probably the largest private collection in existence, and now I'm well known amongst academics and auctioneers. My wife Rebecca tells me I'm being selfish, but I like having a separate space for him. The books up top are for Abington. The ones below are for Rhys. "What will happen when we die?" Rhys always asks.

I tell him I imagine Rebecca will give them all away. That's fine with me. I can't imagine my kids would be excited to inherit a bunch of dusty old almanacs anyway.

Lilly comes by sometimes. She doesn't wear the blue anymore and she doesn't let me call her "Miss." She goes by Grand Master. I always figured there wasn't a man in existence who could stand up to Lilly Celerius but she ended up married to Jack Jacobson of all people. We all thought Thorne had killed him, but thankfully he'd survived the torture and was freed when the rebels liberated the military base. They have a daughter who I hear is twice as deadly as her mother. May she have mercy on us all.

Lilly spent most of her young adult life alone, but between Jack, her daughter, and the travelers who come to train with her, I doubt she will ever be alone again.

Katherine Celerius became our interim President until we formed an election process. She knew quite a bit, spending half her life a noble and the other half in the slums. She was always a serious and reserved person, but it filled me with joy to see her around. To think the wife that Steven Celerius had tried to avenge for so long would end up leading the government he helped form. He was fighting for her all along. Just not in the way he thought.

As for me, I kept reading and learned to write. Sort of odd that the dumbest of the group wrote our history, but now I'm a writer and live for ironies like that. Cartwright and Rhys helped with the language, and I gathered every piece of information I could. I talked to Neil and Lilly. I found the Wolf's journals and even Carlin's. Harold Thorne recorded everything, hoping he might light the way for future generations. I don't think he came across as well as he might have liked. It took me years, but I wove together a little patchwork of our journey with some artistic interpretation here and there. Cartwright told me he thought the first one wasn't too good, but he confessed that the next ones weren't so bad. I get why he might be upset. I outsold all of his works combined. Sometimes he lies and tells me it doesn't bother him. I dedicated the first one to Rhys for teaching me how to read, and the last one for everything else.

Rhys still hears the voice, but we take it a day at a time. Some nights he and I leave the library and go find Nikolai in the woods. "Just Darius and his monsters," Rhys always says.

But we both know the truth. Neither of them are monsters, no matter what anyone says.

And of course there's Neil. I kept waiting for him to get fat or for his hair to go gray, but he's stayed annoyingly youthful. We begged him to be President for a while, but of course he wanted no part of that. He recommended his wife, who was elected with near unanimous support. She alternates weeks running the nation and taking the short trip to see him at the Golden Mug, where he lives and works. Her Vice President, Robert, doesn't mind.

We all enjoy no small amount of fame in this era. People always ask Neil to produce a flame, but he never does. Some people think he's lost the fire, but that's not true. Everyone who knows Neil knows it's on the inside. Flickering away. Always.

AUTHOR'S NOTE

Dear Reader,

I hope you enjoyed *The Ashes* and the conclusion to *The Feud Trilogy*. I have to say, it is bittersweet to say goodbye to these characters. I changed the ending a few times, so I'd love to hear if you felt satisfied with how things turned out. If you'd like to share what you liked, loved, or even hated, I'd love to hear from you. You can write to me at kyleprue@kyleprue.com.

Finally, I need to ask a favor. If you enjoyed the book, I'd really appreciate it if you'd leave a review. I'm sure you look at reviews when deciding to make a purchase so you already know that reviews are incredibly important. Readers can make or break a book. I appreciate your help to spread the word about my books.

If you'd like to hear what's next, please join my newsletter at kyleprue.com. I am giving away a free prequel to the series.

Since you are a reader, you may also care about the literacy crisis in America. Did you know that one third of 8th graders can't read? That 7,000 high school students drop out of school everyday? That only 1 in 300 underserved kids owns a book of their own?

I started a non-profit, Sparking Literacy, that offers author visits, literacy programs and free books to teens that are at-risk and underserved. We are a volunteer organization and all donations are used to provide programs and free books. Illiteracy is the most solvable disability. Please help us. Find out more and donate at: sparkingliteracy.org.

Thanks for reading. I hope you enjoyed the journey.

Gratefully,

Kyle

ABOUT THE AUTHOR

Kyle Prue is an award-winning author, actor and comedian. Kyle wrote *The Sparks* when he was just 16 years old. The next two books in the series are *The Flames* and *The Ashes*.

The books have won numerous national and international awards for Best Young Adult Fiction and Best Young Adult Fantasy including: Presidential Awards from the Florida Authors and Publishers Association; Florida Book Festival; New England Book Festival; Midwest Book Festival; Southern California Book Festival; and International London Book Festival. Kyle also won an International Moonbeam Award and a prestigious Indie Fab award for Best Young Author.

He is a popular keynote speaker at conferences and his assemblies are a huge hit with teens. To book an event, email Kyle at kyleprue@kyleprue.com.

Kyle is the founder of Sparking Literacy, a non-profit dedicated to lowering the high school dropout rate by inspiring teens to read, write and follow their dreams. You can learn more at sparkingliteracy.org.

Follow Kyle on social media:
Facebook: KylePrue
Twitter: @kyleprue
Instagram: @KylePrue

ACKNOWLEDGMENTS

I considered copying and pasting my Oscar speech into this document, but I want to finish up on a high note.

I wrote the first words of the *Feud Trilogy* when I was sixteen years old, and from the moment my fingers hit my keyboard the trajectory of my life changed. Almost seven years later, seeing *The Ashes* going to print fills me with melancholy. The series that changed my life is coming to an end. Though the era is in its final days, I will never forget the people who defined it.

My parents, of course, come first. They deserve the lion's share of the thanks. Without them, I'd be nothing but a stain on the publishing industry's lobby floor.

I was lucky to attend a high school that supported my creativity and encouraged me to follow my dreams. I wish every kid could attend a school like Seacrest Country Day. It really is a magical journey.

The editors who helped me fine-tune my drafts are indispensable. Huge thanks to Owen Gemmer. He is always my first reader and gives notes that are spot on. His friendship is the icing on the cake. It takes a long time to find an editor who is the best fit. I am lucky to have met Julie Mosow so early in my career. She always understands what I want to say and offers great insight into how I can do it better. A big thanks to my high school teacher and mentor, Howard Schott, who is always my last reader, as his copy editing is unparalleled.

Thank you to Ashley at Cardboard Monet for the great covers for the series. Thank you to the Prue Crew Street Team for being my early readers and helping spread the word about my books. I'm as big a fan of you as you are of me.

No one would know about my books without the work of a lot of great marketing people. Thank you to Melissa Storm and her team at LitRing for all their help and advice. Thank you to Penny Sansevieri and the team at Author Marketing Experts. They shared a wealth of knowledge, and I'm grateful to have such great partners for the release of *The Ashes*. Also, thanks to Sari Cicurel my PR superhero.

Another huge thanks to Scott Bowles. The fact that he took the time to read my first book and give me a review before I published *The Sparks* gave me credibility when many publishers doubted anyone would want to read something written by a teen. Scott is one of the coolest, most fascinating guys I have ever met. He definitely makes the list for my dream dinner guests, dead or alive.

I didn't know about the literacy crisis until I started speaking in middle and high schools around the country. I am so grateful for all the donors who support Sparking Literacy and help lower the high school dropout rate by improving literacy in teens. As we like to say, we may not change the world, but we may change the world for a child. Thanks for helping us make a difference.

I would be remiss if I didn't shout out to my beautiful, talented friends in Midnight Book Club. You've been the bedrock of my college experience and a constant built in feel-better button. You're all so deeply funny, unique, and weird and I love you for it. You're the only club I ever wanted to join and I am so glad I did.

Some other randos who put up with my brief insanity once a year when I had to buckle down and write: David, Courtney, UMich Acting, Goose Patrol, Joseph, Whoville, Weird House, Bay Harbor, Diva Dragonfly, etc. These names will sound like gibberish to the vast majority of you, but those named will think it's funny they booked the acknowledgments.

Thanks to all the students I met on book tours for always making me feel so welcome. And most of all, thanks to my readers. You are the reason I write. Thank you for sharing my books and spending time in this fantasy world with me. I hope you enjoyed the ride.

CPSIA information can be obtained
at www.ICGtesting.com
Printed in the USA
LVHW091740110122
708307LV00023B/1064/J

9 780999 444979